W9-ABK-076

GODDESS CROWN

SHADE LAPITE

WALKER BOOKS

This is a work of fiction. Names, characters, places, and incidents are
either products of the author's imagination or, if real, are used fictitiously.

Copyright © 2023 by Shade Lapite

All rights reserved. No part of this book may be reproduced, transmitted,
or stored in an information retrieval system in any form or by any means,
graphic, electronic, or mechanical, including photocopying, taping, and
recording, without prior written permission from the publisher.

First US edition 2023

Library of Congress Catalog Card Number 2022922924
ISBN 978-1-5362-2652-2

23 24 25 26 27 28 APS 10 9 8 7 6 5 4 3 2 1

Printed in Humen, Dongguan, China

This book was typeset in Arno Pro.

Walker Books US
a division of
Candlewick Press
99 Dover Street
Somerville, Massachusetts 02144

www.walkerbooksus.com

For my mum, Grace Bolaji Lapite.
For modeling how to be a strong, purposeful woman
while remaining loving and generous.

THE FOREST

THE SUN WOULDN'T SET FOR ANOTHER FEW HOURS, BUT EVENING came quickly in the forest, and Aunty had made Kalothia promise to be back at a decent time so they could enjoy her age-day meal. *This last one and I am done here,* she promised silently.

The scent of loamy earth filled her nose and the warm air bathed her skin. It had been a beautiful day. As though the forest knew she would be leaving in a few hours and had put on a show to wish her well.

She braced her feet, sighted her arrow, pulled the rawhide string back, and released. The arrow sliced through the air. The hare keeled over, dead before it knew it had been hit.

Kalothia strode over to the body, whispered a prayer to the Goddess, thanking her for the blessing, then added the hare to a hunting bag that already contained two squirrels and a grouse. Her vervet monkey, Ye-Ye, swung down from a tree branch and landed in his favorite spot on her shoulder. She'd rescued him after his mother was killed by a snake when he was only a few days old. Under her doting care, he'd matured into a mischievous creature who never listened and never left her side.

"Are you done?" Clarit called from her perch on a boulder. She slapped at a mosquito and sighed.

"I am." It comforted Kalothia to know she'd be leaving Aunty and Teacher with a fully stocked provision room. Though Aunty clicked her tongue and grumbled about the unseemliness of Kalothia hunting, they all knew there'd be little meat on the table if she didn't. Teacher was unskilled at anything beyond his books, and Aunty's simple traps only caught the smallest forest animals. Kalothia was glad to use her weapons training to supplement their meals, Goddess knew she'd never had to use the training to fight off intruders. She knew she was worrying unnecessarily; Clarit could also hunt when she was gone. In their practice combat sessions, her bodyguard wielded her cudgel with lethal precision. Kalothia had no doubt the woman could provide game for the table.

Except there'd be no reason for Clarit to remain in the forest once Kalothia was gone, she reminded herself. Clarit would rejoin her army unit wherever they were stationed and probably breathe a sigh of relief that her annual three-month tour of duty protecting a minor royal in the middle of a strange forest was finally over.

"This way!" Kalothia called to Clarit, deciding on a shorter route back to the house.

Clarit grunted unhappily but followed.

When she'd been younger, Kalothia had enjoyed teasing her bodyguards by choosing the most difficult routes whenever she was allowed out of the house. She knew every log, every bush, every beehive, every alcove—it was impossible for her to get lost. The delight of that had waned eventually. She'd grown tired of the forest she'd been forbidden to leave and that she was not allowed to traverse without an escort. She longed to visit the towns and villages she knew were nearby, but they were off-limits. "Only if you're attacked, and then you run and don't look back." Nahir had made her repeat the rule so many times.

Sixteen harvests and they'd never been attacked. Sometimes a brave outsider would venture into the forest, shaking and fearful, braced to encounter the dead souls that were said to live there. Most of the time it was just her, Aunty, Teacher, her bodyguard, and Nahir on his occasional visits.

Nahir.

Thinking of Nahir made her kick mindlessly at a tuft of grass and sigh. Would she see him before she left? He never forgot her age day, but there'd been so much trouble on the eastern border recently, he might be unable to leave. It was better this way.

She kicked at another cluster of grass. If he came, he'd ask probing questions and look at her with those eyes that saw too much. Clarit would tell him about the strange hunters who'd ventured so much deeper into the forest than usual a moon ago, and Nahir would start making paranoid sweeps of the forest and putting her through fighting drills. He took his job as head of her security under his father, Lord Godmayne, painfully seriously. It was actually ridiculous, as she'd told him many times. He was only three harvests older than her. She could still remember the lanky boy of thirteen harvests who'd accompanied the series of stern-faced army men sent to manage her rotation of bodyguards. He'd tried to imitate his unsmiling seniors, but she could see his pleasure when they'd gone fishing and she demonstrated how to spear fish in the lake, or when they'd laid hog traps and caught one of the fat, fierce creatures.

Nahir had changed when he had passed the combat tests and become a captain at seventeen. By the time he was made head of her security, he had become quiet and sober with the weight of responsibility. She found she couldn't read him the way she once had. His world was so much bigger than hers, his concerns so numerous. She missed the boy he'd been and felt victorious whenever she managed to tease him out. But the last thing she needed on this age day was Nahir sniffing around, seeing far too much.

"You should be happy on your age day."

Kalothia jumped at the sound of Clarit's voice. The woman rarely started a conversation. Kalothia looked back at her.

"You've been quiet today," Clarit observed. "I can listen if you want to talk."

"I've reached sixteen harvests. I'm supposed to be reflective at such a milestone."

Clarit grunted again. Kalothia summoned up a smile. She did not want to trigger Clarit's concern. Kalothia began prattling about how they were running low on salt and how she hoped Nahir would bring some if he managed to make her age-day celebration so they could preserve the game she'd caught. She kept the steady stream of words flowing until they reached the compound gate.

The gate was overgrown with vegetation, impossible to find unless you knew where to look. She stepped aside so Clarit could enter first, waited the mandated minutes while Clarit did her checks, then followed her inside. The sandy ground was bathed in golds and reds, the evening sun streaming down into the clearing. The house stood at one end, a cluster of connected circular rooms made from red, sunbaked mud bricks and covered with thatched roofing. A vegetable patch sprouted cheerily beside it, and before it a long, rough-hewn wooden table had been set with goblets and bowls covered with squares of fabric.

Teacher wandered out of the hen house, a handful of eggs balanced precariously in his hands. He was a small, dark-skinned man with a shock of white hair he always forgot to comb and large spectacles. He stood in the compound and looked around as though he'd forgotten where he was heading, then catching sight of them, he smiled and called, "Welcome back! How was the hunt?"

Kalothia smiled in answer and ran to join him so they could stroll inside together. "Two squirrels, a grouse, and a hare," she boasted.

"Excellent work!" Teacher reached for the front door, jiggling the eggs dangerously. Alarmed, Kalothia dove forward to open it for him, certain Aunty would kill him if he dropped them.

Inside the house, the air was rich with spices, but there was no sign of Aunty. Kalothia breathed a sigh of relief. If she bathed and dressed quickly, Aunty might not mention her late return. She dumped the bag of game on the parlor room table and hurried for the door.

"I said be back at a *decent* time!"

Kalothia jumped at the crack of Aunty's voice. She winced, turning back slowly.

Aunty stood in the doorway to the provision room, dressed in a yellow kaftan with matching headscarf, one hand fisted on her hip.

Kalothia took her in: the small, round-faced woman who had fed, scolded, hugged, and cared for her since her birth. The fist on hip signaled swift action was required. She shot Aunty a sweet smile. "I'm just wondering, if I had to pour all my love for you into bottles, how many would I need? I don't think there'd be enough."

Teacher grinned.

Aunty chuckled then tried to hide it, remembering she was annoyed with her charge, but the smile hovered stubbornly at the corners of her mouth. "Your mouth is sweeter than sugarcane! Your mother was the—" She cut herself off, but it was too late. The playful mood dissipated.

Kalothia often thought there was nothing Aunty and Teacher would deny her—after all, they'd moved to the middle of the Faledi forest to care for her. Quite a change from the royal court, where they'd lived before. There was nothing they would refuse her, except the truth about where her parents were.

Silence sang through the room until Teacher nodded toward the corridor. "Hurry and wash up!" The eggs shifted in his precarious hold.

"Hey, la!" Aunty cried. "Put my eggs down immediately!"

Ye-Ye cried with delight and leaped off Kalothia's shoulder to closely observe the endangered eggs. Kalothia smiled at Teacher and rushed off to bathe.

»—→ ◊ ←—«

THE MUD WALLS HAD BEEN ABSORBING HEAT ALL DAY, KEEPING the house cool. Now, as evening fell, they released the stored energy, warming the rooms, keeping the house a pleasant temperature. Kalothia took a refreshing cold bath. When she emerged, she found Aunty in the sleep room they shared, perched on the bed, fixing a hole in one of Kalothia's dresses.

"What am I wearing?" Kalothia asked.

Only on her age day did she allow Aunty to indulge her desire to see her in dresses. The rest of the time she lived in the tunics and shokoto that Nahir brought her from the North, since the South didn't make such items for women. Aunty pointed at the sky-blue dress she'd hung over a chair.

Kalothia oiled her skin with shea butter scented with lavender, then slid into the dress. She crouched so Aunty could button the back. Aunty hummed in satisfaction when Kalothia rose and the fabric fell elegantly to the floor. Dresses were nice enough to look at but decidedly impractical when you were planting in the garden, hunting, rethatching the roof, climbing trees, or any of the other things Kalothia liked to spend her days doing. She made an effort to tolerate the annual discomfort.

"Now sit and I'll do your hair," Aunty instructed.

Kalothia grabbed two wooden combs and a small looking glass from the table, then lowered herself to the handwoven floor mat, wedging herself between Aunty's legs. Aunty worked deftly, her hands gentle and soothing as she unbraided the week-old cornrows, combed the knots out of Kalothia's thick afro, then rebraided the hair.

When she was finished, she tapped Kalothia's shoulder. "Let's see you."

Kalothia raised the looking glass and they both studied her reflection. Her dark red hair had been twisted into four thick cornrows that marched around her head like a crown. It was a style Aunty liked to do on her age day. As usual, she could see Aunty's eyes misting and her mouth puckering as she tried to contain her emotions.

"Do I look so much like her?" Kalothia said. When she asked about her parents, she found the best approach was to do it gently, like a fisherman dangling bait to hook a catfish.

"Yes," Aunty said. "If only she could see you."

Kalothia touched the cool glass of the pendant that hung at her throat to calm herself. It was the only thing she had from her mother.

Well, that and her coffee-rich skin, wide eyes, and full lips. She knew her red hair came from her father. These weren't useful details. Having your parents imprinted on your face and hair was not helpful when you'd never met them and barely knew where to start the search to find them.

Aunty made a visible effort to shake off her melancholy. "One day, when your parents are no longer fearful of the king, they'll come and get you. Now let's go and eat before the sun sets."

Kalothia trailed Aunty outside, trying not to feel bitter about the promises that never came to fruition, and the waiting that seemed to have no end. She had one last night with Aunty and Teacher. She didn't want to waste it feeling angry or wondering about her absent parents.

She'd lived in the forest for sixteen harvests, ever since her parents had fled the royal palace during what Aunty and Teacher called the Great Upset. They had supported Queen Sylvia (a fellow Northerner like them), who had been accused of adultery and treason. After her execution, Kalothia's parents had fled for their lives, fearing King Osura's anger.

Kalothia had been only days old, and they'd quickly realized that running and hiding was too dangerous for their newborn. They'd left her in the safekeeping of their dear friends Teacher and Aunty and had marshaled support from the lord of the Northern Territory to provide a home and bodyguards for her. Since then, there had been no news of them at all. She didn't know if they were alive or dead, but she had remained in hiding ever since to prevent the king from killing her or using her to lure out her parents.

This was the story Kalothia had been told repeatedly, with very little variation or any added details. It troubled her that Teacher could lecture for hours on how the value of cowrie shells rose and fell or why Galla would never be provoked into war with Padma though its eastern neighbor made frequent raids along their border, or myriad other topics, yet he had so little to say about the Great Upset and her parents. It made her certain they were hiding something.

The sun had entered its golden phase. It bathed the compound in yellow light. Citronella candles had been lit and arranged along the table. Kalothia suppressed a sigh. Nahir would not make it for her age day. Disappointment dragged at her shoulders and sadness clogged her throat. If he arrived the next day she would be gone. Would she ever see his solemn, thoughtful face again?

Aunty began uncovering the dishes, revealing fried rice, steamed bean cakes, roasted plantain, spicy gizzard, and baked fish. Ye-Ye saw an opportunity and leaped onto the table to inspect the bowls.

"If you touch anything, you're going in the pot!" Aunty warned the small monkey.

He chattered unhappily at her and bared his teeth.

Kalothia wagged her finger at him. "Stop that! You know she always feeds you. There's yours!" His bowl was made from half of a dried melon husk and sat at the end of the table. It had been filled with more chopped fruit and nuts than Ye-Ye's tiny body could hope to accommodate. "See! You should say 'Sorry, Aunty!'"

Ye-Ye blew out his lips, making them vibrate noisily, then scuttled over to sample the items in his bowl. Kalothia laughed at her pet's antics. They were a welcome distraction from her thoughts. Clarit appeared and took a seat at the table, resting her ever-present cudgel by her feet.

"Teacher! Come say the prayer!" Aunty called.

Teacher ambled out. He'd washed up and changed into a tunic and shokoto that were only slightly wrinkled. He moved to the head of the table, adjusted his glasses, and raised his palms in the air. "We thank you, Goddess, for eyes to admire, a mouth to taste, and a heart to appreciate your goodness. We thank you for Kalothia and pray that you cover her in your celestial light."

"Let her will be done," Kalothia and Clarit murmured in affirmation. Kalothia lifted her palm to her mouth in the gesture that would seal the prayer.

"Is that all?" Aunty demanded.

Teacher widened his eyes innocently.

"You didn't pray for her health, for her safety, for an increase in wisdom . . ."

Teacher was already sitting and filling his bowl with food. "I said 'cover her in your celestial light,'" he argued. "The Goddess has better things to do than listen to lengthy prayers."

Kalothia laughed. The two of them would never change. Aunty was the most devout person in the house, yet she refused to pray over the meals because the Goddess's third precept was "The burden of learning and leadership falls on men." Teacher wasn't sure the Goddess existed, but as the only man in the house, he was forced to lead the prayers if he wanted a peaceful life.

Aunty grunted with irritation. She grabbed Kalothia's bowl and began scooping a generous portion of everything into it.

"I nearly forgot!" Teacher drew a small package from the breast pocket of his tunic. "Happy age day!" he called, passing it down to Kalothia.

Tears sprung up in Kalothia's eyes. For a moment, she couldn't speak. Who would give her age-day gifts once she left the forest? Would her parents? Would they apologize for the sixteen age days they had missed?

She shoved the thoughts away and pulled the cord on the parcel before unfolding the fabric. Inside was a small book bound in leather soft as butter. She flipped it open and gasped. It was filled with beautiful hand-drawn maps of Galla. Each of the four territories occupied a separate page. She traced her fingers over the lines of the Eastern Territory, slid them to the area that symbolized the Faledi forest, her forest, a place she would finally leave. She fingered the book of maps and turned up her smile a few notches. "It's perfect, Teacher! Thank you."

Sadness rushed through Kalothia. This was the last time they would sit here like this. The last time Aunty would overfill her bowl to ensure she ate well. The last time she would watch Teacher gobble his food with cheeks puffed and sweat beading on his forehead. The last time Aunty would pour her lemon water and wait for her to begin her meal before filling her own bowl.

If Kalothia found her parents, maybe they could all eat together. Once the danger from the king passed, of course. There were so many ifs and maybes it all seemed so unlikely. Still, she could hope.

THE ATTACK

KALOTHIA WOKE TO BLACKNESS. THE OIL LAMP HAD BURNED itself out, indicating it was close to dawn. The waxy-sweet smell of the geraniol oil Aunty liked to sprinkle around the bed to repel mosquitoes hung thick in the air. It clogged the back of her throat.

Beside her, Aunty slept noisily, her breath sucking in and out like the rumble of thunder. Tension clutched every muscle in Kalothia's body. It was time.

She slid out of bed. Aunty slept on, her noisy rhythm unchanged. Kalothia paused for a moment. She couldn't see Aunty in the deep blackness, but she pictured her round face, the features she knew as well as her own. She said a silent farewell.

The clay floor was cool beneath her feet. She inched across the black room until her outstretched hands made contact with a chair. Running her fingers along its carved back, she felt her way down to the seat where she'd folded her clothes up in a wrapper. She scooped the bundle up and inched a little sideways until she felt the warm wood of the sleep room door. A soft weight landed on her right shoulder.

Ye-Ye chirped gently against her ear then snuggled against her neck. She patted her vervet's furry body and paused by the door to check Aunty was still asleep. One breath, two breaths, three breaths, the gusty boom of Aunty's exhalations continued in a steady rhythm. The room was still.

She slipped out.

There was no point creeping past Clarit's room. The woman had ears like a cat. She had decided her plan had to include Clarit following her out of the house.

The washing room glowed with the dim light of an oil lamp turned to its lowest setting. Its flickering yellow flame painted the walls gold.

Kalothia placed Ye-Ye on an upturned bucket then washed up quickly, impatient to be on her way. After dressing in a shokoto and a simple tunic, she wound the brightly printed wrapper around her head, ensuring her red hair was tucked securely away, as she always did when she left the compound, to protect her identity. She'd always been told red hair ran only in the royal family and would give away her identity as a minor royal if discovered. When she was ready, she scooped Ye-Ye onto her shoulder and left the washing room, taking the oil lamp with her. Outside, a cockerel called loudly across the yard.

She found her cloth bag behind the scroll shelf, dropped two knives inside, pulled the strap over her head, then tucked a third dagger into the waist of her shokoto. What did you pack when you were leaving your home forever? She grabbed a handful of cowrie shells from a bowl on the scroll shelf. Once she was out of the forest, she'd hitch a lift. Anything going west. In her heart, she was clamoring to go south. She knew she'd make far more progress on finding her parents in the capital, Port Caspin. All the people who'd known them and might know something of where they'd been for the last sixteen harvests were in the South. But the royal court was also there. That part of the country would be teeming with the king's supporters. She'd be walking straight into a hornets' nest. No, she'd go west first, adjust to the outside world, test the waters, then see if she could edge toward the South for real answers to her questions.

In the provision room, she filled a banana leaf with nuts and dried fruit. She broke off a piece of the bread Aunty had baked the night before and handed it to Ye-Ye. "Don't get crumbs in my tunic."

She put the rest in her bag along with an empty waterskin. On her way back through the parlor she stopped, considered for a moment, then turned toward the scroll shelf. Her new leather map book sat among the parchments and rolled hemp scrolls. She slid it into her bag.

Her favorite spear stood tucked into a nook beside the scroll shelf. A deft twist of the shaft allowed her to slide the parts into one another until the weapon was reduced from six feet to one. At the door, she gave the house one last look. "Please, Goddess, in case you're listening, protect this home." She lifted her palm to her mouth to seal the prayer, then opened the door and slipped out.

OUTSIDE, THE AIR SMELLED OF THE NIGHT'S RAIN. THE CLEAN dampness eased the constriction in her throat. She forced herself to smile. She would be brave. She would not be fearful.

"Took your time." Clarit's dry voice spoke beside her.

Kalothia swallowed. Just one more hurdle to clear.

The sky had lightened enough to see the circle of trees and the outline of Clarit's broad shoulders and low-cropped hair as she leaned on a post by the vegetable patch.

"You don't have to come, Clarit." Kalothia said it for form, to avoid suspicion. She layered in a little exasperation for authenticity. "I'm just going to the stream to check on the fish baskets. I'll be back before the second milking."

Clarit snorted, as she knew her bodyguard would. "When I'm hauled before a court and found guilty of disobeying an order from Captain Godmayne himself and I'm sentenced to walk the Northern desert and die under the fiery heat, you'll plead my case, no doubt?"

Kalothia rolled her eyes. She had expected this. "You're so dramatic, Clarit. Fine. Let's go." She led the way across the yard.

The hens squawked in their hutch as they passed, their wings flapping excitedly against the wire mesh that kept out predators. Kalothia stepped aside when they reached the gate and let Clarit pass through first, to check it was safe. After several long moments, a low whistle sounded. Kalothia opened the gate and stepped out into the forest.

She took a moment to orient herself in the dim light. The earth was soft beneath her feet, still thick with rainwater. Songbirds chorused loudly in the treetops. She breathed in, tasting moabi blossoms, damp wood, and ashy soil on her tongue.

"Are you planning to stand there all day?" Clarit asked.

Kalothia had to hold back a nervous laugh. If Clarit knew what she was planning, she'd lock her in the house and never let her out. Instead, she was urging her on.

Kalothia took a deep breath and set off. Over the years she had forged a web of pathways through the tangled foliage that were invisible to others but made her journeys easy. She led them along one. It crossed through the clearing where a storm had downed two large cashew trees during a long-ago rainy season. Kalothia had always told Clarit to use it as a marker for the way home. Once they'd passed it, they plunged back into the dense vegetation for a furlong before reaching the cluster of palm trees where the tiny talapoin monkeys liked to play in the branches and hide among the coconuts.

As always, Clarit looked up and exclaimed, "Don't these creatures grow tired?" The excitable mammals were endlessly fascinating to her.

While Clarit was distracted, Kalothia stepped back, unnoticed, and blended into the forest. Just as she'd planned. Ye-Ye muttered against her neck.

"Shush!" She said as she walked steadily away, her feet silent in the undergrowth. She wouldn't wait for Clarit to notice she was missing and start searching for her. It was too dangerous; Clarit was too good at her job. She had to put distance between them, and quickly. Eventually, Clarit would give up, find her way back to the cashew trees, and use them to guide her home, where she could send word to Nahir.

She walked through the dawn quiet, imagining the new life that awaited her. It was terrifying to think of fending for herself, meeting people outside the tiny circle of guardians who'd cared for her, but she was determined to adjust. She would travel to the nearby town of Illupeju and begin her journey there.

She'd been walking briskly for several minutes when a finger of unease slid over her. Something was wrong. Her eyes searched the layers of green and brown, her nose flared for unusual scents, her ears strained. Nothing. Then . . . something. Slashing. Somebody was hacking their way through the forest. Multiple somebodies. Dread scratched at her stomach. Something told her that it wasn't Clarit.

She pulled her spear from her bag and hurriedly retraced her steps, moving back in Clarit's direction.

The attackers had reached her first.

It took a long moment to absorb the scene under the palm trees: the two people ranged around Clarit, their lethal-looking weapons raised, ready to kill. It took another second for the defensive training she'd learned over the years but never had cause to use to click into place. Then a flash of movement in her peripheral vision had her spinning to the right while her hands twisted her spear to full length. She threw Ye-Ye up into the branches of a tree and barely raised her spear in time to block the sweep of a cutlass.

The blade was wielded by a large man rearing up beside her. She blocked on instinct; there had been no time to think. He swung again and she deflected. The force of the impact shivered up her arm.

Pain flared in her shoulder. She tried to step back, to plant her feet more securely, but the cutlass flew at her again, curving toward her head. She raised her spear to block it, but the jarring contact threw her to the forest floor.

The spear fell from her hands.

Ye-Ye scampered back and forth on a branch above the man, chattering at him loudly.

The attacker ignored the tiny animal and grinned down at her. "That was more fight than I expected." His accent was so thick she could barely make out the words.

Kalothia lay sprawled on her back, her spear inches away. He reached down and tore the wrapper off her head. At the sight of her hair, he grunted in satisfaction and hoisted the cutlass above his head with both hands. His eyes were hard and pitiless. He meant to kill her.

Before he could swing down, Kalothia hooked a foot around his ankle. She used the leverage to drag herself up against his legs. With the speed of a rattlesnake, she whipped her dagger from her belt and buried it in the man's fleshy calf. The sensation of the sharp metal tearing flesh made her gag. She'd never injured a person before.

The man howled and dropped to his knees.

She tore the blade free and scrambled away. Still on her knees, she snatched up her spear and held it defensively.

The man who had attacked her was clambering unsteadily to his feet. She risked a glance at Clarit. Her bodyguard had drawn blood on both her opponents, one was limping badly. There was no time to see more. The man roared and leaped toward her. It was as though he had channeled all the pain of his injury and anger into his cutlass. He swung at her ferociously. But the pause had given her time to remember her training. Years of sparring with Nahir had forced her to learn ways to overcome stronger opponents. She'd learned to think fast and move faster.

When the man swung at her and she ducked and dodged, her evasion enraged him further. His swings grew harder but less accurate. She let him herd her backward until her shoulders pressed against a tree. When he swung for her again, she dropped to the ground. Above her, the cutlass blade sank into the trunk with a sharp crack. While the man worked to free it, Kalothia darted away from the tree, sprung to her feet, and swung her spear with all her might, slamming it against the back of his skull.

The man went down like a felled tree, raising dirt and leaves. He was unconscious. Or possibly dead. Kalothia didn't stop to determine which. She spun back to Clarit.

The two attackers—a man and a woman—were strong fighters but nothing compared to Clarit. They were sweating and panting in the swampy heat. Clarit was barely winded. Kalothia let out a relieved breath. Clarit would win this.

When Nahir had assumed management of her security, he'd reduced her bodyguards from two to one. Each guard would come and stay for three-month stretches, a secondment from the Northern army. She'd asked if he made the change because she was in less danger. He'd told her no, she would never be in less danger, but he now assigned only his elite fighters, which was why she only needed one.

She watched Clarit feign a left dodge, jump right, and swing her cudgel at the man with a force that lifted him off his feet and sent him flying before he crashed into the brushwood.

The woman was losing blood from multiple wounds and had no hope of holding Clarit alone. Clarit bore down on her, knocking her to the earth with terrifying speed.

"Help me!" the woman cried. She was struggling to get up.

It took Kalothia a second to realize her words were not Gallan but Padman.

Who were these people?

Kalothia had always been told the danger was from the palace, from the network of spies the king had deployed across the country to seek out any supporters of his dead wife. But this woman was from Padma, the neighboring country. Why would they be in the forest? There was nothing here, except for her.

"Help me!" the woman cried again.

An arrow whistled through the air. A streak of black in the muddy light. Clarit twisted and it grazed her arm. Barely a scratch. She'd been lucky.

Clarit ducked. "Get down!" she shouted over her shoulder to Kalothia.

Kalothia dropped down too. She scanned their surroundings for the source of the arrow. A man stood by a nearby tree. His hair was shaved close to his scalp and a short beard covered his jaw. His black clothes fell in unfamiliar lines from his tall, lean body. His hands worked swiftly, nocking a new arrow into the large bow he held.

Had Clarit seen him? She glanced back at Clarit and frowned. Clarit was no longer crouching but on her knees, swaying oddly. What was she doing?

"Clarit?" Kalothia called. They had to move before the man shot again.

Then Clarit fell backward.

Kalothia darted forward, keeping her body low, rushing to Clarit's side.

White foam bubbled from her mouth. A strange, rancid scent stung Kalothia's nose. She watched the vein pulsing in her body-guard's throat as though Clarit was struggling to breathe. Clarit's eyes were wide and terrified, but she lay inert, paralyzed. Horror spread through Kalothia's body like ice.

"Clarit?" Her voice trembled.

Clarit began to convulse, her body rolling violently until she stilled. Her brown eyes were wide open, staring at the sky, as white foam ran in rivulets from her mouth, slid across her smooth brown cheek, and pooled in the earth beside her.

"No!" Kalothia's breath became short and choppy. Something squeezed tight in her chest. She grabbed the front of Clarit's tunic. "No!"

An arrow whizzed past, thudding into the ground a handspan

away. Kalothia turned. The man in the forest was watching her, his hands nocking a new arrow.

There was movement beside her. The injured woman was on her feet again.

Kalothia needed to move, but she was frozen.

Move! A part of her brain was screaming at her. But Clarit wasn't moving. Disjointed thoughts tumbled through Kalothia's head.

The twang of the arrow launching echoed through the air. Kalothia threw herself to the ground. The arrow thudded into the earth beside her.

A hand grabbed her and hauled her to her feet. Kalothia's brain was still frozen in horror. It was ingrained training and muscle memory that drew her dagger from the waist of her shokoto and rammed it into the belly of the woman holding her.

The woman's eyes widened with shock as Kalothia pulled her blade free. Then she fell to her knees and doubled over. Kalothia ran, plunging into the woods.

NO WAY HOME

SHE RAN UNTIL HER LUNGS BURNED. UNTIL HER LEGS SHOOK with fatigue and sweat drenched her skin. By the time her senses returned, the sun blazed high in the sky. Kalothia crouched in a patch of deep shade and watched the stream that ran through the open meadow. She panted in and out. The noise made it hard to listen for danger, but she had given up on trying to regulate her breathing. Just as she had given up on trying to still the violent shake in her hands. Something vital had broken loose in her chest, and the rest of her body was desperately trying to hold itself together but might well collapse at any moment. While she waited for that to happen, she watched the stream.

She needed water. She needed to wet her parched throat, then fill her waterskin so that she could return to the house and protect Aunty and Teacher. She needed to move, but the image of Clarit's lifeless body crowded her head. *What happened?* The arrow had barely grazed Clarit, there had been no blood. Her brain churned in confusion. She could see her bodyguard's face, slack and unresponsive, the white foam on her lips . . . A shudder ran through her. Poison. The arrow had been poisoned.

The long grass waved in the breeze. Birds sang brightly from the trees that overlooked the clearing. Animals scampered around the area, going about their business. She stayed beneath the shade of the trees and tried to gather herself. Ye-Ye mewled by her ear and gently batted his head against her neck. He was thirsty too. She needed to get up.

Besides, the longer she sat there, the more chance one of the attackers would come upon her. And what about Aunty and Teacher? Neither of them was a fighter. The attackers could be at the house at that very moment. The alarming thought propelled her to her feet.

She looked around once more. Saw nothing but the green forest and the empty meadow. She sucked in a breath and willed her shaking hands to still. "Let's go!" she whispered to Ye-Ye.

Keeping her body low, she left the shelter of the trees and ran toward the stream. Every bird cry, every rustle and crunch of foliage registered in her brain. She forced herself to keep moving through the open field until she reached the edge of the water. Crouching, she sank her waterskin into the clear depths. It was blessedly cool against her skin.

When her flask was full, she pulled it free and raised it to her parched lips. The glint of sunlight on silver scales beneath the surface barely registered. She had opened her mouth and swallowed a mouthful before it struck her that the fish were floating upside down.

She dropped her waterskin and dragged Ye-Ye back onto land.

Burning erupted on her lips and tongue as though they were being attacked by a swarm of angry bees.

The stream had been poisoned.

She ran for the cover of the trees.

As the fire in her mouth burned hotter, it became harder to think. Her stomach began to clench. Agonizing ripples pulled her to her knees. She fell to her side doubled up into a ball, her mind blank of everything but the pain burning her up from the inside.

>——— ◊ ———<

"SHE'S NOT HERE."

"Her flask is in the water. She's nearby. Find her!"

The voices drifted through her head. Garbled words. The ground was hard beneath her head. She had the vague feeling she'd lost time, but everything outside the pain was a haze. Until she heard footsteps crunching through the brush. The attackers were here. That thought registered.

She focused on the nearest tree and clawed her way closer to it. She couldn't tell where the voices and footsteps were, wasn't sure if she was moving toward danger or away, but instinct made her huddle into the tree trunk, burrow into the long grass around it.

Time had no meaning, only pain. She clutched the pendant at her neck. Tears streamed down her face, a poor outlet for the screams she fought to silence. The voices continued, calling out to each other. The footsteps circled, echoing inside her head. She didn't see the coconut until Ye-Ye pulled her eyelid up so that the brown gourd filled her vision. He had rolled it up to her face. Once her eyes were open, he chirped quietly at her; his little arms pushed the fruit so that its hairy skin batted against her forehead, the water inside swishing quietly.

Finally, she understood what he was telling her to do. She gritted her teeth, pulled herself to a sitting position, and drew her dagger from her belt. Her stab was awkward but strong enough to make a hole. Desperate for relief, she tipped the fruit up to her mouth. She rinsed her burning lips, then drank in deep mouthfuls. It cooled the burning like balm. Too quickly the gourd was empty, but the pain had eased. It was a bearable throb, instead of the debilitating agony.

On all fours she crept through the long grass until she could see the two men searching for her. She didn't recognize either of them from the earlier attack, but they both wore the same tight, black clothing. One stalked through the meadow whacking a thick branch aggressively through the grass. The other had ranged farther out and was peering up into the branches of the trees that ringed the clearing.

"She's not a monkey!" the first one called to him. Padman again. She wasn't fluent in the foreign tongue, but she had always been good at languages. She'd grown up speaking Common Galla like Aunty, but Teacher had taught her basic Padman. "She's not going to be hiding up in a tree."

"How do you know?" the other man said. "She's been living out here in the forest all her life. Maybe she's half beast now."

Coldness spread through Kalothia's body. They knew so much about her. How? Why were men from Padma, Galla's enemy, searching for her? How had they tracked her down? Had they found the house yet? She began to crawl quietly, deeper into the forest, until she thought it was safe to stand, and then she broke into a lumbering run.

An alcove at the foot of a hill marked the route back to the house. She shared another coconut with Ye-Ye, relieved when it swallowed up the worst of her pain, then considered her options. The dangers

Nahir had warned her about—the bodyguards, the training, the rules, and the hiding—she had resented all of it. Now there truly were people here to kill her.

She could hear Nahir in her head almost as clearly as if he were standing in front of her. He was telling her to run. To follow the escape route that he'd drilled into her head. East to the large odon tree where she would shelter for the night. At sunrise she would continue east until she found the river. She was to stay parallel but not too close and follow it to the nearby town of Illupeju. There she would wait for him at an inn until sunrise. If he didn't come, she was to get a horse and travel north to his father, Lord Godmayne. "Everybody's job is to keep you alive," he had said. Melodramatic as always.

She sighed and ran a hand over Ye-Ye's fur. The vervet nuzzled against her. She had lost Clarit. It was her fault they had been out so early. Her fault Clarit was dead. Guilt mixed with the queasiness in her stomach. She couldn't run. She couldn't leave Aunty and Teacher to face these terrible people alone. She couldn't follow Nahir's rules. She had to go back to the house and save them.

She edged through the trees that surrounded her home. The air felt too still. She jumped at every whisper and crack. Her skin prickled with awareness as she scanned the woods for movement.

She didn't use the front gate, the opening that she and Clarit had used just a few hours earlier. Instead, she crept toward the tight knot of trees that lined the back of the fence. She slipped between them, then paused and listened. Nothing moved.

She put a hand to her throat, felt the smoothness of her pendant, let it calm her galloping heart. She thought of Aunty, of her wide smile, her gentle hands, her eyes that could flit from admonishing to cheeky humor in the blink of an eye. She thought of how good it would feel to be held by her. She steeled her nerves and stepped up to the fence. Ye-Ye whined gently against her ear.

"Shush, it will be all right," she murmured to him.

There was no secret way in. After all, Nahir's instructions were if there's danger, run. She boosted herself up the wall until she could brace the tips of her slippers against the wood and then climbed by wedging her fingers between the wood slats. At the top, she hurriedly scanned the compound. The chickens squawked from their cage. The house stood peacefully at the back. The sun's glare made it impossible to see inside the windows.

She levered herself over the fence, then dropped to the ground and stayed crouched there. Nothing moved. She darted to the side of the house and peered into the provision room. Empty. Aunty wasn't there preparing the morning meal as was her usual routine.

Kalothia's heart lurched. She drew one of her daggers with trembling hands and gripped it tightly. Her steps were silent as she crept around the house to the parlor window. Pushing down the fear, she forced herself to look inside.

The room had been destroyed. The eating table lay on its side, stools were broken and scattered, the floor mat was bunched in a corner. Aunty and Teacher lay amid the mess. Aunty was twitching slightly, white foam spilling from her mouth. Teacher was still. Too still. A moan crept up Kalothia's throat and out into the still air. She raced around the house to the front door and wrenched it open.

"Aunty! Teacher!"

She flew inside and dropped to the floor beside Teacher. His glasses lay cracked nearby. His eyes were open, unseeing. Tears blurred her vision. Sobs rose in her throat. He was dead.

She turned and crawled to Aunty. Her throat was still working.

Hope rose in Kalothia's chest. "Breathe, Aunty!" Foam kept bubbling from her mouth.

A man's voice rang out in the compound. *"She's here!"*

She ignored it. Cradled Aunty against her body. She could smell a bitter scent in the air. "Please! Please! Please, breathe!"

Heavy footsteps sounded behind her, then pain flared across her scalp and her pleas turned to a shout. A hand grabbed her hair, wrenching her away from Aunty and throwing her across the room. She crashed into the scroll shelf, rolling in time to see the large man who had attacked her in the woods stalk toward her with a cutlass. She looked past him to where Aunty was convulsing, her head and heels drumming against the ground, more foam spilling from her mouth.

"No!" Kalothia cried. She shot to her feet, despite the pain. She had to get to Aunty.

The man with the cutlass bent his head to the side and his neck joints cracked. His hands clenched into fists as big as mangoes. He lunged, quicker than she'd expected, landing a punch against her shoulder that sent her sprawling to the floor again. He grabbed one of her feet and towed her back, ignoring her desperate kicks. "Maybe I'll take that troublesome red hair as a trophy." He grinned at her. "Now, behave!"

He grabbed her hip with a meaty paw to draw her closer to him. She kicked out, and his eyes narrowed as he swung his leg back for a kick of his own. He didn't see her adjust the grip on her dagger and angle it just so. A heartbeat before his foot connected with her chest, it met her dagger, the force of his kick pushing the blade so deep the hilt met the leather of his slippers. He howled in agony and let go of her.

She stumbled to her feet and over to Aunty. Her face was slack. Her chest was still. White foam spilled and pooled beside her head.

"No!" Kalothia wanted to fall to her knees, but the man was bearing down on her again. Through the window, she caught a blur of movement in the compound. They were coming for her. There was nothing here for her now. Aunty, Teacher, and Clarit were dead. If she wanted to save herself, she had no choice. She ran.

4

REPRIEVE

KALOTHIA SAT IN A FORK OF BRANCHES. THE ODON TREE NAHIR had selected as a hiding spot wrapped around her, its thick branches curving out of the wide trunk. The night was a sheet of blackness. She couldn't tell if her eyes were open or closed. She didn't know if she was asleep or awake. She didn't care. It felt like the inside of her body had been scraped out, like all the tears she'd spilled had left her hollow.

The only family she had known was gone. It was all she could do to keep breathing.

The night stretched out, endless as air.

When she heard the soft scuffle below, she didn't react. Whether it was a wildcat searching for its evening meal or the attackers had tracked her down, she was too exhausted to run. Ye-Ye chirped against her ear, then his warm body disappeared. She sighed and reached out blindly, hoping he was nearby.

"Kalothia?"

It wasn't the sound of her name that had her breath catching. It was the voice. The warm rumble of his voice.

"Nahir?" she breathed and sat up.

The tree creaked as he climbed. A series of soft scuffles that grew steadily closer. Moments later, the thick branch she'd settled against groaned under his weight.

She reached out into the blackness, her hands seeking desperately. "Nahir?" Panic was in her voice, sharp as broken glass. Had she imagined him?

"Yes." A hand brushed one of hers.

She grabbed it and traced her way up the arm until she felt the soft locks of his hair. She wrapped her arms around his body, dug her fingers into his back, and nestled her face against his neck, breathing in the familiar scent of shea butter, saddle oil, and leather.

He held himself stiff and rigid against her for a moment and then she felt him pat her back awkwardly. The world could end and Nahir would still be Nahir: reserved, aloof, uncomfortable with physical contact. She held on to him regardless. Let the warmth of his body seep into her. Let him anchor her. It helped.

"I thought you might be here. Are you hurt?" He sounded discombobulated. "I was at the house. I saw—"

She shook her head, clutched him closer. "I'm whole." The unfairness of it, of escaping the dreadful day mostly unharmed, burned in her throat as she spoke. "But they're all gone. Because of me." The tears she thought she'd finished shedding began to spill again.

He pulled away from her, and she shivered, feeling confused by his reason for moving and desperate for his warmth. Then the branch she sat on pitched slightly as he moved closer and lifted her in a firm grip onto his lap. He wrapped his arms around her, enveloping her in his warmth. Relief flooded her. She burrowed into him and cried, silently, so that the killers hunting her in the darkness would not hear. She cried until she fell asleep.

STRANGE BEASTS

KALOTHIA WOKE SLOWLY. SHE WOKE WITH A HEAD THAT pounded and a mouth as dry as parched earth. Soreness radiated from her neck to her back to the soles of her feet. She slitted her eyes open grudgingly, planning to ask Aunty to prepare one of her healing teas, but the sight of curving branches and a gray-white sky stopped her. She stiffened and snapped to full consciousness. Ye-Ye was curled in a ball in her lap and a thick arm was wrapped around her waist holding her firmly. Why was she—?

Aunty.

The memories flooded back. Pain tore through her chest, making her breathing ragged.

"Shush!" Nahir's voice whispered against her ear.

She tried to move, desperate for space, for room to catch her breath.

He tightened his grip. "Don't move. It hasn't spotted us yet."

What was he talking . . . ? She stilled, catching sight of a creature carefully sniffing the air, balanced on a branch in the opposite tree. Its brown fur was half hidden by leaves and the gray light made it hard to get a true picture of it. Yet she made out a wide head surrounded by a thick mane, a long jaw, and a narrow body. It was a strange, misshapen animal that did not belong in her forest. She was not sure it belonged anywhere. More worrying was its stare. There was a hungry interest in its gaze, especially when its eyes stopped scanning the foliage and fixed on their position. She tensed. Had it seen them?

A whining call came from below, and the creature in the tree turned its head in response, then rose on its two hind legs, like a hyena. It had the long powerful body of a lion and a monkey's flicking, ropelike tail. Kalothia shuddered. The Goddess had not made this creature.

The animal dipped its head and snarled. Slowly, Kalothia eased her spear out of her bag. She held her breath, expecting an attack. But the thing simply leaped from its perch, using its tail to swing from branch to branch, racing downward with ease.

"Dammit!" Nahir said. "It's a scout! Come on!" He started clambering after it.

Ye-Ye woke with an offended cry when Kalothia scrambled to her knees. "Sorry!" She tucked him into her shoulder and began climbing down after Nahir. A scout? It took her a few seconds to understand. The creature had not planned to attack them, but to alert its pack so they could attack as a group. Like a swarm of bees.

A howl tore through the air. Dread crawled over her skin. In the distance, a chorus of howls rose in answer.

Kalothia jumped the last few feet to the ground. The animal

stood snarling. Though it held back, its shoulders were low and its claws scratched at the earth. Kalothia snapped her spear out to its full length.

"They usually terrorize the little villages along the Galla-Padma border. I've never seen them so deep into Galla's interior." Nahir held his sword at the ready. "We call them kiyons." He stepped closer to Kalothia, and the kiyon tracked his movement with a cold stare. When he took her arm and began to ease backward into the forest, it growled and snapped its huge jaw.

"It's holding us here," Kalothia realized.

A high-pitched screech ripped through the trees. Closer this time.

"You have to go," Nahir said.

It was the first opportunity she'd had to look at him. Under his leather chest armor, he wore a black tunic and shokoto decorated with orange thread, a color that marked him as a Northern soldier. Despite spending the night wedged in a tree, he was as tidy and contained as ever. His black, locked hair was tied in a neat tail and hung down to the middle of his back. The three silver hoops he wore in his left ear proudly declared him a son of the North and contrasted with the dark coffee hue of his skin.

He stuck a hand into the pocket of his shokoto, pulled out a handful of cowrie shells, and handed them to her. "Take these. I'll hold them off; give you a head start. The town I told you about, Illupeju, is east of here. If I'm not there by sundown go north, to my father."

She rolled her eyes, fear making her short-tempered. "I'm going to ignore that since you've clearly lost your mind."

"The rest of the pack will be here any minute. Take the cowries and go."

She could hear the crash of foliage and growls of the searching animals, yet here he was wasting time. "If I go, they'll eat you, then hunt me down next. Stop being ridiculous! They're a pack. We have to fight them together."

The scout kiyon growled, its gaze switching between the humans and the surrounding foliage. Answering snarls and grunts came from all around them now.

"We need a plan," she added. "And fast."

A muzzle poked out of the bushes, its large jaws snapping loudly. Adrenaline rushed through her as, one by one, the other kiyons padded out to surround them. All right, the plan would be: stay alive.

She and Nahir moved without speaking, shifting until they were back-to-back. The kiyons closed in, their misshapen bodies unnerving, their postures poised to attack.

"Strike to kill, blind, or maim," Nahir said.

A flash of the woman Kalothia had stabbed the day before filled her head. She recalled the woman's wide eyes and the horrible give of her flesh beneath the knife. Her stomach turned. She swallowed and took a series of shallow breaths. She'd never fought people before, and she'd never had to defend herself against animals that behaved in unnatural ways. She hated these firsts, but she had to face them if they were to survive. If she had to kill these creatures she would.

There were six kiyons. They surrounded them now, growling low and gnashing their huge jaws. The first darted at Kalothia in a blur of fur. She swung her spear and it connected with a sharp crack. The animal shrieked in pain and backed away. Two more rushed at her.

It was muscle memory, hours of the same drills that moved her feet so she could snap the spear back and forth in a whirl of movement connecting with anything that came close. The kiyons fell back, howling with anger. She swiped a hand across her sweaty forehead and barely caught the shadow of movement that had her tilting her spear upward just in time to catch the kiyon launching itself at them from the trees. She let the momentum of the blow send it crashing into a nearby tree. It tried to stagger up but fell back with a whimper. Behind her, she could hear Nahir's steps crunching over the earth and the ragged sound of his breath as he fought.

One of the kiyons tried to slink toward her from the side while another raced at her, slid to a stop, reared back, then repeated the action. She smiled grimly at their tactics. It was a risk to shift the spear to one hand and reach for her dagger with the other, and sure enough, when she threw the dagger at the slinking creature, catching its foreleg, the other kiyon immediately leaped at her. She had to swing her spear with one hand.

Without the other hand to stabilize the spear, the kiyon was able to grab it in its powerful jaw and wrench it violently. She was dragged forward, away from Nahir's back, leaving him exposed and barely keeping her balance.

Immediately, a kiyon darted forward, teeth bared, to attack Nahir's blind spot. There was no finesse in her response, just a wild fumble for another dagger, a desperate throw, and a second of relief when the blade found the kiyon's throat and it crashed to the ground. She spun to the other kiyon, still fighting for her spear. Yanking it back, she drew the creature close enough to aim a hard kick at its chest. It screeched and released the spear.

Swiftly, she swung the weapon, catching the kiyon with a hard blow against its head. It staggered back. She was breathing hard. Every inch of her ached. But she straightened and braced her feet, ready for the next assault. The kiyons were panting too. Their next attack was slow and less coordinated. She gritted her teeth and struck fast and steady, hitting whatever flesh she could.

The kiyons had weakened further. Their attacks slowed until one gave a final shriek of anger and plunged into the woods in retreat. Its companions lingered for a moment, uncertain, before deciding to follow suit. They slunk back off into the woodland, cradling injured jaws and paws.

Kalothia waited, tensed, alert for their reappearance. She stayed that way until Nahir put a hand on her shoulder. "Anything broken?" His gaze swept over her, checking for damage.

She shook her head. Her legs wanted to collapse beneath her, but she willed herself to stay upright. "Can we go and find that town now?" Her words were slurred with exhaustion. "Before anything else comes looking for us."

ILLUPEJU

THEY'D WALKED FOR HOURS BEFORE SHE STOPPED SPINNING toward every creak and tensing at every animal cry.

"They're not following," Nahir told her.

She nodded, tried to let his certainty sink into her bones. It was easier to think when she wasn't twitching with nerves. But then her mind began to drift back to Clarit and Teacher and Aunty. A trembling started in her legs and traveled upward until her whole body shook. She forced her mind away, turning it toward other thoughts. "Tell me again. What is the plan?"

He looked her over carefully as though verifying she wasn't about to burst into hysterical tears. "We'll stop at Illupeju for supplies, then go north to my father."

Just a few days ago, she would have pointed out the folly of this plan. Galla's four territories maintained a careful balance of power. Teacher had told her that she could not live in the North, though it was Lord Godmayne—lord of the Northern Territory and Nahir's father—who financed her living arrangements. He'd said a royal in the North, regardless of how minor, would antagonize the other three lords. Furthermore, Lord Godmayne would appear a traitor if he took in supporters of the late queen and it would anger the king. She would have reminded Nahir of this and argued that she didn't want to go from one hiding place to another; she wanted to find her parents. But all that had changed now. Because she'd realized something.

"You weren't lying."

Nahir looked at her, a frown creasing his forehead. He said nothing.

"All of y-you, about my p-parents." Her words tumbled out in a stutter. She looked away, stared ahead at the trees—which were beginning to thin—and the soil that was turning from coffee to a deep red sandy texture. "There really are people trying to kill them . . . and me." She drew a breath, glanced at Nahir. Something passed over his features, a flash of something that was gone before she could decipher it. "I thought you were all lying to me, making me afraid, so I wouldn't try to leave the forest and find my parents. But you weren't." She thought of how often she'd sighed and sulked and grown angry when they'd repeated the same lines about the danger she'd been in. She'd been so difficult. Shame and grief burned hot in her stomach.

"The king is dead," Nahir said.

She stopped. Frowned. Shook her head to clear it. That was not the reply she'd been expecting. "What?"

Nahir's hands clenched into fists, then relaxed. His eyes met hers. "I came to tell you all . . . the king has died."

She blinked. Thoughts moved sluggishly through her head. The king was dead. Just like that. "I wished for his death," she confessed, unsure whether she thought the words or said them aloud.

Nahir watched her steadily but said nothing.

Ye-Ye swung from one of her shoulders to the other, sensing the change in atmosphere. He nuzzled against her, and somehow the movement soothed her. It occurred to her that Nahir had responded in sorts to what she'd been saying.

"My parents can stop running. I can stop hiding," she said.

Something swept through her at the realization. Relief? Hope? The buoyant emotion, whatever it was, was quickly crushed by new fears. "But the attack . . . ? Those people wanted me dead. Were they from the king?" Nahir was watching her with unreadable eyes. Had the king really ordered the attack just before his death?

"How did he die? Was it sudden?" Kalothia asked.

Nahir frowned. "The palace sent a messenger bird. I don't know the details. He'd been bedridden for years."

Yes, she'd heard that. Bedridden, yet still intent on hunting down her parents. On causing pain, right up to his last moment. She thought of Clarit, Teacher, and Aunty. She hoped his death had been painful: punishment at last for killing his wife. She would not mourn him. But how had he found her, and right before his death? It all seemed so . . . convenient.

Confusion, pain and joy, relief and distress: discordant emotions clanged inside her.

Nahir watched her for a long moment, but "Let's walk" was all he said.

A part of her was relieved that he didn't press her to talk anymore, and walking helped. It swallowed up some of the wild energy coursing through her. Soon the trees began to thin and the sky became visible in swaths of blue. They were nearing the edge of the forest.

"Cover your hair."

She turned to find Nahir holding out a white kerchief. She put a hand to her head, touching the cornrows. "Oh!" She thought of the big man with the cutlass who'd torn her wrapper from her head. How had she forgotten so quickly? "Do you think they're still looking for me?"

Nahir paused and seemed to consider his words. "Yes, but they probably weren't expecting you to survive. We might get a head start. It could take a few days for them to receive new instructions from whoever conscripted them."

She glanced at him. "'From whoever conscripted them'?" she repeated. "You think someone other than the king . . . ?"

He shook his head and shifted his feet uncomfortably. "No. The king would have sent the order through an underling, though. Someone from the Gallan court that he trusted."

Kalothia nodded. "They were speaking Padman. The attackers."

Nahir stared at her. "Padma hates Galla."

Relations between Padma and Galla had been bad for decades, and Nahir had often complained that the king's illness kept him from dealing with the Padman attacks in the East, which then grew worse when nothing was done to repel them. It made no sense that the king would recruit Padman assassins. Galla had its own spies and fighters; there was no reason for him to join forces with a hostile neighbor country. Was it possible that whatever illness had plagued the king and caused him to withdraw from public life after the queen's execution had also affected his state of mind?

"Although," Nahir added after a moment, "there are plenty of Padman mercenaries who would do anything for money. The same goes for the state forces at times. They are said to act with equal dishonor when it suits them. Either way it would explain that kiyon attack. I think the Padmans are crossbreeding them to use as hunting dogs. I did wonder why they were so far from the border." Nahir scratched his head. "I'm not sure. I need to think."

She tied the kerchief quickly with deft fingers. "Shouldn't we search for my parents now . . . ?" Now that the king was dead. Her mouth couldn't say what her brain was still processing.

"No." He didn't even pause to think.

She gave him a sharp look. Then was forced to ask "Why?" when he failed to elaborate.

"Because a new ruler brings uncertainty. We'll go north and wait for the royal court and the country to settle down. My father will be on his way to Port Caspin by now. All the lords will gather for the funeral. But he doesn't have to be in residence to cover you with his protection in the North."

She sighed, exasperated by his determination to hide her. She tried to tamp her frustration down and look at the situation from his point of view. If her parents had been in such grave danger, maybe the king's death wasn't an automatic switch that fixed the problem, maybe things needed some time to settle. And the Padman connection was new, as far as she could tell.

Nahir knew the world better than she did. It made sense to trust his judgment, but didn't he understand how desperate she was to see her parents? How waiting made her want to crawl out of her skin?

"Do you think they'll stay in hiding?"

Nahir didn't answer. He didn't even look her way.

A sudden fear clutched at her throat. Could they be dead? No! But she couldn't bring herself to ask. Instead, she mused, "Teacher always said it would cause trouble if you took me north."

His mouth tightened, stubborn now. "Don't worry about that. The North can defend itself."

Teacher had also scoffed at the idea that the East could keep her any safer, but she didn't voice that thought. She didn't like her concerns being so casually dismissed; she liked it even less that when she opened her mouth to argue, Nahir motioned her to silence, his eyes on a nearby tree.

She followed his gaze and was surprised to spot a man perched high up the trunk of a palm tree. "What is he doing?"

"Palm wine tapper," Nahir explained briefly. "Probably harmless, but we have to stay alert. The attackers could be anywhere."

She shielded her eyes with her hand and tried to get a better look at the man. She was fascinated. She'd read about the men who climbed trees and extracted the sweet tree sap for fermenting, but she'd never seen one. The man, bare except for a length of fabric looped about his hips and tucked around his legs, did not notice them. He didn't look dangerous, but Nahir hurried her along until the tapper had disappeared in the trees behind them.

It was then she realized that, over the sound of birdsong and their crunching footsteps, she could hear a distant rumble. Gradually, the rumble turned into voices, the rattle of wheels, and grunting animals. They emerged from the tree line to find themselves at a road. It was wide and paved with red bricks that matched the red sand on either side. The road was a hive of activity: wagons drawn by horses, men and women on horseback, herds of animals, people on foot pulling carts.

"This is the King's Highway," Nahir told her.

She nodded. She knew this road. She'd seen it on numerous maps, including in the book of maps Teacher had given her for her age day. Teacher had been diligent about teaching her history and geography.

It was the longest road in the Eastern region, running as it did from the Northern desert to the Southern Sea. Yet she'd never seen it. She couldn't have pictured the red dust that billowed in clouds under the wheels of tens of wagons pulled by teams of horses. The wagon beds that bulged with goods and animals. The smell of sweaty fur and dung that stung her nose while the rattle of wagon wheels and clop of hooves filled the afternoon. The way the road dipped and rose, stretching off endlessly in either direction.

King Osura had paved it, turning it from a worn dirt path into this magnificent thing. The work had been done the year he traveled the length of the country with his new wife, Queen Sylvia. The builders had been tasked to pave the road just ahead of the journeying couple, so they could see it happening. The history scrolls Kalothia had read talked of the king's brilliance and foresight but had made no mention of how several years later the same king had executed his then-pregnant wife and mother of his son, Prince Olu, thereby fracturing the royal court and stoking deadly tensions that still rattled across the country.

Nahir took her hand. "We have to cross."

It didn't seem possible with so many vehicles traveling at all kinds of speeds in both directions, but he pulled her out into the road. She wasn't sure if wagons slowed for them or if they just timed it well, but they managed to dodge the traffic and hurry across.

On the other side, a wooden board had been carved out to read ILLUPEJU. A beaten path took them into the woodland and then to a deep, wide trench. It abutted a wall of earth: muddy red sand packed tight to form a solid fortification over ten feet high. Kalothia stared in fascination. She'd lived in the forest for as long as she could remember. She'd never entered a town.

"It's built for defense," Nahir explained, nodding at the wall. He pointed up at a tree that towered over it from the far side. It took a moment for her to make out the man who sat deep in its branches, watching their approach. "They'll know we're coming before we reach the gate."

Illupeju's gate was a short walk along the wall. The man guarding it was tall and broad. His shokoto and tunic were white. The short sleeves of the latter revealed muscled arms that bunched as he searched the people waiting to pass through the gate. He asked questions of each one, and his face was hard and unyielding as he assessed the answers. A jittery man with a wild forest of hair was turned away as were two men with sheathed swords who claimed they'd come to visit a sister but could not agree on her name.

Kalothia was too intrigued by the process to wonder what explanation they would give for their visit until they were shuffling forward and the guard was looming over them. She hoped Nahir had a decent lie prepared, but was startled when the gatekeeper stepped back, bent, and touched his right hand to the ground in a bow of respect. "Welcome, Captain," he said in a quiet boom. "My apologies for the wait."

Ye-Ye chose this moment to leap from her shoulder. Kalothia didn't even have time to cry in alarm before Nahir had snatched the vervet from the air and secured him in a firm grip.

The man gave Ye-Ye a chiding look, then shifted his gaze back to Nahir. "If he's yours, you'd better keep a tighter rein on him, or he might end up in somebody's cooking pot."

Ye-Ye grumbled unrepentantly and blew his lips noisily at the guard.

"Behave!" Kalothia hissed, taking him from Nahir's hands.

"Don't linger on the streets." The guard was speaking to Nahir again. "When a king passes with no heir, people grow agitated and bold." He accepted the cowrie Nahir offered for the toll and waved them through.

"How did he know you?" Kalothia asked.

Nahir gave a rueful smile and shook his wrist where his army beads hung. "Should have removed these." He did so now, slipping them into a pocket in his shokoto.

Kalothia was only half listening. There was so much to take in. The round, red-baked mud huts with thatched roofs; the children who ran around, kicking up sand and screaming; goats and chickens wandering about leisurely. The women who walked with swaying hips, wooden bowls balanced on their heads filled with food or colorful wares, women pounding huge pestles in mortars in a steady rhythm, women cooking over open-air fires.

"They're all wearing white," she said.

"The color of mourning," Nahir replied. "If we don't want to stand out, we'd better change."

They moved farther into the town, and the huts gave way to red-brick buildings larger in size. "Where are the men?" Kalothia asked, suddenly realizing all the activity was being conducted by women.

Nahir cast her a baffled glance. "They're there."

She frowned, looked closer. He was right. The men sat in huddles, or slept, under the shade of canopy trees, or they stood chatting in the shade cast by buildings.

"'The burden of learning and leadership falls on men,'" Kalothia quoted one of Aunty's favorite Goddess precepts. "But it seems the burden of working falls on the women."

"Southerners," Nahir grunted. He and Clarit came from the North and referred to all Gallans below the Northern lands as "Southerners," often in the same dismissive tone. Clarit said that in the North, the Goddess and Mother Nature met head-on and the Goddess was forced to give way.

The harsh climate, rugged terrain, and bordering desert made survivalists of all the Northern inhabitants. Both men and women were educated; they worked the land together, tended the children, and defended the borders. Clarit joked that anything less would be like fighting with one hand tied behind your back. Women held leadership positions in the names of fathers and brothers, an artful concession to the Goddess's rules. In the North, the precepts were interpreted in ways that meshed with daily life.

Kalothia watched with annoyance as a woman with a baby tied to her back, a small child clutching her hand, and a basket filled with baked bricks balanced on her head strolled past a circle of seated men in deep discussion. It seemed to her that you could learn and lead while also pitching in with the work.

A man's deep voice singing a plaintive melody cut through the afternoon heat. As they moved farther into the town, the owner of the voice came into view. He was also dressed in white and his voice was pure and clear. It was as inviting as a cool breeze, and people stopped in the street to listen.

"King Osura, son of King Osuji, son of King Olatun, right back to the Book of Kings has departed for his celestial home.

"He delivered rice to the poor, he forged alliances, he perfected the King's Highway, he married the beautiful Queen Sylvia, and he cried himself sick when she betrayed him."

Kalothia jolted in surprise at the suggestion of the late queen's infidelity. It was so different from the way Teacher and Aunty had told the story of the Great Upset. They had always stressed the queen's innocence. An unhappy murmur rippled through the crowd. Kalothia noted the upset expressions and wondered that Queen Sylvia seemed to have supporters, even here. The singer sensed his audience's displeasure and quickly moved on. Nahir tugged her arm. "We don't have much time."

She followed him reluctantly, her ears straining to hear the end of the song.

"He raised a boy, our next king, lost in a fire. Goddess save Galla and grant us a king . . ."

SHE KNEW IMMEDIATELY WHEN THEY REACHED THE TOWN'S temple. It was a round, red clay building. The shape and construction reminded her of home. The temple's curving walls were punctured with gaping doorways where men dressed in white crossed in and out. Aloe vera grew prodigiously around its walls, conspicuously skirting a section where the precepts had been carved. Above them was the symbol of the Goddess: two spheres intersecting, representing the circles of nature and humanity. It was a symbol that had adorned her own home, thanks to Aunty. She didn't need to read the precepts to know what they said. Aunty had recited them from memory every morning:

1. Look for me in nature. I live in all things.
2. Follow my priests, the bridge between earth and sky.
3. The burden of learning and leadership falls on men.
4. The modest and peaceful woman will be crowned with blessings.

They had rounded to the back of the temple when a woman stepped out of the dark interior and into the bright sunshine. She was the most magnificent woman Kalothia had ever seen. Her hair was a thick black cloud around her face. Her skin was dark as obsidian stone and glowed with energy. Her eyes were large and clear, and shaped like almonds. It was impossible to tell her age: she seemed both youthful as a new adolescent and old as a village elder. She wore an indigo wrapper tied under her arms that hugged her long body and fell to graze her ankles.

"What?" Nahir asked.

"That woman . . ." Kalothia breathed, awestruck.

Ye-Ye leaped from her shoulder and bounded forward. The woman bent to rub a gentle hand over his head, but her eyes were fixed on Kalothia.

"What woman?" Nahir asked.

"She's right th—" Kalothia said. But the temple doorway was empty. The woman was gone.

Ye-Ye mewled unhappily.

"Where?" Nahir asked.

"She came out of the temple . . . I just saw her . . ."

Nahir looked at her strangely. "Women aren't allowed in the southern temples unless it's a feast day."

She knew this. And yet, the woman had been right there, and she *had* come from the temple. But where was she now? It didn't make any sense.

"Come on. We should hurry." Nahir took her arm and pulled her down the street. He led them to a large, dusty courtyard packed with horses and donkeys drinking from troughs. Men sat at tables throwing dice and pebbles, or they stood around the courtyard walls drinking from tankards and watching the play at the tables.

She caught Nahir giving her a quick once over. She was certain she looked as rough as she felt. Her clothes were rumpled, torn, and covered in dried mud. Her skin was dry and scratched in numerous places. It was some kind of witchcraft that Nahir still managed to look clean and composed.

"We'll get a room, clean up, find horses and supplies, then head north." He laid out the plan succinctly. "Try to keep your pet quiet. Monkeys are rarely kept as pets, and we don't want to draw any unnecessary attention to ourselves."

She stroked Ye-Ye's back as they crossed the courtyard and whispered "Shush" to him. He lay docilely against her neck, and she hoped this meant he planned to behave.

Behind the gaming tables, they entered a low doorway that said GUESTS. The door led to a cool and quiet room. An elderly man, also dressed in white, sat at a table pruning a small plant with a sharp knife.

Nahir greeted him. "Good afternoon, sir." He bowed, touching his right hand to the floor, and the old man nodded in acknowledgment.

Kalothia slid to her knees in the respectful bow Aunty had taught her for elders. The owner raised his brows in surprise.

"She's from the village," Nahir explained, tugging her back to her feet. "You can just dip your knees instead of the full bow," he murmured.

Kalothia tensed with embarrassment. It was so difficult trying to apply theories Aunty and Teacher had taught her about the real world when she had never gotten to use any of it before now.

The owner smiled warmly at her. "It's nice to see a young girl who values the old ways."

"How is the day treating you?" Nahir asked in a friendly tone she had never heard him use before. It wasn't that he was an unfriendly person. He was just—direct.

The man sighed and flapped his hand at a noisy fly. "The Goddess has taken our king. Who will take the throne now?" He shook his head. "We pray the Goddess grants us peace."

Nahir and Kalothia pressed their palms to their mouths to seal the prayer. "Her will be done," Nahir agreed. "Can we trouble you for a room? It would be a blessing to get out of this heat."

"Of course." The man leaned forward, joints popping loudly, and cracked open a large book on the table. "One room?" His eyes swept over them curiously.

"Yes, one room."

"For you and . . . ?"

"My wife," Nahir supplied.

Kalothia twitched with surprise. She coughed to cover up her reaction.

The man gave them another searching look, but merely said, "Your name?"

Nahir looked around, eyes falling on the ink jar. "Hetti," he said, giving the Northern word for ink.

Kalothia coughed again. This time to cover a laugh. He was so bad at this. It was nice to see him out of his element.

"Hetti," the man mused as he wrote. "Not a name I have heard before. You have not traveled far." He eyed the small bags they each held.

Nahir paused, looked blank.

"We were robbed," Kalothia blurted.

The man's eyes narrowed in suspicion. "You were robbed?" he asked doubtfully.

"Yes!" she squeaked, wishing she'd left Nahir to do the talking.

"The rest of our possessions were taken," Nahir said apologetically. "My wife was quite shaken."

Kalothia looked at the floor, hoping her embarrassment doubled sufficiently as distress.

"Hey, la! I hope you are unhurt." With Nahir's confirmation, the owner was suddenly all concern.

"We are well. But if a bath could also be drawn, that would be helpful," Nahir said.

The man rose creakily to his feet. "Of course! We usually ask guests to use the bathing room out back or the bathing house down the street, but you have been through enough. *Elebata!*" he bellowed in a loud voice that belied his stiff movements and bent frame.

A young woman came running, slippers slapping noisily against the floor.

"Oh-ya! Show this couple to a room in the guesthouse. Then have the boys take the cast-iron tub up and ready it for a bath. Quick! Quick!"

The girl hurried to obey.

A few minutes later, they were settled in an airy room on the third floor. Kalothia watched as the girl flitted about the room, checking the bedsheets and candles, while men filled the bathing tub. She sensed Nahir's impatience. His face was placid, but she could read restlessness in the tense set of his shoulders and the occasional tap of his index finger. As soon as the tub was full and the servants gone, he rose.

"I'm going to find horses, clothes, and food for the journey north. Have a bath and rest. I won't be long." He walked over to where she stood by the balcony doors and reached over her to close the drapes.

She could smell the sweat and shea butter on his skin. Something about his proximity made her skin heat. She scooted back, trying to put a little distance between them. When he glanced curiously at her, she looked away, embarrassed and confused by her own strange reaction.

"Lock the door behind me," he instructed before slipping out.

SETTLED IN THE BATHING TUB WITH WARM WATER LAPPING around her, Kalothia let the shell she had constructed to keep the horrors of the previous day at bay crumble. Once again, she saw Clarit's wide, terrified gaze as she lay paralyzed, fighting for breath. Kalothia's mind filled with Teacher's open, unseeing eyes, his cracked glasses out of reach.

Tears coursed down her face and splashed noisily into the bathwater. She gagged and choked when the room's scent was overlaid with the rancid smell that had surrounded Aunty as she drew her last breaths. Their bodies would still be there, she realized. Lying on the hard ground in the heat, at the mercy of predators. Sobs shook her. After all their love and care and sacrifice, there was nothing she could do to protect the people she loved most in the world. There would be no funeral pyre, no blessings to ease their way to the Goddess. She sat in the tub and cried until the water cooled and her skin pebbled with goose bumps.

When she was wrung dry, she rose from the tub and tied a bedsheet around her chest. She stood in front of the mirror to fix her hair. Ye-Ye explored the room while she worked. As she unpicked the cornrows Aunty had braided, she stared at the red thickness, then down at the pendant around her throat. Did Aunty, Teacher, and Clarit die because of her heritage? Because her parents had defied a king?

Guilt coiled around her lungs, strangling her breath. She had to find her parents, to make the sacrifice of those she'd lost worthwhile. She twisted her hair back into four thick cornrows. She thought of Nahir's terse answers when she'd suggested starting the search immediately. She hated that he'd rejected her ideas and made decisions for her while refusing to share his reasoning. It would be easier to accept not getting her way if he opened up a little more and explained why. She sighed. She didn't want to cause Nahir or his father any more problems or get caught up in a civil war. She would follow his lead for now. She would go north, just as he had insisted; she'd wait for a new ruler to be chosen.

The knock on the door made her jump.

"It's me." The low gravel of Nahir's voice calmed her instantly.

She opened the door, wrapped in the bedsheet. Nahir blinked at her and seemed to freeze for a moment, then he coughed and turned away, busying himself with closing the door.

A wave of awkwardness crashed over her too. It was bizarre— she'd walked around the house dressed only in a wrapper without a thought every day, the bedsheet offered just as much coverage, but something about the small room and it being only the two of them made her feel naked. "Did you bring me clothes, or should I get used to this wrapper?" she asked to cover her unease.

Her tart tone broke him out of his discomfort. He tossed a dress and matching wrapper on the bed. "Put these on." Then he walked over to the closed drapes that concealed the balcony and drew them back. He stared down at the courtyard making a determined show of ignoring her presence.

She wasted no time slipping into the simple white dress. Nahir had judged her size correctly, and it fit easily. She turned the wrapper into a headwrap. Nahir seemed to be absorbed by something in the courtyard.

"What's so interesting?" she asked, trying to peer around him.

His gaze still on the window, he reached behind himself to push her back into the room. "Something's changed out there," he warned. "I think they've found us. Get your things. We need to leave."

She barely heard him. His hand pressed against her chest and it felt like the skin there had been branded, and her heart was fluttering in a curious and thoroughly uncomfortable way. What was this stupid feeling that kept overtaking her?

"What's wrong?" Nahir asked.

She shook herself out of her stupor and began shoving her few possessions into her small bag while Nahir strapped on his armor.

There was a noise in the corridor. "Quick!" Nahir said. "Move the bed! Block the door."

She hurried to help push the bed until they had it wedged against the door.

The door handle rattled loudly.

7

ESCAPE

THE RATTLE TURNED TO POUNDING. THE DOOR SHOOK IN ITS
frame from the force. Another crash, and it began to splinter. Ye-Ye
screeched in fear and burrowed against Kalothia's neck. She didn't
feel the terror she'd felt in the forest. Maybe because there was day-
light. Maybe she'd reached her emotional limit. She reached into her
bag and began to pull her spear free.

Nahir shook his head. "If we fight it gives them time to gather
reinforcements. We'll be trapped here." He threw open the balcony
doors and stepped out. "Fire! We need water!" he yelled down at the
courtyard. Below, men leaped to their feet and ran for either the well,
a pump, or the horse trough.

"We're going up." He tugged her bag out of her hands and drew
the strap over her head and shoulder, then put his hands on her waist
and lifted her enough to reach the bottom of the balcony above them.

In the room behind them, the doorframe gave way with a crack.

The years of annoying Aunty by climbing trees suddenly proved their usefulness. Kalothia swung herself easily up and over the balcony. While Nahir climbed up behind her, she let herself into the room.

Furious voices speaking in what sounded like Padman drifted up from the room below. She put on an extra burst of speed as Nahir joined her and they took the back stairs up two flights and burst out onto a flat roof.

The sun had not yet reached its midday peak but it blazed furiously overhead and Kalothia felt sweat running down her back. Nahir looked over the side of the building, down at the tall kaplor tree that reached halfway up the guesthouse, then across it to the neighboring building. She could see the calculations running through his head.

"I couldn't make the leap to that building." She nodded at the next roof. "But I could use the tree to climb down."

Nahir shot her a skeptical look.

On the far side of the roof, two men appeared from the staircase. The strangers sprinted forward, halving the distance within heartbeats. They were out of time and options.

She took three steps back, pressed Ye-Ye tightly against her chest, ran, and leaped off the roof. Air rushed by as her body arced through the air. Her stomach turned over. The tree grew in her vision until it was all she could see, until she was tumbling through layers of leaves, branches stabbing, scratching, and clawing at her. Finally, she came to a stop. She was wedged in a nest of branches, dazed and stunned but unharmed. Ye-Ye was safe too. She breathed a sigh of relief that was cut short by a crash above her. Leaves and wood rained down.

Nahir. She began to scramble out of the way. The lower part of the tree had no branches so she had to grip it with her arms and legs and shimmy down.

Finally, her feet touched the ground. She stood, swaying, her breath panting in and out. People watched curiously from doorways, but nobody looked dangerous.

Ye-Ye swung out of the tree to land on her shoulder.

A few seconds later Nahir jumped down. "Quick, we have to get to the horses."

He led them in a stumbling run down the side street, around the corner away from the guesthouse, and then down a series of alleys and streets. She kept up, her ears and eyes alert for followers. At last, they turned into an empty stable yard, where two horses had been tethered. Nahir put a hand out to halt her on the edge of the space. He scanned the area. The horses whickered impatiently.

Kalothia caught a flash of indigo blue in the corner of her eye. But when she whirled to get a better look, there was nothing. Her pendant suddenly felt hot against her skin. She tugged at it uneasily. "I feel like we're being watched," she murmured.

"Me too. But I think we'd draw more attention if we went looking for new horses. Let's mount quickly and ride for the gates."

She nodded.

"On three," he said.

She braced herself, ready to sprint across the yard and leap onto one of the horses.

"One . . . two . . ."

The walls of the stable yard exploded.

8

KIDNAP

KALOTHIA CAME TO SLOWLY. HER HEAD FELT FOGGY AND PAIN speared through every part of her body. When she opened her eyes, it felt like sharp blades were being shoved into her head. She hurriedly snapped them closed and tried to get her bearings with her other senses. She was on a horse: the large, warm body beneath her jolted in time with the steady clop of hooves. Her wrists were tied, she suddenly realized with sharp horror. They'd been bound together and secured to the saddle of the horse. Which meant the hard body pressed up behind her couldn't be Nahir. Now that she was paying attention, she realized it reeked of old sweat.

She slitted her eyes open. The blinding pain was less this time. She was on a horse that was trotting along a dirt track that wound through a farm of some kind. Rows of plants surrounded them on both sides, arching over the path so that leaves slapped her face as they rode. She tilted her head back slightly and saw that the sun now hung directly overhead. It should have reassured her that only a short amount of time had passed. But in that interval the town of Illupeju had disappeared along with Nahir. She had no idea where she was or who she was with.

She began to struggle. A rough hand grabbed her neck and squeezed violently. She tried to twist free, but the arms held her firmly in place; she tried to breathe, but the hand at her neck was too tight. Just as black spots began to color her vision, the hand released her. She coughed and dragged air into her body through her aching throat.

A blast of hot breath slapped against her ear. "If you struggle again, I will break your neck." It was a man's voice, his accent thick, with a lisp.

She stilled.

Nahir! Where was he? The thought sliced through the physical pain, the growing fear; it cut through everything, slashing at her insides like a machete.

There'd been an explosion in the stable yard. She remembered the walls collapsing on them.

"Nahir?" she said. Her voice was a croak.

"Your guard?" her kidnapper said. "The Goddess has him now." A rumble of laughter filled his voice.

Dread rushed through her. "No."

"I planned to finish him off myself, but the building that fell on him had already done the job. An army captain. Such a loss." His voice was sarcastic, and he shook his wrist to draw her attention to the colorful array of beads that hung from it. Nahir's army beads.

Pain sliced through her. It was leagues beyond the physical discomfort she felt. It dragged on her limbs, tightened her throat, blurred her eyes. She tried to reach her pendant but couldn't manage it with her bound hands. The thick cords of bamboo rope wrapped around her wrists bit into her skin when she tried. This man was lying, she told herself. He had to be. But the pain throbbed through her all the same.

"Who are you? Why are you doing this to me? To my family, my friends?" She spat the questions through parched lips.

"Somebody in Port Caspin wants you dead. They'll think you died in the rubble back there. Meanwhile, you're still worth a lot of money. I'm going to sell you to the highest bidder."

A shiver ran through her. The plants grew thicker and taller, blocking off any view of the world beyond. It was as though she'd been snatched from the earth and it was just her, this dangerous man who would either kill or sell her, and the crushing pain of losing everything. The plants danced and whispered in a faint breeze. Where was Ye-Ye? Was he buried beneath rubble too? A whimper crawled from her belly and slipped from her mouth.

"Yes. Be afraid!" said the faceless man behind her.

They did not travel for long. The plants came to an end and the horse trotted out across a sparse wood into a clearing, where it stopped. A man stood waiting. He was big and brawny with a face that glistened purple like a washed grape. Fury was in every rigid line of his body. "Have you lost your mind?" he shouted. "You were supposed to kill her! Why is she here?"

The man on horseback dismounted but kept one hand clamped around her wrist, holding her in place. When he spoke again, Kalothia saw that he had lost most of his teeth. The gaps gave his words the pronounced lisp. "Have *you* lost your mind? Do you know how much she is worth? Her soldier is dead. She won't give us trouble."

Her soldier is dead. The words were boulders blocking all other thoughts in her head.

"Why are you complicating this job?" the other man shouted. "Our orders were to kill her. We kill her. That is the end."

"Maybe for you, Gati! I am not a sheep, mindlessly following its shepherd. We can get a second fee, then leave Padma and Galla behind." Something tucked into the waistband of his shokoto caught her eye. It was the handle of Nahir's favorite dagger. That blade was as precious to Nahir as his own life. The bracelet, the dagger, the man's words, it was too much. Grief crashed over her. It was a whirlpool sucking her down. She couldn't breathe. Couldn't move. Couldn't feel. A numbness spread through her body. She watched her captors argue and felt nothing.

"She has to die," the brawny man—Gati—stated.

"If you have enough money and can afford to pass up something as valuable as this"—the man with the lisp gestured at Kalothia— "then leave. I will manage the matter myself." His hand moved to the hilt of his sword.

Gati's face tightened. "Our orders were to kill her. To remove any obstacles. That is why we killed her guardians. To remove all traces. Are you an obstacle?"

The lisper's hand flexed on his sword hilt.

Gati drew his sword.

And then they were on each other, iron clanging against iron, feet kicking up dust.

Kalothia looked on dispassionately. She felt exhausted. What did it matter which one of these men survived? One was going to kill her;

the other sell her. She'd fought hard to survive, but maybe this was her fate. Despair wrapped around her. Maybe the Goddess meant for her to lose everybody and finally her own life.

A furry body slipped out of the saddlebag. Tiny paws scuttled up the fabric covering her thigh until a soft weight landed on her arm. It wasn't until Ye-Ye climbed to her shoulder and hung from her hair to peer into her face that she recognized him.

"Ye-Ye!" she breathed.

His little features were scrunched with worry. Tears bloomed from her eyes and streamed down her face, dripping from her chin. Ye-Ye brushed his hairy cheek against hers. She tried to reach up, to touch him, but a tug of the thick bamboo rope against her wrists warned her that she could not.

A desperate grunt dragged her eyes back to the fight. Gati was bearing down on the other man now. His sword was swift and ruthless. The other man was trying to block the blows, but his technique was weak. Suddenly, he gave an animal-like cry of pain, high-pitched and wild. Gati had skewered him in the side. He fell to the ground, blood pouring from the gash. He clutched weakly at it while Gati brought his sword down, separating the man's head from his body.

Kalothia gagged and turned away. He would come for her next.

"Run!" Kalothia whispered to Ye-Ye. He gave a piercing cry, scurried down her body, and raced off. She was alone.

The man called Gati approached her now. His mouth was set. His eyes hard and emotionless. He flexed his hand on his sword.

This is it, she thought. Under the numbness was anger. There would be no justice now for Aunty, Teacher, Clarit, or Nahir. Even for herself. They would disappear and whoever had ordered their deaths would crow with triumph. And she would never find her parents.

Ye-Ye yipped behind her and the man stiffened. Surely, he wasn't afraid of a small monkey?

"Who are you?" the man asked.

Kalothia frowned. Who was he talking to? She half turned and jolted when she found a woman standing in the clearing with them.

It was the woman from the temple. She wore the same indigo wrapper tied under her arms, her hair fanned out in a thick black cloud, just as it had earlier, and she glowed with energy. Where had she come from?

"Who are you?" the man shouted again. "What are you doing here? If you value your life, you'll leave now." He raised his sword.

The woman smiled at his threat. Yet there was no humor in her large, clear eyes. They shifted to look directly at Kalothia, and it was as though the air had been sucked from Kalothia's lungs. It was as painful as trying to look directly at the sun. Kalothia closed her eyes against the powerful gaze.

She could hear the man shouting. Suddenly, there was a brush of cool skin against hers. She opened her eyes in time to see the ropes fall from her wrists. She stared in shock, confusion. She looked up. The woman was gone. Nothing but trees, soil and open sky, and the man with the sword. He was blinking, dazzled, like she had been. It took a moment for her to understand the opportunity she now had. Immediately, she slid off the horse. By some miracle her bag was still draped about her body. She pulled her dagger free.

She dismissed the mystery of the woman, focusing her attention on the immediate threat.

Play to your strengths, Nahir's training came to her. Her heart squeezed. Nahir! She pushed the thought away and focused on her opponent. He was mid-height, well-built. Close combat—close enough to use her dagger—would favor him and his superior strength. However, he had just fought a tough battle. His chest still rose and fell with the exertion.

She scanned the ground. The dead man's sword lay nearby. If she could reach that . . . She patted the horse on its rump so it moved off in a trot, safe from danger, and waited for Gati to make the first move.

He lunged. A fierce thrust. She ducked, came up, and threw her dagger.

It flew true, thudding into the shoulder of his sword arm. He grunted with pain.

Kalothia scooped up the dead man's sword. She brought it up in time to block Gati's blow with a clash. It was significantly weaker than his previous one. The knife was still embedded in his arm and he was struggling to wield his sword. Beads of sweat dripped from his forehead. He clenched his teeth. He knew he was in trouble.

She jabbed and thrust to get him moving and force him to block. Then she arced her sword in a decorative butterfly pattern that Nahir had taught her and the man's sword flew out of his hand while her blade went to his throat.

"Who sent you?" Kalothia demanded.

The man's face was harsh with fury. His mouth a hard line of granite. He did not reply.

"Who sent you?" she asked again, this time in Padman.

The attacker raised an admiring brow. "She speaks the enemy tongue."

She pressed the point of her blade into the soft skin of his neck. The apple in the man's throat bobbed reflexively. His eyes hardened. "Answer me," she said. "Who sent you? Why?"

He grinned at her. His teeth were dull yellow slabs in his mouth. Crooked and uneven. But he stayed resolutely silent.

She groaned with frustration. She wanted to ram the sword into the man's throat. She wanted to punish him for the events of the past few days. For all she had lost. The huge well of pain inside her was big enough to slice his grinning face clean off his body.

She had to drag herself away. Pull her sword arm back with steely determination. The man's smile widened. Before she knew it, he'd torn the dagger from his shoulder. Blood gushed from the wound. He staggered then fell to his knees.

There was too much blood. He wouldn't survive it, but he couldn't die. She needed answers. She looked around for something to bind the wound. Finding nothing, she tore the wrapper from her head.

When she reached for him, he slapped her away. "I hope you meet an early death like your mother," he spat, his voice a rasp now. He glared at her with hate. "I hope your cowardly father never finds rest."

She shrank back from his words. "What do you know of my parents?"

He closed his eyes.

"Tell me!" she shouted, shaking him.

His breath rasped in and out, his fingers twitched, and the blood pool grew and grew.

She kept shouting at him, but he said no more.

Finally, he was still and silent.

She watched, unmoving, for several minutes, her body in shock. Then Ye-Ye chirped beside her. She bent and picked him up. She rested her face against his soft, furry body as she cried. What did all this mean?

She reached a hand for the pendant around her neck. What had that man known about her parents? She shook her head. It was so full it ached. What should she do now?

She stroked Ye-Ye and tried to think. The kidnappers had talked of Port Caspin. Her parents had fled from the royal court in Port Caspin. It was the most obvious place to go for answers. It was also the most dangerous. Nahir would have been appalled, but he was gone. There was nobody to stop her.

She sucked in a deep breath and drew herself up. She would go to the capital and search for answers. She had nothing left to lose. If whoever had orchestrated this was in Port Caspin, she would find them and make them pay. She wiped her tears and tied her wrapper back over her hair. She had to approach one of the dead men to retrieve Nahir's army beads and dagger. It was a grisly job, but she refused to leave any part of him with these thugs. She searched the ground for her dagger, cleaned it, and slipped it into her bag. Finally, she hitched up her dress and mounted one of the men's horses, kicking it into a trot.

NEW FRIENDS

KALOTHIA FOUND THE PLANT-SHROUDED PATH THAT HAD LED her to the clearing. She followed it in the opposite direction. When she emerged on the other side, she was still in woodland, but she could hear distant sounds of life. A short ride later and she was standing again at the wide, bustling King's Highway, probably just a furlong from where she had stood with Nahir hours earlier. Tears prickled her eyes. She blinked them back and shoved down the desire to collapse beside the road and howl. The sun had slid from its zenith but was still hours from sunset. She needed to start moving south.

For several long minutes she watched as vehicles rumbled past. There were men on foot leading horse-pulled wagons, men on horse-back steering herds of animals, men riding solo and men riding in packs. Occasionally, she would spot a woman, always accompanied by a man. She recalled Aunty scolding Clarit each time she arrived for her scheduled posting by herself. "The East is not like the North. Women here do not travel alone." Aunty would quote the Goddess precept: *"The modest and peaceful woman will be crowned with blessings."*

Clarit would roll her eyes. "I'm peaceful until others trouble my peace," she'd retort, stroking the cudgel that she wielded so expertly.

Kalothia could see the courage it would have taken for Clarit to ride these roads unaccompanied. Maybe a courage nurtured by growing up somewhere where women's freedoms were broader. The way some of the men looked at her as they passed made her question if she had a similar courage. She was grateful for the weapons in her bag, though she prayed she would not need them again for a while. The food she'd packed had been eaten in the forest, but she still had the cowries Nahir had given her and she had a healthy horse. Her situation was not desperate. But the thought of traveling the vast, busy road alone terrified her. She resolved to join a group.

She stood uncertainly on the shoulder of the road, feeling the time pass with each breeze that shimmered by. Her horse stamped impatiently. It flicked its tail at a fly, then blew out a gust of breath.

At last, a long convoy appeared in the middle of the highway. Wagon after wagon roped together, driven by men. But toward the end of the train was a group of mounted women. They were young, her age. Three had babies tied to their backs. Something anxious inside her released. Without thinking, she tightened her knees against the horse's sides and urged it forward, out into the mad scramble of traffic.

She had to weave deftly around the sea of travelers; at one point she feared she'd lost the convoy, but when she reached the middle of the highway, she found the distinctly roped wagons still streaming by. From there it was a simple matter to trot alongside it until she reached the women.

"Welcome, sister!" one of the women ducked her head politely and called to her. She had two horizontal scars on each cheek. Her hair was parted into triangles, each partition wrapped in black thread like a spider's leg, then all the legs were tied together in a crown. Her skin was the soft brown of cork wood.

The other women echoed the greeting, dipping their heads, then raising them to welcome her with smiles and curious eyes.

She smiled back, immediately at ease. "Thank you." She fell into step alongside them. "Do you know the way to Port Caspin?"

The curious gazes sharpened. "Who are you traveling with?" asked the woman with the threaded hair who had greeted her first.

Kalothia wondered if she should pretend to have friends; she didn't want to draw attention to herself. But she felt safe under the woman's gentle smile, it was a tiny piece of comfort in the whirling chaos of her life. "I'm alone," she admitted.

The women's expressions changed to shock. One clucked disapprovingly.

"I am meeting my husband in Port Caspin," Kalothia added hurriedly.

"Oh!" The woman with the threaded hair looked skeptical. "He did not arrange travel companions for you? A woman cannot travel the King's Highway alone."

"No." Kalothia shook her head meekly.

More tongues clucked. All the women were disgusted by the neglectful, imaginary husband.

"You will travel with us," another of the women decided. She too had the horizontal scars, and a wide smile. She wore wooden bracelets on her wrists that clanked cheerfully each time she moved her hands. "We are going to Port Caspin now."

"Thank you!" Kalothia agreed immediately.

"I'm Bisi," the first woman who had greeted her offered. "This is Chidera." She pointed to the woman with the wooden bracelets. She turned and named the other women.

There was a pause and Kalothia realized they were waiting for her to supply her own name. Ah. Did she tell the truth? Probably a bad idea if there were still men searching for her.

"I am Clarit," she said, swallowing the frisson of pain that speaking her dead bodyguard's name caused.

"Oh! You are from the North! I always love the simplicity of their names," Chidera said. "Which part?"

All eyes looked to her again. Kalothia guessed the women were probably tired of one another's company and excited to have somebody new to discover. She searched her mind for details of the North from her conversations with Clarit and Nahir.

"I'm from a small farm near the Red Desert. Oshodi. You probably don't know it."

"I know it." One of the other women was giving her an assessing look. "We travel all over the North buying cassava from small farms. Very few people there speak Common Galla." The woman switched to the Northern dialect and added, "You speak Common like a Southerner."

Kalothia smiled and, in the same Northern tongue, said, "Thank you. My uncle was a trader and I learned from him." She'd learned the thick, guttural Northern Gallan dialect from Nahir and her bodyguards.

The woman cocked her head. "You speak both tongues like a native," she said admiringly. Kalothia felt the woman's eyes travel over her scarf, her pendant, Ye-Ye, and her dress. "You travel with a monkey and no extra clothes? No food? What is it your husband does?"

Kalothia cast around for something plausible that would discourage further questions. "Um, he's a . . . glassblower. He found work down south."

It seemed the right answer. The women nodded and conversation turned to other topics.

They rode for hours down the King's Highway until the air turned cool, the mosquitoes buzzed noisily, and the sun reddened and began to slink closer to the earth. The women talked of many things, leaving Kalothia's mind to drift aimlessly. When talk turned to the king, she tuned back in.

"Barely a year after the prince's death. Such bad luck. The family is cursed." Bisi shook her head.

"It was his conscience that killed him," another woman declared before she was hastily shushed.

"It's not for us to speak ill of the dead," another woman added.

"My mother still talks of the time when Queen Sylvia and King Osura toured the country," Chidera declared.

"Lower your voice! Do you want to get us all arrested?"

"Calm yourself! Do you think royal guards hide on roadsides waiting for somebody to mention the queen he executed?" Chidera sighed wistfully and returned to her story. "My mother says the royal carriages swept along the King's Highway in a convoy that went on for miles. The builders were laying the paving stones barely cubits ahead of them. It was a beautiful sight. Every family in our village was given a bag of rice and two chickens as part of the celebration. Queen Sylvia had insisted. A few years later she was dead."

A quiet settled over the group. Kalothia listened, rapt. Aunty had told her these stories. How the queen had loved her people. How they'd revered her. Hearing these women speak of her made her real. She was warmed unexpectedly by the thought that her parents had defended such a good woman. Then another of the women said, "No man will keep an unfaithful wife. Least of all a king."

The other women tutted and hissed at her.

The woman shrugged. "There were witnesses." The tutting grew louder. "Her own guard!"

"With the right resources, you can persuade anybody to say anything," Bisi said.

"Why would a guard lie? The rumor was already rife across the palace—I heard—before he felt obliged to come forward."

"Obliged or compelled? He could have been paid or forced. People say morals in the palace are as dirty as a latrine. Where is the man they claim bedded her? Untraceable! Because it was a lie!" Bisi pushed back.

"The king wouldn't have executed her if he wasn't certain." The woman's voice had risen with annoyance.

Bisi scoffed. "I've seen men sacrifice many things to maintain their pride."

Kalothia was glad someone had spoken in the queen's defense. Her parents had believed the queen innocent, even though so much of the court had turned against her. They had believed it so vehemently that they had decided to go into exile and abandon their only child rather than betray her. She wondered what had prompted the queen's own guard to lie against her. She hadn't heard about that before.

"You all talk as if you've stepped foot in the royal palace. Let the rich solve their own problems," Chidera chimed in.

A woman began to sing a mournful prayer for the dead. Kalothia did not know the words, but the other women slowly joined in, one by one, until the warmth of their voices filled the air.

THEY ATE THE EVENING MEAL IN THE SADDLE USING A FEW lanterns to bolster the waning light. Steamed bean cakes, fried chicken, and baked plantain were unpacked quickly and consumed just as rapidly. Night had fallen when they turned off the highway and followed a worn path until they reached a wide river. Its grassy shore was lit with oil lamps and crowded with traders negotiating with boatmen or disembarking from boats. The moon lit the river, revealing the crowd of vessels still traversing the waters.

It seemed impossible that their huge contingent of horses, wagons, and people could navigate through the bustling throng, but somehow it was accomplished. They moved through the crowd, past docking posts, where lanterns hung next to signs with names like Clear Waters, Swift Sail, and Ocean Wave until they reached a post named Beneath the Waters.

"I hope that's not a prediction for our journey," Kalothia muttered nervously. She had never traveled on water before. The row of flat-bottom boats tethered to the post looked sturdy enough, but who could tell.

"What prediction?" Chidera asked.

Kalothia pointed to the post. "Beneath the Waters," she read.

Chidera gave her a confused look of dismay. "You read?"

Kalothia had been worrying about the boat, but the change of atmosphere pulled her back to the conversation. Chidera was holding her body stiffly as though she'd just heard that Kalothia had a communicable disease.

Kalothia chided herself. How could she have forgotten about the Southern attitude toward female education? She had to be more careful. "I overheard some people talking," Kalothia hurriedly lied.

Chidera nodded, but her body remained stiff, and Kalothia had the feeling she did not believe her. She still recalled Aunty's bitter objections to her learning to read. Aunty had talked of curses, of madness and infertility. But Aunty's anxiety was no match for Kalothia's quick, curious mind. She was deciphering symbols at five harvests and sounding them correctly at six when Teacher had insisted that he teach her properly.

◆

THEY BOARDED THE FLAT BOATS IN GROUPS. IT TOOK THREE OF the huge rafts to accommodate the convoy. They cast off and quickly left the shore behind, buoyed by a brisk wind that filled the raft's sails. The women settled down on the rush mats that they had laid out.

Kalothia stood watching the captain maneuver the rudder that dictated their path. Absently, she touched a hand to her pendant. She needed to form a plan for Port Caspin. But it had been such a long day, her brain was foggy with fatigue. She sat and settled Ye-Ye in her lap thinking she would close her eyes for a few moments then give the problem some serious thought. The next thing she knew somebody was shaking her awake. She opened her eyes to a leafy shoreline, illuminated with lamps and busy with people. It was still night, yet there were guards in red uniforms patrolling—tall, well-built, brown-skinned men with hard faces. She could sense that the women around her were nervous. The presence of guards was obviously unusual. What was happening? The women began to speculate. Was it another census? Had there been more problems with smugglers? Were Padman terrorists operating along the shore?

"But none of these activities would summon the king's personal guard," noted one of the women.

When they reached their dock, more guards stood waiting. They scrutinized each member of the convoy as they disembarked, holding smoky lamps up to faces and assessing with unblinking stares. They opened and checked the wagons. They searched the panniers that had been strapped to the horses. Kalothia could tell from the bewildered faces around her that this was not usual. She heard the words *throne* and *war* breathed several times by the wary traders. It seemed the lack of an heir for the throne was already breeding tension.

"You should persuade your husband to return to the North." Bisi spoke beside her while they waited for the guards to conclude their search.

"What? Why?"

"I travel these roads many times a year, and I've never seen anything like this, especially at this time of night. These guards . . ." She tutted. "A country without a leader is like a chicken running with no head. It becomes wild and unpredictable. The North will be more stable. The unrest may not spill that far."

Kalothia thought of the guard's words when they entered Illupeju. *When a king passes with no heir, people grow agitated and bold.* Even the innkeeper had been worried. *We pray the Goddess grants us peace,* he had said. Kalothia had been thinking of the king's death in relation to her own life; she had not thought of the stability his rule had brought to Galla.

Bisi went on, "The four lords are probably all in Port Caspin right now. They are pledged to protect the throne. They should find the best candidate to rule." Bisi clicked her tongue. "But ego and power will guide their every move."

Kalothia nodded. Teacher had said the same thing. How arguments over territory boundaries, trade, and proximity to the throne made it impossible for the lords to work together. It was one of the reasons that no official heir had been named in the year since the prince's death.

"And if they can't agree on a successor for the throne?" Kalothia asked the question aloud, but she knew the answer. Each territory had its own standing army. The path from dispute to war could be as short as a drawn sword, Nahir had often said.

"It's better you don't stay in Port Caspin too long," Bisi advised, her voice somber in the night.

Kalothia looked out into the darkness. She would not get caught up in the politics of the royal family. They had already stolen her parents and sixteen harvests with them. She would not sacrifice anything else. She would search out those who had known her parents in a bid to find their location and learn the truth about their fate. And she would discover who had sent the attackers responsible for killing Teacher, Aunty, Clarit, and Nahir. She would focus on her own goals.

PORT CASPIN

PORT CASPIN WAS THE NATION'S CAPITAL, THE SEAT OF GOVERN-ment, home to the royal family, and the heart of Galla's trade and culture. When Kalothia had dreamed of her parents' return, of them all finally leaving the forest, she'd dreamed of walking the streets of Port Caspin with them, of wandering through the bustling markets and buying trinkets for friends like the characters in her books did, of eating sweet cakes at the port and watching the ships sail in and out. Her favorite line from her favorite poet, Mishi, went: *When the Goddess returns, she'll fold up the world and leave only Port Caspin as a tribute to humanity.*

Instead of joy, she carried grief and vengeance in her heart and the barest hope that somebody in Port Caspin would be able to help her find her parents. The assassin in Illupeju had suggested her mother was dead. What did he know of her family? Had the attackers targeted her parents first? The frustration of so many unanswered questions pounded in her brain. Though she had slept on the boat it had not been restful. Weariness pulled at her limbs and yawns tumbled from her mouth. She breathed in the heavy night air and reached for calm.

The ride from the river to the city was long and slow in the darkness. After a few hours most of the women had found places to rest on the wagons. Only Kalothia and Bisi remained mounted. The road had begun to narrow and the sky to creep from pitch-black to navy when the earth to the left of them seemed to tilt and shape itself into mounds with peering eyes. An eerie singing filled the air, carried on the breeze. Kalothia squinted into the night, trying to understand what she was seeing.

"The Ibeso Caves," Bisi spoke unexpectedly, making Kalothia jump.

Ye-Ye, who was sleeping in a sling around her chest, grumbled at her abrupt movement. "Sorry!" Kalothia soothed him. The caves stirred a dim memory in her head, but she couldn't place it.

"They're guarded by kori birds that sing at night," Bisi went on. "It's said the birds' song lures lost travelers into the caves and they never emerge."

Kalothia nodded, remembering now where she'd heard the name before. "My Aunty used to warn me she'd send me to the caves to be eaten by spirits if I didn't behave," she recalled.

The air around the caves was cool and strange. In the near dark it did seem like spirits might be watching them from the gloom. Kalothia shivered. She was grateful when they finally drew clear of them.

The sky had lightened to dawn-gray when the lights of the city appeared in the distance. Gradually the clomp of their horses' hooves were overpowered by a new sound.

A rhythmic noise.

shoosh shuuush

shoosh shuuush

shoosh shuuush

It was like a noisy exhalation followed by a slow indrawn breath. It seemed to roll in from all sides at once. Kalothia looked around, trying to trace the sound. The road sloped upward for a short while. Eventually, as they topped the summit, sunrise illuminated the tops of a towering pair of black, wrought-iron gates.

Beyond the gates the morning light touched a crowded scattering of rectangular white buildings, brushing them with gold. The flat roofs looked like stepping stones, trailing outward until they met a blue expanse of water that sparkled like glass and stretched so far into the distance it seemed to drop off the end of the world. The *shoosh shoosh shoosh* noise grew louder. It was the waves breaking against the shore. Kalothia could taste the gritty sea salt on the air.

At the top of the gates, the metal had been bent to form the letters PORT CASPIN. Kalothia breathed out in awe.

Nahir had always spoken of Port Caspin with disdain. Kalothia had dreamed of visiting it then writing to tell him all the ways he was wrong. There would be no letters now. No celebration or enjoyment of this city. Instead, Kalothia realized with a jolt, she would have to tell his father that his youngest son was dead. How would she deliver such news? She tried to picture Lord Godmayne's face. She hadn't seen him in many harvests, and the memory of him had dimmed. Had he been kind? He'd ensured she had all she needed, but he'd also left her care entirely to Aunty, Teacher, and her bodyguards. She was unimportant, a minor royal, and the child of traitors, while he was the lord of the Northern Territory. She did not expect him to have time to visit a young, helpless dependent. Still, the inattention stung a little. But it might have hurt more had Lord Godmayne not sent his own son along on visits and then made him head of her security. A decision that had now cost his son's life.

She sighed and stared up at the Port Caspin gates, thinking again of all the time she'd dreamed of coming to this city. Sorrow filled her chest. She had lost the anchors in her life in just a few days. Lord Godmayne was the only person left who cared for her, and she found herself yearning to see him, even though she would have to share such terrible news. When she found him, she would ask him about her parents. Maybe his own grief would make him sympathetic to her desperate need for answers and he would finally tell her the truth about their whereabouts. Then together they could find out who was responsible for the attack on her home. He'd have a better idea of the possible suspects and their motives. With his wealth and contacts, she could get answers to her questions, find her parents, and get justice for those she loved.

A crowd was clustered around the closed gates. Many lay sleeping on straw mats, others were waking slowly and sharing food or moving to the edge of the gathering to perform morning ablutions with flasks of water and chewing sticks.

"The gates will open soon," Bisi said, looking at the rising sun. "The city markets will be clamoring for our goods, the gate solders know better than to delay."

Kalothia gave the crowd a second look and found she could distinguish the traders among them; they sat with baskets filled with eggs, nuts, spinach—all manner of delicacies. They had roped cows, goats, and donkeys to nearby trees. Some had camped in the nearby field with teams of hogs or flocks of sheep. But there were others, people with no goods, dressed in white for mourning. The crowd was steadily beginning to rouse, and she noted that many of those dressed in white were kneeling in prayer. They held candles. One elderly woman was crying, her hands raised palm-up to the sky.

They had come to mourn the king, she realized with a jolt. They had camped outside the city gates waiting to pay homage. A middle-aged man beat a fist against his chest, his head bowed in prayer. Kalothia wondered what these people had found to admire in a king who had executed his pregnant wife, caused factions of the royal court to flee in fear, and spent much of the last sixteen harvests in his bed. Maybe it was stability; as Bisi had said, power changes could be uncertain.

Suddenly, the huge, black city gates began to swing open. A burst of chatter rippled across the crowd, people surged to their feet and edged forward. Kalothia's horse danced nervously in place and Ye-Ye screeched unhappily. The mass of people seemed more densely packed and unwieldy than moments before. Kalothia realized that she would not be able to proceed with the traders. Their wagons and number would make it hard for them to maneuver through the crowd.

She thanked Bisi for her kindness and then, waving off the women's concerns about her proceeding alone, steered her horse out of the crush.

She trotted around the edges of the throng, watching as the gate opened and closed at intervals to admit small groups of people. She remembered the questions the guard had asked at the Illupeju gate. Without Nahir, what kind of reason could she manufacture to enter? She rode along the wall, searching for an alternate route that wouldn't take her past the guards.

Perhaps there was a quiet spot where she could climb the walls. She soon saw that this would be impossible. The earthen walls were high. The height of three men. And on top of that the earth around the wall's base had been dug away in a deep trench. Just like at Illupeju. There were other gates, but all were almost as crowded and equally well guarded. On the road beside one of the gates, a man was selling something that gave her an idea. She returned to the main entrance with a plan.

She sold her horse to a trader for three strings of cowrie shells. After exchanging two cowrie shells to purchase what she needed, she began to light a fire.

SHE WAS CLOSE TO THE GATES WHEN THE AIR EXPLODED INTO A cacophony of loud pops. The noise boomed, causing animals to howl and scatter. People were shouting, pushing, scrambling. Some of the crowd surged toward the gates to escape the confusion.

Kalothia felt a moment's concern that she'd caused such panic. Nobody seemed to realize that it was just popping corn going off. Completely harmless. She tucked the concern away—there was no time to waste. She shoved people aside, elbowed her way forward, and struggled to remain on her feet when the crowd lurched sideways, but she was, in fits and bursts, able to slip through the gates into the city of Port Caspin.

Inside felt like another world after the noise and activity beyond the gate. There were no guards, only an innocuous, deserted street that curved up to a slightly busier thoroughfare where workaday wagons rattled along and the occasional elegant carriage rumbled past. Ye-Ye's head whipped around as he took in all the interesting new sights. The handful of men and women out and about were dressed in the finest clothing Kalothia had ever seen. Shokoto seemed to come in all sizes— long and short, baggy and tight—decorated with colored stones and sewn with bright threads. Most people wore white, just as the mourners at the gate had. But the fabrics were rich, dazzling even, in the morning light.

Everything around her called for her attention. Taking it all in, she could see the buildings were uniformly white. Some were narrow, some were vast. There were windows made of colored glass, while their wooden doors were etched with delicately carved figures, and there were contraptions that spilled water when a lever was pulled, and gutters that carried wastewater away. Traders walked with goods piled high on their heads, shouting their wares loud enough to be heard by slowly rousing households. The city pulsated with color and movement and the scent of cooking food.

It was overwhelming. Fatigue from a night spent on the road rushed in, and Kalothia swayed on her feet. She had planned to find a place to wash up so she could immediately go in search of Lord Godmayne, but exhaustion wrung the last dregs of energy from her and she decided it was critical she find a bed and rest for a few hours. She'd look for a guesthouse, she resolved, thinking of the cowries that still remained from selling the horse. Later she would find a way to contact Lord Godmayne.

As she walked deeper into the city, the calm atmosphere began to change. Soldiers started to dot the road, patrolling in pairs, their faces hard and inscrutable. Some looked rumpled and red-eyed, as though they had spent the night far from their beds.

A wooden bowl slammed into the bricks at her feet. "Red earth!" Kalothia swore and leaped back, then scanned the street in shock. She found the culprit several cubits away. It was a large man clothed in a black military uniform decorated with green thread. An Easterner. He was facing off against an even larger man wearing the same attire except for the white thread. Southwestern. They both began yelling.

The Eastern soldier could barely stand upright; he'd clearly been drinking. Passing soldiers paused and drew closer to the melee. They called encouragement to their clashing colleagues, a kind of wild, eager energy radiating off them. This was the restlessness that Bisi had spoken of. Kalothia could see how these men of differing armies might serve as a tinderbox and set things off. A handful of city dwellers had wandered closer to watch the scuffle. Kalothia was edging away when something spooked the motley collection of bystanders and suddenly people began to run.

Panic caught like a wildfire, and in seconds everybody was running. A large man with an immense belly brushed past her and knocked her backward. Ye-Ye yelped and clutched at her hair. She would have fallen beneath the racing feet but a firm hand grabbed her and pulled her upright.

"This is not a safe place," a stern voice said.

She could feel Ye-Ye trembling, so she pulled him into her arms and cradled him close as she turned to find she had been saved by another soldier. From the North this time, distinguished by his orange threading. He kissed his teeth—a noisy sound of contempt— but kept his eyes on the now wrestling soldiers. "I see the Eastern army still picks their men from the chaff left after the harvest," he grumbled in the flat Northern tongue.

"If only they would brawl in private," she replied in the same Northern dialect.

"You're from the North? Good morning, sister." He gave a quick bow.

Kalothia bent her knees in a shallow bow of her own. "Good morning."

People were still brushing past them. The shouts from the fighting soldiers had increased in volume as their colleagues joined in the fray.

"You are far from home," the soldier said.

She had to fumble for the story she had told the traders earlier of the girl from a Northern farm meeting her husband in Port Caspin, but she dredged it up. "I'm looking for an inn where I can rest for a few hours. Later I'll find my husband."

The soldier wanted to be useful. "I have a wagon. I'll take you to a trustworthy guesthouse."

Kalothia smiled, grateful and relieved. She didn't know if she could have walked much farther. "Thank you."

"Let us go before these fools kill each other."

THE WALKING DEAD

THE SOLDIER SAT UP FRONT IN THE WAGON WHILE KALOTHIA made herself comfortable in the back. Ye-Ye climbed down from her shoulder to peer over the edge at the passing landscape. They took a broad road out of the center of Port Caspin. It connected with several smaller streets before beginning to climb sharply up a hill.

They were stopped briefly by a guard dressed in the bloodred royal guard uniform. After giving the wagon a cursory check, he allowed them to continue.

"I have to collect a friend!" the soldier called to her in the back. "Then I'll drop you at the guesthouse."

The wagon rounded a corner, climbed an incline, crested, and began to descend. Kalothia caught her breath at the white building ahead of them. It stood on a shelf of rock overlooking the sea. It was perfectly circular, the roof a dome. The white walls shimmered in the sunlight and the blue sea behind it seemed endless.

"What is this place?" Kalothia called. Her eyes were wide with wonder. She had never seen so much splendor in her life.

"The Temple of the Goddess," the soldier called back. The road had grown busy and he slowed to maneuver around a line of waiting carriages. "It's busy because of the king's funeral."

"Already?" Kalothia asked, surprised that the king's funeral should take place so quickly. It was customary to wait eight days before burial when monarchs and dignitaries died, to allow time for preparations and for their elite guests to gather.

"I hear some of the lords were concerned about having so many soldiers in Port Caspin at a time of uncertainty. They shortened the timeline."

It made sense, especially after the unruly behavior she'd witnessed earlier.

As the wagon drove forward, Kalothia caught the faint sound of drumming carried on the breeze. It grew in volume until she spotted the source: a line of men with white fabric tied around their waists, their bare upper bodies ebony black and glowing with sweat. They were beating drums of all sizes in complex rhythms.

The wagon turned off the road onto some grassland near the temple.

"We'll wait here for my friend," the soldier said.

Kalothia nodded and settled in to watch as exquisitely dressed people exited from beautiful carriages. A flash of movement caught her eye. When she turned toward it, she was shocked to see the woman in indigo tending to the profusion of aloe vera around the temple walls.

Kalothia's heart began to race. In all that had happened since the fight in the woods, she'd almost forgotten this woman, but an idea had begun to form in her mind of who she was. It was so terrifying that every time it sprang into her head, she thrust it away. Ye-Ye gave a cry of excitement at the sight of the woman. He launched himself out of the wagon and scampered toward her.

Kalothia stared after him in horror. "Ye-Ye! No!" She vaulted over the side of the wagon and took off after her pet at a run. "Ye-Ye!"

Ye-Ye turned back and gave a cheeky grin before scampering past some finely dressed people and disappearing inside the temple.

Kalothia groaned. She gave an extra burst of speed, but then a royal guard stepped into her path and she had to skid to a stop to avoid crashing into him.

The soldier was hard-faced, hard-eyed, and the hand at his sword hilt said that he'd brook no nonsense. "Who are you?" he demanded.

"I'm . . . I . . . I just need to get inside for a quick—" She tried to step around the guard, but he grabbed her shoulder and used the heel of his hand to give her a strong shove back. At least that was what he intended. Much of her practice sessions with Clarit had involved countering heavier weights and stronger opponents. She leaned back. His shove never connected and in the split-second it took for him to regain his balance, she ducked. Her swift footwork had her dodging around him. It was the yank on her headwrap that slowed her, but a sweep of her hand and she'd shaken free.

He grabbed her wrist in a standard army hold, one she easily reversed. After which she jerked him off-balance, kicked his foot, and nearly toppled him. He managed to remain on his feet, but he couldn't stop her from snatching his sword from its scabbard and turning it on him. He looked stunned and stood silent, panting.

In the pause, her sense returned. She had just attacked a royal guard and stolen his sword. So much for not drawing attention to herself. She lowered the sword and held it out to him, hilt first. But he didn't move. He was staring at the top of her head. She put a tentative hand to her scalp and felt . . . not the cotton of her wrap but her soft, braided hair.

Whispers rippled around her like a breeze, and she realized she stood at the center of a crowd. Some looked troubled. Some confused. A few shocked. An older man was clutching his chest as though he might collapse. The drums had stopped.

A middle-aged woman broke from the body of the crowd. She wore a headwrap of white and gold that opened like a fan around her head. Her hands were outstretched, and she was crying. "Kalothia!" she breathed.

Kalothia stepped back. The woman didn't look dangerous, but the force of her emotion and her desperate outstretched hands made Kalothia wary. How did this strange woman know her name?

And then Kalothia caught sight of an impossible face in the crowd. No. It was . . . No. Her head began to spin. How could it be?

Everything in her clenched with longing.

It was . . .

"Nahir . . . ?" she said. The dizziness increased. She felt light-headed. The world went black.

REVELATIONS

THE WORLD CAME BACK SLOWLY. LAVENDER, CITRONELLA, AND grapeseed lamp oil teased her nose. Two people were speaking close by. An unfamiliar voice and one so familiar her chest ached.

"She doesn't know. She has no idea! Just as you ordered. We can't tell her like this." There was anger in the voice. The voice that made her heart pound. She wanted to soothe it away.

"We don't have the luxury of time. Galla is in crisis. Tell her the truth and what she must do." She didn't recognize the second voice. It was quiet, measured, and implacable. There was no arguing with a voice like that.

"Let me take her away from here. Break it to her slowly and let her decide what she wants to do. We haven't given her any choices."

"You've had a long couple of days and barely rested. You're being too emotional. She doesn't have choices. She has a birthright."

A warm weight landed on Kalothia's chest. She caught the wet-fur smell of Ye-Ye a moment before he nuzzled against her face, making her sneeze. The voices cut off abruptly.

"Please leave. I'll talk to her." That voice! One she thought she'd never hear again. Fear and hope twisted in her chest. She tried to find the lever that would open her eyes. While she struggled, she heard footsteps pass her, then the creak of a door.

Fingers touched her face. They smelled of leather and shea butter. "Kalothia?"

But Nahir was—

Her eyes flew open.

Nahir was looking down at her, concern etched along the furrow of his brow. A white bandage ran around his forehead, cuts and scratches covered most of his face, but it was him.

"Nahir?" she whispered, afraid that if she spoke loudly, she would wake from whatever dream this was and he would disappear.

He smiled. The dimples that she rarely saw peeked out. "Yes," he answered, and it was the deep, gravelly voice she knew so well.

She tried to pull herself up. He helped with a hand against her back. As soon as she was upright, she threw her arms around him. Ye-Ye screeched in protest and Nahir grunted in pain. She loosened her arms hurriedly. Ye-Ye wriggled out with a squawk. She laughed, joy fizzing up in her like bubbles in boiling water. He was alive! He was solid and real in her arms.

"I thought you were dead," she said against his shoulder. "They said you were dead."

He patted her back and that made her laugh again. It was so typical. Then he pulled back and looked at her. "When I woke up after the explosion . . . you were gone." His voice dropped on the last words. He cleared his throat. "I searched Illupeju and the surrounding area. You'd just vanished. It was too dangerous to ask the locals—word might have passed to the attackers following us. So, I came south to request my father's help and gather men for a search. Then you appeared. Here. In the temple." He took her hands. Nahir, who rationed physical contact, held her. She couldn't help smiling, despite his obvious suffering.

"What happened?" he asked.

"A man took me. He was paid by someone in Port Caspin to kill me. But he decided to try for more money by selling me." The words sounded absurd even as she said them. "His partner insisted I had to die. They fought." She remembered how the brawny kidnapper had bled out, the hate in his eyes and voice. A shudder ran through her. "The man said he hoped I died early like my mother." She stared at Nahir. "What was he talking about? How would he know about my mother?"

He shifted, looking uncomfortable. "Were they Padman, like the others?" he asked.

She nodded. "Why are Padmans after me? I don't think the king was behind the attacks. But who else could it have been?"

"I asked my father. He's looking into it. At this stage, we don't know who sent them. You have to be very careful with the people here." He shook his head. "I can't believe you came to Port Caspin."

She frowned. "I know you insisted I go to the North, but I couldn't! I need to find out who attacked my home; Teacher, Aunty, and Clarit will not rest until I do. And now that the king is dead, I have a chance to find my parents."

He didn't respond, but a nerve twitched at the side of his jaw; she sensed that he wanted to remonstrate with her further and was fighting to quell the urge. She didn't want to fight with him. It was such a relief to have him back, to be able to touch him and share her fears with him. Now his father could help with the logistics of finding answers. It was remarkable the difference a day had made in her life. She held up her arm and looked at the string of colorful beads that circled her wrist. She had expected to hand them to Lord Godmayne in apology. It felt wonderful to slide them off and offer them back to Nahir along with his dagger.

"Where did you find this?" he asked, surprised out of his worries.

An image of the assassin she had killed flickered in her mind. She shook her head, shoving the painful memory away.

"One of the attackers," she said simply.

Somebody knocked on the door.

"Wait!" Nahir called. There was a tension in his voice that made her look at him in surprise. Once again, he shifted uncomfortably on the sofa. It was so uncharacteristic of him to be nervous or restless, she stared at him in alarm. "What's going on, Nahir? What's worrying you?"

He winced as if she'd struck him.

"Nahir?"

"Listen. I have to tell you something."

The tension wasn't only in his voice now, it was in the stiff line of his shoulders, in the grip of his hands, in the intensity of his gaze. A seed of anxiety bloomed in her chest.

"What?"

He sighed. He looked away as though searching for the words. The anxiety spread through her. Suddenly her hands felt cold even as they rested in his. This was going to be bad. Whatever it was.

When he spoke, his words were short, direct, like a medicine man setting a bone. "King Osura was your father," he said.

"What?" The words made no sense. "What?" she said again.

He drew in a breath. "Kalothia. I don't know how else to say this. King Osura and Queen Sylvia were your parents. Prince Olu was your brother," he said, slowly. "I know that will be a shock . . ."

She stared at him. At the cuts that marred his face. The brown eyes she knew so well. The grave expression. Was she dreaming? Was this really happening? "You're jesting."

He frowned. His grave expression shifted a little. Sympathy.

No. He wasn't jesting. "I don't understand what you're saying. My parents . . . they loved Queen Sylvia. They took her side during the Great Upset. They've been hiding for sixteen harvests while the king hunted them. They . . ." She stopped. The stories had all been lies.

"I'm sorry," he said. "This narrative was already in place when I . . ." He shook his head and squared his shoulders. "I was ordered to keep you safe. It was easier for me to do that if I kept you away from the world. You wouldn't have stayed hidden if you knew the truth."

She gaped at him. "So, you *lied*? To keep me locked up in the forest, you *lied to me*!"

Her hands clenched and unclenched; she was pulsing with anger. Goddess damn them! She'd known something was wrong. Hadn't she told herself for years that the stories they spun felt . . . wrong? But she would never have guessed this. Never. *Never.*

"That means . . . my parents are . . . dead." Myriad thoughts clamored in her head, but that last one screamed loudest. Her parents weren't hiding, they weren't longing for her, they weren't anything. "All this time . . ." she whispered. An anvil pressed on her chest.

Nahir looked away. A nerve twitched in his jaw.

The door opened and a man walked in. He was gray-haired, tall, and striking. There was something familiar about him, but her mind was too troubled to pin it down.

The man bowed his head. "Your Highness." He'd been the one

talking earlier, she realized, the voice she'd heard as she woke. He had the same deep brown skin as Nahir, the same well-proportioned features. "I'm Lord Godmayne, you may remember me."

Nahir's father! Over ten harvests had passed since she'd last seen him, but she recognized him now.

"I'm sorry this has come as such a shock," he said. "Our intention was always to keep you safe. I ordered all those around you to hide the truth, only for that reason."

He was so casual in his revelations. She sucked in a breath, then another. Why was it suddenly so hard to breathe?

He looked at her with concern. Then he crouched, so they were eye level. "You look so like her: Sylvia. Her eyes carried all her emotions, just like yours do. Her father was my second in the army. When he died, he entrusted me with the care of his only child. At sixteen harvests Sylvia asked to go south, so I secured her a position in the royal court. The next I knew she'd caught King Osura's eye." He sighed and rose back to his feet. "Osura seemed to be in thrall to her. If she was in a room he couldn't look away. He found her every thought fascinating. Maybe his attraction burned too bright. When it soured, it was just as fierce. His jealousy matched his ardor. I couldn't save her. But I did what was necessary to protect you. You may be angry, but ignorance kept you alive."

Nahir sighed.

Kalothia flushed with fury.

"You are still angry." Lord Godmayne nodded, acknowledging the obvious. "You don't have my experience and you don't know the dangers of this court. Believe me, it was for the best. Anyway, what's done is done. Now we must restore your place in the court. You are

Princess Kalothia. You must dress and attend the king's funeral. The prayers have begun."

Princess Kalothia. Just like that. She clenched her fists. Too many emotions swarmed in her mind to identify any single one.

Nahir reached for her fisted hands, then flinched when she jerked away. "This is too much, Father!" he objected. He turned to her. "You don't have to attend the funeral. We can leave here, go somewhere quiet, give you time to think."

"Don't be ridiculous!" Lord Godmayne snapped.

Nahir sucked in a breath, visibly trying to rein in his temper.

Kalothia didn't speak. She couldn't. She was concentrating on breathing. On not throwing up.

"She's the only heir to the throne," Lord Godmayne said. His voice was commanding. This was not a request. "She must stake her claim now, or the other lords, Suja, Caspin, and Woli, will snatch it away. Without a throne, she's just a danger to whoever leads the country. A stumbling block to be eliminated. She must take the throne to survive."

Nahir scratched the back of his neck. "You didn't give her a choice before. She deserves to choose now."

Lord Godmayne looked down at his son. "She has no choices." His voice carried a flash of impatience, a tone that said they'd already discussed the matter and he was now tired of it. Had Nahir tried to persuade his father to let him tell the truth before? Lord Godmayne wasn't a man who could be easily persuaded. She shook her head. She would not feel sympathy for Nahir. He had chosen to obey orders instead of being honest with her.

"She is the heir," Lord Godmayne went on. "She must be crowned."

Nahir's response was a frustrated growl she'd never heard before.

She shoved the twinge of concern away. She didn't care about his frustration. Abruptly, the fatigue from all the traumatic events she'd experienced crashed over her. She closed her eyes, trying to dull the roaring in her head.

Cool fingers touched her chin. Her eyes snapped open to find Nahir holding her face gently. She jerked away and stared daggers at him.

"Bukki will help you dress." Lord Godmayne turned from her to the door and called, "Come!" Yet another person entered. The room felt crowded and oppressive, even though it was large and there were only four of them in it. "We'll give you space." Lord Godmayne tapped Nahir on the shoulder. "Come," he said again, this time to his son, but it was in the same imperious tone.

Nahir held her gaze for a long moment, then rose and followed his father out. The door shut behind them with a click.

Kalothia trembled with anger. Lord Godmayne had kept her trapped in the forest with lies and now he planned to continue dictating her life. All for *her* own benefit, of course. Nothing to do with his own ambition. How dare he?

"Your Highness?"

Kalothia stared at the new person. Lord Godmayne had called her Bukki. She was a short, round girl with large eyes and a calm face.

"Lord Godmayne said I should help you dress." Bukki held out a steaming bowl of water.

Kalothia looked away, her thoughts still spiraling. They'd lied about *everything*. It felt like her entire life had been built on a foundation of sand. Now a strong wave had come and washed it all away.

"My mother was your mother's closest friend," Bukki said gently.

Kalothia looked at her in surprise.

Bukki set the bowl down on the floor and reached into the folds of a voluminous white dress that floated like air when she moved. She drew out a small bunch of grapes and offered them to Ye-Ye, who leaped from Kalothia's shoulder to accept them, then sat quietly on the floor eating.

Bukki smiled. "I've never met a pet monkey, but he likes grapes as much as Sezu, my rabbit at home."

Kalothia was touched by her quiet kindness. "Does Sezu eat them until he's ill too?"

Bukki laughed. "Yes, he does. They're like naughty children." She sank a washcloth into the steaming water. "I never met Queen Sylvia, but my mother talks about her often. She has an engraving of the late queen and lights candles for her every year on the day of her death. She loved her dearly." She pulled out the washcloth, squeezed out the water, then pressed it to the side of Kalothia's neck and face. It stung. Kalothia hissed.

"Sorry!" Bukki said. "You're pretty banged up."

"I've never seen a picture of my mother," Kalothia said, not wanting to think about her injuries and what had caused them. She felt the exhaustion rise again. "Or my father. Aunty—the woman who brought me up—said it was too dangerous to have pictures around . . . But now . . ." Kalothia trailed off. She'd never seen a picture of the king or queen either, and now she knew why.

"You could be your mother's twin." Bukki smiled and moved the cloth to the back of Kalothia's neck. It was warm and strangely soothing. "Apart from your hair."

"My hair." Kalothia laughed. A little hysterical. "Red like my father's. Red like the *king's*," she corrected herself.

"It's very unusual. It runs in the king's family but nowhere else in Galla."

"I was told it only occurred in the royal family. I thought I was a peripheral member of the royal family. I had no idea that it meant—" Kalothia cut herself off.

"That you were the princess," Bukki finished for her.

Kalothia nodded. It was odd to be talking to this stranger about things she barely understood, but something about the girl was reassuring, and her movements were gentle and somehow calmed the agitation running through her. "Did you meet him? The king? The man that murdered his pregnant wife?" she added bitterly. Her mother, she realized. The king had killed her mother. Though Kalothia realized suddenly that she *hadn't* been pregnant when she died. She'd already given birth to a girl child and named her . . . Kalothia. Who else had known that? Her mother had gone to her death concealing her daughter's birth. She thought back. Had Aunty ever talked about her birth? Yes. If Kalothia was ever quiet or moody Aunty would worry and fuss. She'd say, "You came into the world bald and somber, like a nervous uninvited guest. You didn't know you were Goddess-blessed." As she was born without hair, the queen would have lacked the evidence to persuade the king. Perhaps it would have made no difference. If the king was overcome with jealousy, he might have been beyond persuading and allowed the execution of his wife regardless.

She touched the pendant that hung around her throat, the only gift from her mother. "How can I be related to such a man?"

Bukki pressed the warm cloth to her forehead. "Let's see, my father married a second wife when I was a child and abandoned my mother to fend for herself. We were living in his small birthplace village when he left. I learned all kinds of crafts to help keep my mother and me fed. We grew medicinal herbs, wove mats, braided hair—we tried everything before my mother managed to persuade the court that as a former lady-in-waiting she had a right to a room in the palace. It was all very dramatic, but I didn't get a crown out of it. Who wins this game of Most Unfortunate?"

Kalothia met the girl's eyes in shock. Yet she spoke so matter-of-factly it was impossible to be offended.

Bukki smiled. "Let's do your arms."

"I don't . . . I don't think I want to go. To the king's funeral." Her father's funeral. She had to keep repeating the words in her mind, trying to understand them.

Bukki sat back on her heels. "I know this must be a shock, but regardless of everything, this will be your only opportunity to be in the same room as your father. This may be your only opportunity to see him. Don't you want that?"

She mulled it over for a moment. Her mother was gone. Her brother was gone. Aunty was gone. Teacher. Clarit. All of them. The only connection left to her past was this man. The king.

Whenever she'd thought of the royal family, she'd thought how terrible for the prince to live with a murderous father. She'd thought a man who could kill his own wife was irredeemable. Now that terrible family was *her* family. She didn't know what to think or feel.

And now she was being asked to go to the funeral of the one who had caused so much misery. The idea of sharing the same space as him, even for a second, made her stomach turn. Yet she knew she had to. She would never get another chance. She had to see this man who had caused her so much pain. Even if only to make sure he was dead, so he couldn't hurt her anymore.

"Yes," she said. "Take me to the king."

Bukki dressed her in a white silk gown, studded with precious stones, that fell to the floor. "Lord Godmayne said your hair should be uncovered. He wants everyone to see it clearly."

Another directive from Lord Godmayne. Kalothia shook her head. But she was too tired to argue. She let Bukki unbraid her hair and brush it. Bukki smoothed coconut oil between the partings as Aunty used to. The familiar scent made Kalothia clench her jaw against tears. Finally, Bukki twisted her hair into two cornrows threaded with gold strands and slid pins in to finish.

Lord Godmayne returned to escort her. When she saw that Nahir wasn't with him, she gave a sigh of relief. She didn't want to see him. The sting of his betrayal had crawled beneath her skin and torn through muscle and now seemed to ache through the marrow of her bones. She would not forgive him. Lord Godmayne made her angry, but at least he didn't trigger disquiet at her core.

When she looked around for a place to keep Ye-Ye, Bukki held out her hands. "I'll hold him."

Kalothia handed him over gratefully, feeling that at least she had one ally in this strange new place.

THE NEXT HOUR PASSED IN A BLUR. THE TEMPLE WAS COOL AND cavernous. Sunlight reflected off white marble walls, white floors, white pillars. Crowds of people dressed in finery parted when Lord Godmayne guided Kalothia to a seat in the first row of the circular prayer hall. Their whispers ricocheted off the walls like a whirlwind. The temple master leading the ceremony ignored the obvious distraction of his audience and plunged on.

After the speeches, songs, and prayers, Lord Godmayne returned to lead her to the raised dais at the center of the hall and the body that lay there. She braced her trembling legs and looked down at the man stretched out on the stone platform. He was still and blanched of life. His red hair had begun to turn white at his temples. His face was slack in repose. Lines crowded around his eyes and the corners of his mouth. He looked older than his years. She looked down at him, wrung dry of energy and emotion, and simply thought: *This man killed my mother.*

SUMMONING

SHE SLEPT BADLY IN THE SIMPLE ROOM LORD GODMAYNE ALLO-cated to her. Her dreams were filled with flying arrows, kiyons with gnashing teeth, and Aunty gasping for breath. When the royal guard stationed by her door woke her with a loud knock and announced that the lords wished to see her in the throne room, it was a relief to rise and splash water on her face.

Bukki came flying in looking harried and anxious. "Wear this!" She shoved a simple white dress at her.

Minutes later, Kalothia was surprised when Lord Godmayne and Nahir barged into her room too. Her chest tightened. Seeing Nahir was like stabbing a finger into an open wound. She focused on Lord Godmayne and willed her eyes not to drift to his son.

Lord Godmayne gestured for Bukki to leave the room.

"Lord Suja has summoned the royal court," he started once they were alone. "He is the lord of the Eastern Territory, and the youngest and most rash among the lords. But Lord Woli follows his lead and Lord Caspin follows the crowd, so his influence can be significant. I left the summoning to him, as I've seen the lords play power games with their attendance when the call does not suit them. It's better Suja calls the assembly. Your appearance at the funeral this morning piqued his interest, as I hoped it would."

Kalothia shook her head, still foggy from snatches of sleep, and struggled to follow all the details. "How . . . how will this help me find the person responsible for the attack on my home?"

Lord Godmayne glanced at his son. "That should not be your immediate concern. I will present you to the court and we will persuade the lords to allow the palace elders to assess your royal status. The elders knew your mother, your resemblance to her is too obvious to deny. And then there's your hair, so clearly inherited from the king. It should be a mere formality to have your position confirmed." He turned toward the door.

Irritation burned in Kalothia's head. Lord Godmayne was controlling the situation again and ignoring her concerns. Defiantly, she stepped back and sank down on the rumpled bed. She was not in the mood to have orders fired at her like an army foot soldier.

Lord Godmayne turned back, surprised. "We must go now."

Kalothia crossed her arms and stared at the man who had saved her life and financed all her needs but had also lied about every aspect of her life and imprisoned her in a forest. "If meeting the royal court is so important, why have you waited so long to bring me here?" It was so difficult trying to understand the older man's intentions.

Lord Godmayne inclined his head, conceding the point. "The king was erratic and depressed. It didn't seem safe to inform him of your existence," he said simply.

What could she do but accept his explanation? She had no evidence that it was untrue. That didn't change her refusal to be ordered around. "Regardless, I didn't come here for the throne. I came for justice for my family."

Lord Godmayne stared at her for a moment. "Is this your doing?" he snapped. He didn't look at Nahir, but it was clear where the words were directed.

Nahir huffed out an amused breath. "Maybe you should take a while to get to know your charge. You'll find she does as she pleases."

Kalothia kept her eyes glued to Lord Godmayne. She would not look at Nahir. She was not interested in his assessment of her. "Did the king order the attack?" she asked. "Nahir said you thought not, but I want you to explain it to me."

Lord Godmayne growled a swift curse. "The king did not. If he'd known of your existence the whole court would have too; he was not a discreet man. I've had my people looking into the attack. We know nothing yet. The Gallans with the means, influence, and interest in killing the future heir of Galla will be seated beside me in the throne room. If that is not reason enough to attend this meeting, let me be clear: without the throne you will be fair game to anyone seeking power in Galla. I've done what I can to protect you, but at this point you must cooperate if you wish to stay alive."

His words were blunt and hit her like a series of blows. She did not like being scolded like a child, but before she could think of a response Lord Godmayne had turned to Nahir and said, "Escort her to the throne room," then stalked out.

She stared at the closed door, considering her options. It made no sense to waste time sitting stubbornly in her room. Especially if Lord Godmayne was right and the people most likely to have ordered the attack were Galla's three other lords. But she'd vowed that she wouldn't get caught up in the palace politics. Learning that she was the king's daughter did not change that. She would not be maneuvered anymore. If she needed to verify her status in order to stay in the palace and find the answers she needed, she would do that. She would not take the throne; she was not interested in being her father's heir. Without looking at Nahir, she rose and left the room.

»—→ ◊ ←—«

WHEN THEY'D ARRIVED AT THE PALACE EARLIER SHE'D BEEN dazed with exhaustion and could only recall that the *swish swish* of the sea had seemed to pour into the building through every window.

Now as she, Bukki, and Nahir followed the guard, she took note of the servers dressed in white mourning who hurried to and fro. She noted the carved ivory stools and tables that decorated the corridors, the silver-framed mirrors on the walls, animal skin rugs, bronze sculptures tucked into alcoves, oil paintings of animals and landscapes, leather settees, and essential oils burning gently above candles, perfuming the air. It was all so sumptuous and beautiful that it felt like walking through a dreamworld.

The guard led her down a blue corridor, then turned the corner. She blinked. Up ahead, a pair of tall, thick trees rose from the tiled palace floor and stretched toward the too-high-to-see ceiling. The guard stopped before the trees and bowed. Beyond him, another guard stood before a pair of huge wooden doors. He opened one, and the babble of voices washed into the corridor.

"It's the throne room!" Bukki whispered behind her.

Kalothia's knees shook a little, but she forced herself to move forward, passing beneath the canopy formed by the overlapping branches of the two trees. She stepped from the quiet corridor into a vast room.

The people continued to talk among themselves, but Kalothia felt a shift in their attention as their eyes latched on to her. They formed a sea of white, their clothing covering every conceivable style. There were tunics and dresses cut at dramatic angles and decorated with beading and jewels; precious metals glittered on fingers, across throats and wrists; headscarves had tassels and shiny threads. Each person looked like they were competing for attention with their neighbor. Kalothia was the pigeon among a flock of peacocks. She moved through the room, trying to ignore their pointed stares.

The people—*courtiers*, she decided—sat on long raffia benches arranged in rows on either side of the room. The placement left a wide corridor at the center. At the far end stood a large, imposing seat carved from bloodred wood, varnished and polished to a gleam. The throne the room was named for. To the right of it sat the four lords, Lord Godmayne among them.

"Hey, la! Someone tell the lost girl to come forward." The youngest-looking lord rose to his feet. He was tall and assured. He should have been attractive, but something in his bearing was so sneering it soured his whole appearance. She knew immediately that she was looking at Lord Suja, ruler of the Eastern Territory. He was barely thirty harvests, but Teacher had told her that his father had died when he was young, and assuming the responsibilities for an entire territory had not given him time to mature. Teacher said he had too much power and too little self-control.

The other lords sat around him. There were three, representing the remaining three territories of Galla. Teacher had been diligent in his teaching of geography and nobility. *Because of this?* she wondered with a jolt. In case she ever found herself at the royal court?

Lord Suja stood in the middle and to his right sat Lord Woli, ruler of the Western Territory. She recognized him by his thick, white hair and white mustache. He was the oldest lord. Teacher had called him "the Grandfather of Galla."

At the far end of the row, the short, squat man was Lord Caspin. "He's small in stature but huge in influence," Teacher had said. The city of Port Caspin bore his family's name, and they took a slice of everything that went in or out of Galla's ports. As head of the family, Lord Caspin had an immense amount of power.

Lord Godmayne sat to the left of Lord Suja.

These were the four men who now ruled Galla in the absence of a king. She remembered Lord Godmayne's words: *The Gallans with the means, influence, and interest in killing the future heir of Galla will be seated beside me in the throne room.* He had clearly meant these lords. Any of these men could have attacked her home. All they needed was a willingness to work with their country's enemy, the Padmans, and access to the information that she hadn't died with her mother sixteen harvests ago.

She stopped at the front of the room, and Lord Godmayne stood. He turned to Lord Suja and raised a brow. Lord Suja chuckled but shrugged and waved a hand toward Kalothia as though conceding the floor. He sat and crossed his arms.

"I present to the royal court of Galla, Princess Kalothia Osura," Lord Godmayne said. He ducked his head in a bow toward her. A flurry of whispers rose from the room at the unexpected act of deference. "The only daughter of King Osura and Queen Sylvia, and the only heir to the throne of Galla."

The court exploded into frenzied conversation. Kalothia held herself still. The weight of the stares from around the room were like fishhooks dragging at her. She wanted to curl up and disappear, but she willed herself to stand tall.

The lords had leaned over to whisper among themselves, all except Lord Godmayne, who still stood. He signaled at a drummer in the corner of the room and a swift series of thumps brought the volume back down.

"The princess has grown up away from the court as a consequence of her mother's execution for adultery," Lord Godmayne went on. "I ask that the palace elders be assembled and instructed to assess the princess's claim, as is customary."

Lord Suja clambered to his feet, and Kalothia braced herself, nerves twisting in her stomach. It felt very much like facing off with a predator in the forest.

Lord Suja grinned, revealing a gap at the front of his teeth, but there was no warmth in his expression. "How convenient that, though the king's body has barely cooled on the pyre, we already have a candidate for the throne."

The court tittered nervously.

Lord Godmayne sighed. "This is not the time for jesting, Lord Suja."

"Then let me be serious." Lord Suja met Kalothia's eyes. "You claim to be the king's daughter?"

She wanted to speak, to confront the sneer in his tone and face, but she couldn't. She hadn't had time to digest any of the things that had been revealed about her heritage. She did not feel like the man who'd lain on the dais in the temple was her father. She could not claim what still felt unreal to her, so she said nothing.

Lord Godmayne shook his head. "You might be too young to recall her mother, Lord Suja, but she is the spitting image of Queen Sylvia. Her hair is the color of the king's. What further proof do you need of her parentage?"

"Well, let us hand her the kingdom, then," Suja declared, a razor edge in his voice. The room laughed. "Before we bring the crown, maybe we should learn a little about you. Where were you raised?"

Kalothia felt her body flush with shame, but she raised her chin when she answered, "In a forest in the East."

Lord Suja frowned to hear his territory named. "In which village in the forest?"

Kalothia resisted the urge to wince. "No village, just in the forest."

Lord Suja snorted. "You were raised in the forest? Like a wild animal?"

The court roared with laughter.

Kalothia's heart thundered and her skin felt hot enough to catch alight.

"This is not relevant!" Lord Godmayne called.

"Of course it's relevant." Lord Woli, the nation's grandfather, pointed his cane at her. "Galla has never considered a woman for the throne. It's an insult to the Goddess's precepts. Not only do you bring us a girl but one who was raised like a jackal in the forest. Why not crown a puma?"

Lord Suja shook his head. "Where are the guardians that raised you?"

The noise and wash of shame and anger fell away. Kalothia met Lord Suja's eyes squarely. Was he asking what he already knew? Or would her answer provoke a telling response from one of the other men before her? "My home was attacked." Her voice rose above the hubbub. "My guardians were killed."

She moved her gaze from Lord Suja's raised brow, to Lord Woli's cold gaze, to Lord Caspin, who stared at her as though she'd been caught on the bottom of his sandal. None of the men looked concerned, or surprised. But they were politicians and experienced in the art of lying and concealing their true feelings. And they could just as easily have been wondering why she'd survived.

"You appear to be extremely unlucky," Lord Suja went on without emotion. "Your adulteress mother was executed and now your guardians have been killed. Maybe *you* are the curse, the one ruining the lives of those around you."

Kalothia absorbed the cruel barb in silence, though she was sure the hurt showed on her face. Yes, a man this callous could have sent assassins to her home, she decided.

"*Suja!*" It was Nahir's voice, low and warning.

Kalothia glanced toward the sound of it and found him standing against a wall. His face was composed, but tension radiated from every line of his body.

"Insulting her won't change the facts," Lord Godmayne added.

Lord Suja rolled his eyes. "And what are the facts? She bears a strong resemblance to a woman executed for being loose. Is it inconceivable Queen Sylvia had a bastard child?"

The crowd stirred at this thought, murmuring among themselves.

"There are village women practicing all kinds of dark arts, who could find a way to fake the distinctive red hair. Imagine if we crowned this nobody only to find in a few moons that her hair returned to its customary hue. Until this intrusion, we all believed Queen Sylvia's child—regardless of its paternity—died with her, unborn. Now we are to believe the baby miraculously survived?" He paused, dramatically. "Queen Sylvia was Northern. Isn't it more likely that Lord Godmayne is seeking a new avenue to put a Northerner on the throne? A way to seize control of this great nation for himself? Why else do you think he has kept you so carefully hidden all these years?" He glared at Kalothia. "Did he tell you it was for your own protection?" Lord Suja's voice was climbing in volume, his tone rousing. "This lie about your parentage is not simply an opportunistic effort to gain riches, but a dangerous, criminal act of treason." The last words were shouted with such force spittle flew from his lips, and the finger he flung in Kalothia's direction trembled in the air.

She stared at him, shocked.

Lord Godmayne was on his feet, Lord Caspin was debating with Lord Woli, the courtiers were all shouting at once: the room was pandemonium. Lord Suja met Kalothia's eyes. The anger in his face cleared with the abruptness of a summer storm, and he winked at her. Her shock gave way to annoyance. He was insulting her for his own amusement and the pleasure of the crowd.

The chaos raged for long minutes until Lord Woli rapped his cane sharply on the marble floor for attention. He slowly unfolded himself from his chair and stood. The room quieted in anticipation. "Kalothia." He drew out her name ponderously. "Lord Suja is slightly agitated, as you see." The crowd laughed at the understatement. "This is all too abrupt for the usual protocol. We cannot expect the elders to handle such a claim under these circumstances. I propose a solution."

The crowd leaned forward, entranced and eager.

Kalothia waited warily. There was something in his soft, pleasant tone that set her nerves on edge.

"In the days of our ancestors—when the Goddess appeared to

men to give guidance and bestow her blessings—if there was a challenger to the throne, the people of Galla held a simple test."

There was chatter among the crowd now, and sharply indrawn breaths. Some of those gathered had already deduced where the old lord was going. Kalothia had not. She waited.

"The contender was sent to the Ibeso Caves to find a kori egg. If they failed to produce one within three sunrises, they were executed. The kori bird is Goddess-touched and it is only with her blessing that their nests can be found."

The Ibeso Caves. Kalothia's mind ranged back to the ominous wall of rocks and gaping apertures she had passed on the journey to Port Caspin. Her hands clenched at the thought of entering the forlorn place.

Lord Woli tried to add more, but the crowd's chatter rose and crested like a tide, drowning out his voice. He sighed and returned to his seat, leaving Kalothia to stand awkwardly alone, exposed. Anxiety burned in her chest. She put a hand to the pendant at her throat, searching for calm. She wrapped her fingers around it and was struck by the realization that her mother, the queen, might have worn the pendant in this very room. Had she endured the same kind of humiliations? How ominous that history should repeat itself in this way.

Lord Godmayne rose from his chair and crossed to speak sternly to Lord Woli. Lord Woli merely waved a hand and looked untroubled. Lord Godmayne turned to Lord Caspin, but he shrugged and raised his hands helplessly, a smirk tugging at his lips. The noise of the crowd continued. Kalothia shuffled from one foot to another, nervous and self-conscious. She didn't know what to say and was wondering if she could slip back toward the door when a tall man with a thick bush of gray hair strode over to her carrying a small stool. "Sit while you wait," he said shortly.

She nodded, grateful for this small kindness. She noted with curiosity that he moved to retake a seat close to the lords. He obviously had some status in the court.

Eventually, the noise died down.

It was Lord Suja who rose this time. "You don't have to accept the challenge," he told her, humor dancing in his eyes. "You can leave Port Caspin today and not return. However, if you would like to stay and you wish to prove you are the king's daughter, then the only evidence we'll accept is a kori egg. Why don't you sleep on it? Return to the throne room tomorrow and let us know your answer." He smiled as though he'd bestowed some kind of benevolence on her. "While you think, we'll extend to you the best protection the palace can provide." Then he nodded and a guard stepped forward to escort her out.

CONFINEMENT

THE GUARD LED HER BACK TO HER SPARTAN ROOM. WHEN SHE paused on the threshold, he waited with a hand on the hilt of his sword. Perhaps he'd heard about her fight with the temple guard the previous day. Ye-Ye bounded out, delighted to see her. He scuttled up her body until he could nestle in his usual spot on her shoulder. His warm weight was comforting but did little to calm the wild mix of emotion whipping through her.

She felt fury at Lord Suja's insults, especially the painful suggestion that she was the cause of the deaths of her loved ones; rage at being accused of seeking power when all she wanted was justice; humiliation at being paraded and mocked in front of strangers who tittered and heckled as though she were paid entertainment; and panic at the choice she'd been given. If she wanted to stay in the palace, where she was certain she'd find the killer of her loved ones, she would have to risk her life to retrieve a kori egg.

The thought of sitting in a tiny room trapped with her bubbling stew of emotions nailed her feet to the ground. Footsteps sounded on the stairs behind her. With a clutch of panic, she recognized Nahir's measured step. Suddenly, she wanted nothing more than to be locked behind a door where he couldn't reach her. Seeing him had been bad enough. She was not ready to speak to him.

She marched into the room and motioned for the guard to close the door. The hinges creaked as it slowly swung shut. It had nearly closed when a different strain of fear leaped into her chest. If the murderer truly had been up in the throne room, she was prey, easily caught, shut up as she was in this small room with only one guard. She moved toward the door again, wanting to be on the other side of it, where she could run or fight, but also aware that Nahir was right there and she couldn't bear to see him.

The door stopped moving. There was a murmur of voices in the corridor beyond. Her heart twisted painfully. Even as something inside her was soothed by the familiar gravel of Nahir's voice, something else was repelled.

When the door creaked open again, she took a step back, and then several more. By the time he'd walked in she had moved to the window and stood staring out at a vegetable garden two floors below. If she had to escape from this room, she thought vaguely, she couldn't take the window. It was at least twenty-eight cubits to the ground and the walls were made with baked earth that offered nothing to cling on to.

The door swung closed again. This time it clicked into place.

"Kalothia." He said her name softly in a tone she'd never heard from him. Apologetic? Regretful? Conciliatory? She couldn't place it, but it made her chest hurt.

On her shoulder, Ye-Ye twisted to face Nahir. She kept her gaze resolutely turned away.

"I don't want to talk to you." She folded her arms protectively across her chest and tried to reach for the anger that had burned through her body just minutes before. But the anger at Lord Suja had been momentarily banked and replaced by a well of hurt at Nahir's betrayal.

"I know you're angry with me, but I didn't lie to hurt you."

She rolled her eyes. She knew this song already. *It had been for her own good. He'd been keeping her safe from the truth and her desire for freedom.* Pain simmered like a volcano in her body. Her hands clenched into fists against her chest and her nails dug into her palms. Her shoulders were so rigid it felt like rocks had been tied around her neck. Her body began to tremble, and she feared all the emotion would explode any second as tears or screams or some other action she didn't want to perform in front of him. She had to get him out. She would not break in front of him.

He sighed. There was a long pause and she heard him pace the floor. "My father is pushing you toward the throne. I know he thinks he's doing what's best for you—in his defense, he thought the lies were for the best too. None of us knew how the king might react to your existence. During his rare public appearances, the king was emotionally unpredictable; I saw it myself on my few visits to court. He had a distant relationship with the prince—a child he knew to be his. The prince reminded him of Queen Sylvia and that was torture for him. The king would not have protected you, and the palace is vicious. We didn't know who else might wish you harm. My father said it was better to keep you hidden and in ignorance. It took me years to realize that was wrong. I should have spoken up before. I'll always regret that I didn't. However, I'm speaking up now.

"Woli knows the caves are a death sentence. Maybe he and Suja are just throwing their weight around, or maybe they truly want you dead. What I know for sure is they won't accept a woman on the throne. Even if you were a man, they'd find a way to rip you to pieces, because that's what this royal court is: shark-infested waters."

He paused and took a breath. "I know the crown doesn't interest you, so don't get sucked into their games. You can leave here. My father says you'll be in danger from throne hunters, but you're in far more danger here. My father lives in the North. He won't be here to protect you. We can leave Port Caspin and find a new safe place for you."

She snorted. All these years he'd barely spoken and now he wouldn't stop. Why was he pretending to care after everything he'd done? "A new safe place? Maybe a secluded forest somewhere? What about Aunty and Teacher and Clarit? Am I just supposed to forget about them?"

"Risking your life to find their killers won't bring them back."

She whirled around to face him. "How can you say that? How can they rest when their killer walks free? We didn't perform the rituals, we didn't burn them, we just left them—" She cut herself off. "I'm not your responsibility anymore. Your father told you to keep me safe. You did. Your mission is complete." She heard the quiver in her voice and cursed it.

"Kalothia, be reasonable."

She didn't want to hear any more. "You can go now." She turned away. Looking at him was too painful.

Ye-Ye moved restlessly on her shoulder, unsettled by her stiffness and sharp tone. She ignored him. Irritation prickled like ant bites across her skin while tears stung in her eyes.

"Kalothia? Will you look at me?"

She didn't respond. The old Nahir wouldn't have asked; he'd have ordered her to turn around, brandishing their three-year age difference with pride. The old Kalothia wouldn't have needed to be asked. She'd never have disrespected him with a turned back. But they weren't the people they'd been. She couldn't stand to look at him, this person who'd lied to her so thoroughly and determinedly. She bit her lip, pressing down until she tasted blood, until the pain distracted her from that agonizing throb pulsing through her.

He sighed.

Please go, she thought desperately at him.

Seconds passed, excruciating stretches of silence.

"I'll be back later," he said at last.

She said nothing. A few more seconds of marked silence, then finally the sound of footsteps and the creak of the door. She waited until she heard it click shut, until a key turned in the lock, until his footsteps faded into silence. Then she crumpled to her knees.

Ye-Ye leaped from her shoulder in alarm and screeched in distress as she cried, her tears soaking her face and then her dress when she lifted the hem to mop her cheeks. She longed for Aunty's arms; longed for their comfort and safety. But there was nothing but an empty room and the growing heat of the day.

Her tears had stopped by the time a serving girl brought her food. She was younger than Kalothia and dressed in a white kaftan that hung below her knees. She shot Kalothia curious glances as she placed a tray on the floor beside the bed then retreated.

Kalothia hadn't thought she could eat, but her stomach gave a growl of interest at the bowl of ground cassava and water with a handful of groundnuts sprinkled on top. She sniffed the food, worrying that it might have been poisoned. It smelled and looked innocuous. She took a tentative bite. It tasted fine. She took a few more mouthfuls to ensure it was safe before feeding some to Ye-Ye then devouring the rest. She drank most of the jug of water. Filling her stomach helped restore her equilibrium. When she had finished, she was able to think rationally about the options and the suspects before her.

Lord Suja wanted her gone. Looking back, his swaggering arrogance and cutting jibes were so excessively ill-mannered that she wondered whether he was simply hoping to drive her away with insults. She shook her head. As though she could be deterred by cruel words after all she'd gone through.

Lord Woli had been the one to propose a challenge that could easily kill her. He definitely wanted her gone. And Lord Caspin seemed just as sanguine about her death. She recalled his shrug and helpless, raised hands. He was willing to follow the crowd, just like Lord Godmayne had said.

It was clear she had only Lord Godmayne's support, and what could he do, alone, against the three other lords? He couldn't reject the challenge on his own. And, anyway, there was no doubt that he had his own reasons for wanting to prove that she was the heir.

She could refuse to go to the caves, but if she did, she would be banished from Port Caspin. It would be extremely difficult to investigate the deaths of Aunty, Teacher, and Clarit from outside the city. She had to stay in the palace, even if that meant risking the caves. The lords had woven the perfect trap around her. If she was reckless enough to enter the caves, she was unlikely to find a mythical egg nobody had ever successfully retrieved before, and would consequently either die searching or else be executed for returning empty-handed.

She was pacing the room and turning the problem over in her head when a woman's voice rang out on the other side of the door. "She's the king's daughter! You should be ashamed of yourselves, keeping her under armored guard!"

"It's for her protection."

Kalothia moved closer to the door to better hear the tirade. Who could possibly be advocating on her behalf? Had Lord Godmayne sent somebody?

"I can't let you in," the guard went on. "I've been given orders!"

"By whom? I'll go where I please!" the woman huffed. "Come now. You know your mother buys all her tonics and remedies from me. Don't make me bring her here. Let me have a quick word. I'll be in and out before you know it."

Kalothia was so close to the door she had to jump back when the key turned and it suddenly swung open. The guard looked harassed as he ushered a small, slight woman into the room. He hurried back to his post in the corridor and seemed relieved to shut the door on Kalothia and her guest.

The woman tutted after him before smoothly turning to Kalothia and offering a smile while dipping her knees in a shallow bow. It took Kalothia a moment to catch up with what was happening. Then she realized that she was both dismayed by the bow—which was as uncomfortable as being called "Princess"—and that she'd seen the tiny woman before. Her brain raced through the many faces she'd seen since she'd arrived in Port Caspin. The answer came in a burst. She was the woman who'd called Kalothia's name outside the temple before the funeral. She had wondered at the time how a stranger had known her name and then Nahir had appeared from the dead, distracting her completely. Now she wondered again.

The woman straightened and stepped closer. Her eyes roamed Kalothia's face, her expression both incredulous and awed. Kalothia stepped cautiously back. Somebody in the palace had ordered the attack on her home. There was no reason it couldn't have been this woman, who had her cornered in an empty room. When the stranger advanced again, Kalothia retreated once more and brushed a hand over the waist of her dress, where she'd concealed her dagger. The woman stopped. Kalothia braced herself.

"Apologies, Your Highness. I haven't introduced myself. I'm Madame Toks." The woman paused, maybe expecting the name to mean something to Kalothia. She looked disappointed when Kalothia said nothing. "I'm Bukki's mother, and I was your mother's closest friend."

Oh. Kalothia's mind went blank. Her mother. The queen. The woman executed by her husband. Murdered by the king, Kalothia's father. The strange facts that were now her family history made her dizzy when she tried to process them. This woman—Madame Toks—if she was speaking the truth, had been there for all of it.

Kalothia assessed the woman again. She barely reached Kalothia's shoulder and appeared to be between thirty and forty harvests—the age her mother would have been. Her black hair was twisted into long, intricate plaits and gathered into a bun on her head. She wore small gold studs in her ears, and a thin gold chain hung around her neck. Her face was round and pleasant: a rich oak brown. Was this a face her mother had known and loved?

"Life in the palace can be difficult at times, but I'm glad the Goddess brought me back here to witness this day." She gave Kalothia a loving look. "You remind me of meeting your mother. She was preparing to marry the king and I was assigned as one of her ladies-in-waiting. She was outspoken but sweet and had the largest, most curious eyes." She waved a hand, brushing away the memory. "The palace rules say I can continue to live here though my official position is gone. I'm glad I have."

As though sensing her distrust, Madame Toks paused and considered Kalothia. She then thrust a cloth-wrapped package toward her. "Here! Your mother gave this to me for safekeeping a few days before . . ." Madame Toks sucked in a breath.

Kalothia accepted the package warily.

Madame Toks cleared her throat, then added, "Your mother would sketch in it all the time. There's so much of her personality here; I thought you'd like to have it. It's brought me comfort over the years."

At the mention of her mother, Kalothia stroked the cool glass of her pendant.

Madame Toks stared at the necklace for a moment, then her eyes welled up. "Your father gave your mother that pendant the day they wed. She would touch it just like you do." Her voice was cloudy with emotion. She nodded at the package Kalothia held. "Now you have two things of hers."

The package was light in weight and wrapped in cotton fabric dyed with streaks of green and yellow that had faded with age. Had the queen—her mother—chosen the fabric? It was strange to hold something her mother had held. Her stomach tensed with anticipation. She untied the aged fabric. The cloth fell away to reveal a small, leather-bound book. It was pale as honey and soft as fresh dough. She recognized the royal seal, embossed into the cover.

She opened the book and found smooth, white-bleached pages. Each must have cost a small fortune. The first page showed a man of twenty to twenty-five harvests. The king. The youthful face bore no resemblance to the jowly, lined one she'd seen lying in state in the temple; only the flame-red hair connected them.

The image had been sketched with charcoal, smudged in places for coloring and depth, the red added with some kind of dye. The king looked happy. Kalothia couldn't tell whether it was the smile that sat in the crinkles of his eyes, the playful tilt of his head, the arch of one brow, or the curve of his lips, but he radiated delight. That surprised her. Joy was not something that had been associated with the stories of the king later in his life.

The next page showed him again. He sat at a desk writing but had looked up. His emotion was not as overt as in the first picture, but his eyelids fell to half mast, and there was an indulgent smile on his lips that seemed to convey a secret. There were more sketches of him. All with that same secret joy. It was clear they'd been drawn by someone with intimate access to him. Her mother.

The sketches overflowed with love. When Aunty and Teacher had talked of the king who murdered his wife, Kalothia hadn't thought that he had loved her first, or that the queen had loved him too. But it was obvious in the way she drew him. When had the lies crept in? Why did the king believe the accusers of her infidelity and not the woman who had filled pages and pages with sketches of his every expression?

She flicked through more pages, saddened by the joy in the book and the tragedy she knew had resulted. When she came across a sketch of a young woman feeding a goat, she paused. It was Madame Toks, she realized after a moment. She looked up at the woman standing beside her, who smiled. "Ah, yes, that goat was a menace. It was part of the kitchen livestock, destined for the pot. But it escaped from the pen one afternoon and made a mad dash for freedom. Queen Sylvia and

I were taking a walk when it came scampering toward us, chased by five kitchen hands. Of course, Sylvia stepped in and scooped it up. She refused to let the kitchen have it back." Madame Toks shook her head at the memory. "She kept the goat much the way you keep that monkey!" She pointed at Ye-Ye. "Completely impractical—that goat took a bite out of so many expensive dresses! I told Sylvia to hand it back to the kitchen, but she said the goat was too intelligent to be eaten, so she carted it around and hand-fed it and drew sketches when it slept."

Madame Toks laughed. "So typical of your mother. Everyone knew that goat would never learn to behave, but she refused to listen. She could be so optimistic. Just like when she insisted every home in Galla get a bag of rice. Impractical but joyous! The goat lived for three glorious months, then caught its head in a fence in the gardens and died. Sylvia was distraught. The king offered to buy her a whole herd of baby goats. Thankfully, she fell pregnant with you and became occupied by other things." She paused, her mood turning somber. She reached up to touch Kalothia's cheek.

Kalothia instinctively flinched away.

"Sorry!" Madame Toks apologized. She tucked her hands against her stomach. "It's just . . . I've prayed all these years that the Goddess would keep you safe." She touched her palm to her mouth in praise of the Goddess. "And now you're here! They snuck you out of the palace the night you were born. The night your mother was—" Her voice grew croaky, and she cut herself off abruptly. She stared at Kalothia through watery eyes. "Sorry, I didn't think I would get so . . ." She took a breath. "Your mother insisted you be taken away. If you'd been born with this hair . . ." She paused to stare at Kalothia's hair. Kalothia shifted uncomfortably under her scrutiny. "Maybe we could have insisted . . . No! Sylvia was so shocked and shaken by the change in your father that she made us promise to take you away and hide you from the king.

"The rumors of her adultery started like a leak in a boat. A slow sinking. As they reached the king he began to pull back from your mother and she—embarrassed and confused—began to withdraw into herself. The rumors weren't even specific. Sylvia had such a bubbly, friendly demeanor, and someone used that against her. If she spoke to a man or laughed or even made eye contact with someone, it all became a sign of her guilt—that she was a flirt and loose with men. The king was new to the throne and sensitive to criticism. He'd married a girl of no standing from the North. The lies got under his skin. By the time the guard made his accusation, the king had withdrawn his support and left the court to try the queen as it wished."

Kalothia waited awkwardly. When Aunty was tearful, she would hug her and brew her favorite herbal tea, then serve it with dried strips of mango. She didn't know what to do for this unfamiliar woman, who was sniffing and clearly fighting to hold back tears.

"You look so much like her. Apart from your—" She gestured at Kalothia's hair and sighed. "I was sorry to hear your guardians passed away."

Kalothia clutched the book. A wave of pain surged through her. "Passed away" sounded so peaceful and nothing close to the reality of their brutal murders.

Madame Toks put a gentle hand on Kalothia's shoulder. This time Kalothia didn't recoil. Somehow the older woman's touch kept the jagged pieces of her grief from slicing too deeply.

"In the throne room, you said there was an attack . . . ?" Madame Toks prodded gently. "What happened?"

Kalothia explained briefly about the Padman assassins who had destroyed her home. Madame Toks's expression grew graver and graver. "How horrific for you all." She clicked her tongue in sympathy, then drew in a deep breath. "This worries me greatly, beyond the tragedy of what has happened. I felt then and I do now that your mother was framed. The hatred against her rose too fast and too furiously. The guard who gave false testimony disappeared not long after her execution. Now attempts are being made on your life." She sucked in a breath and put a hand to Kalothia's cheek. "I don't know what this all means, but walk with care in this place. There is something rotten here that stinks like a month-old corpse."

A chill ran over Kalothia. She squeezed the book, needing something tangible to hold on to.

"If you need anything, call for me. I'll do all I can." Madame Toks gave Kalothia a last look, brushed a hand along her arm, then stepped away and knocked on the door. "Be particularly careful of Suja and Woli," she said over her shoulder. "They're unpredictable. I'm sure Lord Godmayne is working on winning over Caspin to counter their influence."

A key rattled in the lock and then the door creaked open.

"I'll be back later." Madame Toks gave her a teary smile, then she turned a blistering glare on the guard. "See that she is taken for a walk, or I'll have more than words for you."

The guard sighed and nodded.

The door closed on Madame Toks complaining about the damp air in the room and how it was criminal to keep the king's daughter in such a place. Kalothia almost smiled. Madame Toks reminded her of Aunty, fearless and outspoken. She wondered if her mother had been the same. She crossed to the bed and sank down, opening the book once more.

Ye-Ye, sensing her sadness, scampered over to sit in her lap. As she turned the pages, she tried to imagine her mother sketching. She traced her hands over the delicate lines, pausing at the image of a crib. A few rough lines but still discernible. Her mother had been talented; how sad that her life had been cut short.

Subsequent pages showed a sleeping baby, long lashes resting against round cheeks, a tiny mouth puckered with dreams. Over a series of sketches, the baby grew to a toddler, bright eyes, chubby limbs, a laughing mouth. An aching pain rippled through Kalothia for the young boy who would soon lose his mother, who would never meet his sister.

Toward the back there were sketches of the lords. She recognized them immediately, although they were younger here, of course. There was Lord Woli; the arrogant curl of his lip was unmistakable. Lord Caspin seemed to have a slyness to him; his face was turned away but his eyes looked toward the artist. An unfamiliar man with pitted skin, a scowling mouth, and Lord Suja's eyes came next. His father, she mused. During her mother's time Lord Suja would have been a boy. Lord Godmayne was there too, his face was unsmiling in this sketch. He shared his son's pleasing features, but the years had hardened lines around his mouth, and his eyes were cold and unreadable.

She froze, her hand on the page. The sketches of the lords were lined up, neatly side by side, as though she were considering a line of suspects. Was there some clue there? It seemed unlikely that a plot against the queen sixteen harvests ago could be linked to the attack on her home—didn't it? After a few more moments, Kalothia sighed. She could see nothing out of the ordinary in the pictures.

She turned the page to a drawing of the old man who had brought her a stool. He was slightly younger but otherwise unchanged. He had the same kind expression he'd worn earlier. Kalothia smiled. She hoped he'd been gentle to her mother too. But who was he? She recalled how he'd stood with the lords, among them yet apart. The prime minister? She would ask.

She thumbed through the last few pages to ensure she hadn't missed anything, that there wasn't a secret message for a daughter to read. Disappointed, she put the sketchbook aside and stretched out on the bed. So much had happened over the last two days, a weariness sucked at her, dragging her down. She closed her eyes to absorb it all. Her mind drifted and the world melted away. The next thing she knew somebody was calling her name. She opened her eyes and nearly screamed when she found a face staring down at her.

BETRAYAL

KALOTHIA SHOVED THE BODY AWAY, ROLLED UP TO HER KNEES, and pulled out her dagger in a quick series of moves. Her heart was pounding and her eyes narrowed when her mind caught up and realized she was staring at the girl who had cared for her before the funeral.

"It's Bukki!" the girl whispered. She'd skidded halfway across the room and barely saved herself from toppling over. She stared at Kalothia with wary alarm.

Slowly Kalothia's heart slowed to a less frantic pace. She scrubbed a hand across her forehead. She hadn't known she was so on edge, so fearful in this tiny room. "Sorry. I'm a bit jumpy."

Ye-Ye grumbled at having his rest disturbed and bounded onto her shoulder, comforting her with his soft body.

"That's understandable, given everything." Bukki smiled. "I didn't mean to scare you. Mama says you need to take a walk."

"Mama?" Kalothia asked quietly, following Bukki's soft tone.

"Madame Toks. She came by earlier."

Kalothia thought back and realized Madame Toks had said as much when she introduced herself, but Kalothia had been too caught up in thoughts of her mother to take note. She scrutinized Bukki and decided the girl shared a number of features, including her diminutive figure and round face, with her mother. Bukki moved forward and pulled Kalothia's leather slippers from underneath the bed. Ye-Ye jumped down, sensing something exciting was about to happen.

"The royal guards are sticklers for rules." Bukki pointed at the locked door. "He'll never let you out without approval. Let's take the window."

She said it so casually that Kalothia thought she'd misheard, until Bukki moved over to the window, hitched up her long white dress, and swung one leg over the sill. Ye-Ye yipped with delight and scrambled over to pounce on Bukki's lap and look out at the world.

Kalothia was perplexed. She'd already checked the distance to the ground. It was too far to jump. "Are you planning to fly?"

Bukki gave her a cheeky grin that lit up her face. She swung her other leg over so that both legs were dangling out the window, twenty cubits from the ground.

Kalothia gasped. "Have you lost your mind?"

Bukki grinned again. "The builders resurface the walls in this part of the palace after every rainy season. All they need to travel up and down are these handy devices." She pulled four rods with hooked ends from her hair and handed two to Kalothia. Then she scooted sideways, ran one of the hooks against the baked earth brickwork and gave a quick flick of her wrist.

Kalothia, who was watching her curiously, gasped in horror when Bukki leaned forward and dropped out of sight. She raced to the empty window and found Bukki hanging from the wall clinging to the single rod, with Ye-Ye perched on her shoulder. Kalothia's eyes widened in amazement.

"The hooks slip between the bricks," Bukki explained as she began climbing effortlessly up the wall.

Kalothia huffed out a laugh. This was something she had to try. Taking the rods Bukki had left for her, she mirrored the other girl's maneuvers until she'd learned how to hook the rods into the wall and how to brace her weight. Then she slid off the windowsill. She moved gingerly at first, testing each rod, but the technique was simple and she was soon climbing the wall with ease.

Ye-Ye let out an excited stream of chatter in greeting as Kalothia swung herself into an empty room, similar in size to the one that she'd occupied below. Bukki stood waiting with folded arms and a wide smile. "I'm impressed!"

Kalothia smirked. "That I didn't fall and break myself into a thousand pieces?"

Bukki laughed. "That you followed so quickly. Mama says you grew up in a forest. I figured you could handle yourself, but you're a fast learner."

Kalothia shrugged, catching her breath. "Doesn't it worry you that anybody can climb into the palace?"

"This trick only works on that one wall and I had to bribe the builders with all kinds of favors to gift me a single one of the climbing rods. Then I had to find a carpenter who could duplicate it. There are definitely easier ways to get into this palace." While she talked, she moved over to the door and eased it open.

"Why do you move around the palace like this?" Kalothia asked.

Bukki paused to turn back. "There are so many secrets in this building. I grew up with a mother who'd been banished from the royal court after her closest friend was executed. I learned early that you see what's coming if you tread in places people don't expect." She poked her head out into the hallway. It was quiet. "Let's go explore. It is only appropriate that the new heir to the throne get to see her palace."

Kalothia grimaced at the words "new heir" but slipped out of the room behind Bukki, feeling lighter than she had in several moons. The corridor they entered was more opulent than the simple one that led to her room below. Paintings hung on the walls, and the floor was decorated with painted ceramic tiles that formed symmetrical patterns and flowed into the distance.

"This is one of the guest wings," Bukki said. "It's only used when the royal court is holding a ball or ceremony, so it's usually quiet. Which is why I thought we could start the tour here."

They turned off from the corridor and crossed a varnished wooden bridge that curved over a mirrored pool several stories below before connecting to a new corridor. Somewhere up ahead a door banged, and Kalothia jumped. She caught Bukki's look of surprise. "I'm a little on edge," she said.

Bukki nodded. "I heard about the attack on your home. I'm sorry for . . . your loss."

Kalothia nodded, unable to speak. Bukki touched her arm gently and Kalothia managed a weak smile.

A door up ahead opened, spilling out chatter, laughter, and music. As they snuck past, Kalothia caught a glimpse of a large room with floor-to-ceiling windows overlooking the sea and men and women dressed in white, drinking from ceramic teacups. Lord Suja sat amongst them. Kalothia looked at Bukki in surprise. The revelry was a sharp contrast to the people at the city gates dressed in faded white and mourning the king's death. His death seemed less significant in the palace where he'd lived.

Bukki put a finger to her lips until they were a safe distance away. "Not many in the palace mourned the king's passing," she whispered. "Least of all the lords. They've been playing power games in secret for years. Now they get to vie for the throne openly."

"Until I arrived."

Bukki hesitated and then nodded. "You should be careful, Kalothia. The attack in the forest . . . well . . . it may only be the beginning. This place . . . it's dangerous, as Queen Sylvia found out. My mother says when your mother was accused of adultery, her ladies-in-waiting began spreading rumors about her, the court women stoked the flames, and the lords urged the king to assert his power. She testified for your mother, but there was such a storm of lies she was accused of abetting the affair. She says it happened so quickly. By the time Lord Godmayne arrived to plead the queen's case, the king was so brainwashed by the lies he refused to listen to anything else."

Footsteps sounded in the distance. They froze and pressed themselves against the wall, waiting. When a serving girl appeared, Bukki breathed a sigh of relief. She waved at the girl, who waved back and continued about her business.

"You get on well with all the servers," Kalothia noted.

"They're worth ten of each courtier. Captain Godmayne's lucky he doesn't have to live here."

"Are the lords at court often?" Kalothia knew they all resided in their own territories.

"No. They visit as needed. It has been less over recent years with the king participating so little in court life. Lord Caspin's main residence is in the city, of course. He barely stays here at all. Did you know that the royal family hasn't always been here either? They used to live in the Eastern Territory. In Lord Suja's lands. But after a royal tour, one of your ancestors fell in love with the cliffs and the sea of Port Caspin and decided to build a recreational palace here. When it was finished, he returned with his family to enjoy the dry season by the sea . . . and he never left."

"I'm sure the Easterners loved that."

"Like cats love water. People say that's why Lord Suja is so bitter. It's in his blood. His grandfather's grandfather lost the royal family to the South and the family never got over it. Suja's father was always trying to reclaim the close proximity to the palace his ancestors had enjoyed. He tried to persuade the old king to marry your father to his daughter, but nothing came of it."

Kalothia thought of the young, sneering Lord Suja. It seemed bitterness and hatred toward her mother, as the woman who had usurped his sister's place, was in his blood. Did that resentment extend to her daughter?

"Does Lord Suja have any links to Padma?" Kalothia asked.

Bukki shrugged. "All the lords do in one way or another. Padma has been a thorn in Galla's side for as long as anyone can remember. Everyone would like to see the hostility resolved. Lord Suja probably has more reason to hate the Padmans than the others since most of Padma's attacks are directed at the Eastern villages, where they share a border. That's gone on for years. They've devastated many of the East's salt mines with their raids. Whenever Lord Suja used to come south, he ranted about the king's ineffectual handling of the Padman crisis. He's always threatening to strike his own bargain with the Padmans."

Kalothia had so many questions, about Padma and life at court, but she was distracted when they stepped into a magnificent marble hallway. Late-afternoon sun reflected off the white stone walls and bounced off the floors, transforming the corridor into a gold prism. Carved jade wall fixtures held unlit candles. Plush settees upholstered in silvery gray fur lined the passage. It made Kalothia think of sun-bright days fishing in the stream when the water was clear as crystal and everything sparkled with life.

Bukki led her to a gray door inlaid with gold. She looked at Kalothia, shuffled from foot to foot, then put a tentative hand on the door handle. She paused again. "This was your mother's suite. Do you want to go in?"

Kalothia stumbled back a step. Something squeezed sharply in her chest. She rubbed it, trying to loosen the ache. She looked at the door, wondering at herself. She'd never known her mother, though she'd dreamed of finding her and was saddened now that she never would, but she didn't expect to feel such bone-deep pain at the thought of being in her rooms. She took a breath. Why was she hesitating? Of course she wanted to know more about her mother. She nodded. "Yes, I want to go in."

Bukki paused, as though wondering if she would change her mind, then she opened the door to bright sunshine.

The suite was beautiful. Fresh-cut flowers sat in glass bowls everywhere. The furnishings were made for comfort—calfskin, fur, silk, wool—and the colors for calm—cinnamon, cedar, caramel, tan. There were deep sofas with bright cushions, elegant wooden tables of all sizes, gold-edged mirrors, and intricately patterned woven mats. Kalothia looked around in awe at the splendor, the luxury.

"The serving girls tell me the king had the rooms cleaned daily but ordered nothing was to be changed or removed. They say the prince would come and sit in here sometimes to read," Bukki said.

Kalothia frowned. "No one else came here at all?"

"The king would allow only the maids and the prince. He once had a maid banished from the city after she dropped one of the vases from this room and cracked it. No courtier would have dared to come in. Of course, the king's with the Goddess now so the old rules may not apply."

Ye-Ye bunched his muscles, ready to leap off and explore, but Kalothia stilled him with a hand. "No. Stay." There must have been something in her tone because he whined but relaxed on his perch.

Kalothia moved through the room, her eyes alert to every detail. The silk dressing gown thrown casually over a sofa, the bulbs of candle wax floating in a bowl on a side table, the leather slippers next to the balcony doors. There were other rooms: a dressing room with a wooden hair comb, gold ear studs, and an amethyst necklace thrown haphazardly on the table; a washing room with a patterned wrapper hanging on a drying rack and silk slippers beside a copper bathtub. In the sleep room, charcoals and chalks sat in a bowl atop piles of white paper on a table beside a large bed. The bedsheets were clean and turned back invitingly.

"It looks like she might return any moment," Kalothia mused.

"Mama says Queen Sylvia thought she would. She didn't think

the king would really go through with the execution until it was too late."

"How was she . . . executed?" Teacher and Aunty had refused to talk about it. Part of her didn't want to know but another part was desperate to find out.

Bukki glanced at her for a moment. "Um, there's a place in the palace grounds called the Sunken Garden. The lords and elders meet there when there's a trial or a serious matter to discuss. It has a ledge that overhangs the sea. It's a very long drop, and when the tide goes out, you can see all the rocks it usually hides." She took a breath. "Traitors are chained and pushed off the ledge."

Kalothia gasped. Nausea roiled through her stomach. "That's a terrifying way to die," she whispered.

Bukki nodded.

Heavy with emotion, Kalothia turned to leave the room when her eyes hitched on a crib. It stood in the corner of the sleep room and was beautifully constructed of sandy wood. A red knitted blanket lay folded inside. Her vision blurred and she realized she was blinking back tears.

Thinking about her mother's execution and then seeing this hopeful, cheery-looking crib was too much. She turned away and stumbled through a door that led outside. The breeze was salty and brisk. She sucked it in and let it fill her lungs, let it restore her. When she could think clearly again, she found she was in a court-yard filled with blooming flowers overlooking the sea. Her mother's rooms were arranged in a horseshoe around the courtyard and at the center stood a life-size statue on a pedestal. She moved closer for a clearer view.

A beautiful woman stood cast in bronze. The proud nose, almond eyes, high cheekbones, and hint of a smile were so lifelike it seemed they would move. Kalothia knew that face. It was the one she saw when she caught her reflection in a looking glass. *How strange,* she thought, gazing at it, *that the man who gave you all this had you executed. Yet he preserved your memory like a flower pressed under glass.*

"Are you ready?" Bukki said gently.

Kalothia turned from the statue at the sound of her voice.

"We can come back another time, but they'll be bringing the evening meal soon and if the serving girl finds you gone . . . Are you ready?" Bukki asked again.

Kalothia nodded. She was so overwhelmed with emotions she feared they'd come bursting out if she didn't go someplace quiet to recover.

They took a different route back, new corridors, new gardens, even an aviary.

"What will you do?" Bukki asked as they walked. "About Suja's challenge? Mama thinks you should just sit tight for a while, let them throw their weight around. Eventually they'll have to let you meet the elders and be assessed. The caves are a death trap. No one who enters comes out. No one has ever brought out a kori egg. They can't make you go."

Kalothia sighed. She didn't want to sit around waiting for the lords to be reasonable. But she couldn't leave; the answers she needed were in Port Caspin. "I think I'll have to wait while Lord Godmayne persuades the other lords." It was painfully frustrating.

"Don't worry, I'll show you the ropes while you wait."

Kalothia smiled at her. There was something so bright and optimistic about Bukki. The palace might be cruel and dangerous, but at least she had one friend. They walked down more corridors. It was all a blur, until she caught a snatch of a familiar voice and her feet stilled.

"What is it?" Bukki whispered. They were crossing a terrace from one part of the palace to another. If somebody approached from the other end, there would be nowhere to hide, yet Kalothia remained frozen, trying to pinpoint what she'd heard.

"This is not your fight." An older man's voice came from a window above the terrace.

"I know."

Two words, but she'd know the gravelly tones of Nahir's voice anywhere. Familiar warmth bloomed in her chest before turning to the sickly anger that he now provoked.

"What did you say last harvest when I offered to assign one of your brothers to manage her security?"

Kalothia strained closer, breath held. She'd forgotten where she was and why she shouldn't be caught lurking. All that mattered was his answer.

"I said I didn't like to leave a job half done."

Sickness roiled in her stomach. A job. That's all she was. A job. Just as she'd suspected.

"The job is done now. She's here. Package delivered. I will instruct her in her duties. Go back to your men."

She didn't want to hear his reply. She took off running, oblivious to the direction, careless of the risk that she might encounter people. Bukki didn't catch up to her until she'd raced up a flight of stairs and turned two corners.

BACK IN HER ROOM AFTER A DIFFICULT CLIMB DOWN, KALOTHIA lay on her bed and let the anger and hurt war within her. She ignored her meal when it came, leaving Ye-Ye to pick at it as he willed. She didn't know what to do and she had no one to turn to. Her family—the only one she'd known—was dead. And she was just a job to Nahir. A duty.

Shame licked her insides. Her thoughts were as lethal as knives handled blade first. She had considered him family, all that she had left. Foolish, foolish Kalothia.

Nahir had a family. Three brothers and one sister. He had parents and likely a legion of extended family members who loved him. She was the one desperate for connections. So desperate she'd cry over a man who'd lied to her for their whole acquaintance. Yet the tears soaked her face and refused to stop though she scrubbed at them furiously. Goddess damn him and this hateful room she was locked in.

Outside, the sky had dimmed to a gray evening light. She stared at the ceiling in the growing gloom. What did she want? Her family was gone. All she could salvage on their behalf were answers and punishment for their murders. She couldn't allow their deaths to go unmarked, unavenged, like her mother's.

She sat up, energy coursing through her. Her attackers had come from the royal court, and she was in that court right now; she needed to make sure this was where she stayed, and that meant proving her claim to the throne.

Also, there was a part of her that wanted to stand up to the lords who thought they could have everything their own way. They were not heirs to the throne. She was.

And there was another part of her, the part that was twisting in pain and crying that she had lost Nahir a second time, that craved the distraction of danger, or taking action.

They'd passed the Ibeso Caves on the way to the palace. She could find her way back there. She'd bring them a kori egg, or she'd die trying. It wasn't like anybody would miss her.

16

THE CAVES

THERE WERE FEW TRAVELERS ON THE KING'S HIGHWAY. THEIR lamps cast feeble pools of light in the growing darkness. Kalothia's ears picked up the eerie birdsong that marked the Ibeso Caves quicker than she had expected. It had seemed much farther away when she had traveled with the convoy.

It had been easier than she'd anticipated to escape from the palace, almost as if someone didn't mind if she chose to leave, so long as she didn't bother coming back. Parting with Ye-Ye had been the toughest part. He must have sensed something because he'd clung desperately to her. But she refused to take him on a journey she might not return from. Bukki would care for him in her absence. Once she'd persuaded Ye-Ye to stay, she'd used the wooden rods still in her possession to climb down to the ground. The courtyard below her room had been deserted, and the guards on the gate had been more concerned about intruders than those wanting to leave; they'd barely given her a second's glance as she'd slipped out. She'd walked quickly down the wide paved road that led down to Port Caspin and bought a donkey off a peddler.

The donkey obeyed when she led it off the paved road and up a stony slope that in the darkness seemed to climb and climb. She recalled Bisi's words about night travelers who were lured off the road and into the caves' depths. Her skin prickled with cold, even in the evening warmth.

She didn't see the first cave until she was standing at the mouth, her lamp useless against the yawning blackness in its depths. She slid off the donkey and gave its back a thankful pat. She hoped it would stay nearby until she returned. The birdsong seemed to echo all around her. She swallowed and gathered all her courage. Before she could reconsider, she stepped inside.

The cave interior was humid. Kalothia paused for a moment, letting her body adjust to the press of heat, to the additional effort needed to draw a breath. In her mind she formed a quick plan of action. Whenever there was a choice of direction she would take a right turn. With luck it would make retracing her steps easier. Resolved, she moved forward. For the first thirty cubits the ground sloped gently, offering an easy descent. Then, abruptly, it tilted downward at an angle so sharp Kalothia found herself involuntarily skidding and slipping down the smooth surface. By the time the ground leveled out and she regained control, the faint light from the entrance had vanished. She didn't know how she would climb the steep incline when the time came, for now there was no choice but to forge ahead.

She turned the lamp down to conserve oil. In the yellow glow, she could see the wet stone walls and uneven worn floor. The air smelled of mildew. Spears of calcified rock hung from the ceiling. She walked deeper into the cave network, her feet slapping on the ground, the noise then echoing ominously off the walls.

The path curved and dipped. After a particular stretch, she was certain she'd walked in a circle, having edged along an awkwardly narrow passage beside a distinctly shaped rock twice. The third time the passage disappeared and she found herself walking through a cavern so wide her lamplight didn't touch the edges, only to exit it and arrive in the narrow passage with the odd rock formation again. A terrifying suspicion entered her head that maybe men disappeared in the caves not because of their labyrinthine layout but because the place was enchanted and impossible to navigate. A shiver ran down her spine.

Up ahead there was a split in the path. One branch led to a wide corridor, the other to a small round opening. She was contemplating her options when she realized she could hear a faint sound. It was a high-pitched vibration that changed note. Was it birdsong? It sounded vaguely like the trill the forest birds would emit as they settled down for the evening. She tried to pinpoint the direction. The sound seemed to grow in volume when she moved closer to the round opening, so she bent and squeezed herself through.

The air on the other side was musty and heavy. Her skin grew damp with sweat, and it was a struggle to breathe. She stood still for a moment, fighting off a wave of dizziness. The trilling sound was louder. She was sure.

The lamp illuminated a corridor that stretched off in two directions. She picked one and took a step, crouching because the ceiling was low. A faint but distinct warble sang through the air behind her and she whirled so quickly the lamp hit the wall, sending a crack of noise rattling through the stale air of the cave's many chambers. She moved in the direction the warble had seemed to come from, eager to find the source, straining to hear it again. She had to crab-walk gingerly around a boulder that jutted from a wall. Just as she'd nearly finished rounding it, one of her feet came down on air. The ground had disappeared.

With a cry, she threw herself back against the boulder, dropping the lantern in her panic. It clanged loudly against rocks as it fell. Putting her weight on the foot that still rested on solid ground, she clung to the huge rock, her arms wrapped around its slimy surface, trying not to slide off and trying to find a place to put the foot still cycling in the air. *I'll just hang on, catch my breath, then edge back to safer ground,* she thought.

Something groaned nearby. She tightened her grip on the boulder and pressed her face into its rough surface. There was a jolt and, with a shudder that vibrated against her face, the boulder tore free from the ground and began rolling, heading for the edge and taking her with it. She reached out, trying to find something to grab on to, but stones tore at her hands giving no purchase.

For a long moment, there was nothing but weightlessness and horror. Then her feet struck the ground, sending pain screaming up the length of her body. It was amplified when she fell on her side and rolled, scraping her face and every piece of exposed skin on sharp rocks. She was still rolling when the boulder crashed to the ground beside her, sending shards of rock flying like missiles.

She crashed into a wall and lay still. Every breath felt like a hot poker stabbing her chest. She tried to move an arm but instead froze with a hiss of agony. Parts of her were broken, she was certain. The lamp had landed in a corner and threw out a weak flickering light.

She prayed it wouldn't go out. Her eyes were on the sickly light when something flashed at the edge of her vison. Something on the wall had moved. Several somethings.

Fear gripped her body, driving the pain up a notch. The somethings were like living, shifting shadows. One of the shadows turned predatory silver eyes on her. She gasped and tried to rise. A tidal wave of pain pressed her face back into the dirt. She lay with her eyes closed, panting, trying to push the pain back enough to move.

AFTER A TIME, LIGHT FLARED BEHIND HER CLOSED LIDS. SHE opened them to see a pair of bare feet. Beside the feet, a bird with gold-blue plumage lay sleeping in a nest. When Kalothia tilted her head back, she found the woman in indigo staring down at her.

The woman bent and pressed cool fingers to Kalothia's temple. The air seemed to crackle, and pressure filled Kalothia's head so swiftly she cried out at the pain. Then it was gone. Sudden as a candle doused with water, the press of power evaporated.

"You should try moving. I fixed everything that was broken." The woman's voice was as deep and dark as black coffee at midnight.

Kalothia lay frozen for a moment, then moved her head experimentally. The blinding pain was gone. She stretched her arms gingerly. Everything felt intact. She sat up. Nothing hurt. In fact, she felt great. When she looked down, she saw her dress was ruined, she'd lost her slippers, and her feet were bare, yet her skin was not even scratched. The woman lowered herself to the ground, so that they sat face-to-face.

Kalothia noted how the woman moved with a disturbing boneless ease, as though she didn't require the flexing and contracting of muscles to direct her movements. A single word was clamoring in her head, but she pressed her lips shut, too fearful to confirm it.

The woman looked at her. "Yes, I am."

Kalothia's eyes widened. "Yes, you are . . . the Goddess?"

The woman nodded.

Kalothia nodded back. There was a beat of silence. What did you say to a goddess? "How did you find me?"

The Goddess was watching her steadily, her large brown eyes unblinking. "I've been observing you. I believe you will be useful."

"Useful?" Kalothia's voice rose in pitch. She didn't like the sound of that.

"Yes. You have an energy that I like." The Goddess smiled. Every rock around them seemed to blaze into life, pouring golden light out into the gloom. "You have a penchant for near-death experiences. I almost missed you today."

Kalothia nodded as though this were a perfectly normal conversation. *Where was the Goddess when she missed things? How had she known to come?*

The Goddess tilted her head, as though she were observing an interesting specimen. "I'm in many places. This world is large and I tend many gardens. I cannot be everywhere at once. That power belongs to those greater than me."

Kalothia's heart stuttered. Had the Goddess just read her thoughts, again? The bird cheeped in its sleep and fluffed its feathers, drawing Kalothia's attention.

"You were looking for an egg." The Goddess gazed at the small bird fondly, following Kalothia's eyes. "I brought the mother too. They don't like to be separated. These secretive birds are my favorites."

Kalothia nodded again. It was all she seemed able to do. This was all so strange. *Did the trilling birdsong draw me to this spot? Am I dead? Is this all a dream?*

The Goddess shook her head. Her cloud of thick black hair swayed gently. "You're not dead. You wouldn't be useful to me dead."

This usefulness again. Kalothia really didn't like the sound of it.

"I didn't mean for women to be lesser," the Goddess said suddenly, as if continuing a conversation that they'd already been having. "If you take the throne, Galla will see that they're not. You'll raise them up to be equal."

Kalothia blinked. Take the throne? No, she didn't like this at all. "'The modest and peaceful woman will be crowned with blessings,'" she quoted the fourth precept.

The Goddess's eyes hardened. "Men have tampered with my writings. That was never the teaching."

"Why don't you just correct it?"

The Goddess tapped a finger on the ground. "There are rules."

Kalothia absorbed this for a moment. "I don't wish to be queen."

The Goddess twitched an eyebrow. "You don't? Your mother did."

Air rushed out of Kalothia's lungs. She straightened. "You knew my mother?" Of course! She was a goddess. "Was she . . . useful?"

"She would have been."

"Why didn't you save her?"

"There are rules," she said again. "I can only bend them so much. I cannot prevent a person's death."

The words cut through Kalothia's chest. "But you stopped that man from killing me in the forest!"

"I loosened your ropes. You did the rest. There was no crowd to witness the change. I did not overstep death's domain. It was the bending of a small rule."

Kalothia rubbed her temples. There was so much she didn't understand. She clambered stiffly to her feet. "I don't wish to be queen." She directed the statement at the wall above the Goddess's head, but her voice was clear and determined. If the Goddess chose to strike her down for being uncooperative, then so be it. She wanted justice for the family that raised her and then to be free to make her own choices.

The Goddess rose in that strange boneless way she had. "You have a kori egg now. The only human to find one. You may discover you have fewer choices than you think." She looked sympathetic. Kalothia resented it. She disliked being useful, being maneuvered and manipulated. She'd spent sixteen harvests in the forest because it suited somebody's plan. She did not wish to be moved like a piece on a game board.

The Goddess smiled. Light blazed. "This is the energy in you I like. So independent. One final thought for you, Kalothia Osura. The easiest way to find the answers you're seeking is from the palace. Ideally, from a position of power. You know this. It's the reason you entered the caves. When you fight destiny, things go awry." She turned and walked deeper into the cave. Within seconds she was gone, blending into the darkness beyond.

Kalothia watched after her, annoyed. She hated that her words made a semblance of sense. Finally, she bent down and examined the sleeping bird. "Will you wake if I lift you?"

The bird stirred sleepily. She recalled how Aunty had taught her to gather eggs by putting a finger under the bird's body, tilting gently but decisively. The bird stirred again, waking with a yawn, then pecking with annoyance at her hand. But she'd already caught a glimpse of the blue egg below its body. She let the bird go so it could fluff its feathers and resume its restful slumber.

"Let's see if you'll let me carry you." She lifted the nest carefully.

The bird cracked an eye to watch her warily, but it remained still. When she left the cave room, she found a distinctive path remained lit with no discernible light source. "It makes no sense to leave your 'useful' new tool trapped in a cave," she grumbled to herself as she followed it. The path led her up slopes, through low-ceilinged caverns, around endless corners and through narrow tunnels. Finally, she spotted a bright shaft of light that grew, became a fresh breeze, then opened into twilight.

17

TRIUMPH

KALOTHIA STUMBLED OUT OF THE CAVES INTO EVENING LIGHT.
She blinked against the red and orange rays, wondering how long
she'd been gone. Had an entire day passed? Slowly the scene before
her registered and her confusion became a frown. Nahir sat kneeling
before a fire, his eyes closed, his head bent. Was he . . . praying? Her
jaw dropped; her eyes narrowed with disbelief.

As though he'd heard her thoughts, his head shot up and whipped
around in her direction. He was on his feet in a blink. There was a
stiffness to his movements and he walked with a limp. Still he was
in front of her before she could speak, hauling her into his arms,
enveloping her in a hug. For a few moments she let him hold her,
grateful and comforted by the warmth of his body. Then she remembered the kori bird cradled in her arms, and immediately after, the
words he'd spoken that had broken her heart. She wriggled until he
released her.

He cleared his throat, clearly embarrassed. "Are you hurt?" He scanned her torn clothes and disheveled hair.

"I'm fine." She took a step back. "Why are you here?" She kept her voice cold, neutral. If he grew angry and left that would be fine, she told herself, after all, she was just a task for him.

The kori bird chirped unhappily. Unsure whether it was due to the evening light or having been sandwiched in a hug, Kalothia rocked it reassuringly and bent her body to block out the setting sun.

"You found a bird?" There was shock in Nahir's gravelly voice. She didn't want to look at him. He was absolutely not forgiven. But he moved close enough to peer down over her shoulder. He was so near she could feel the heat from his body, smell the scent of his skin, hear his quiet breaths. She had to will her feet to the ground and reject the urge to retreat.

"Is there an egg in there, too?"

He shifted even closer. She held her breath.

"That task was blessed-near impossible, Kalothia." His tone was so serious she glanced up at him. He was studying her, his eyes dark and intense. "I'm beginning to think you were destined for the throne. You are Goddess-touched."

She jerked. What would he say if she told him she'd just spoken to the Goddess? Would he call her crazy, or would he believe her? A yawning fear was opening inside her, a sense of dangling over a cliff edge. Just days ago, she'd been a minor royal with missing parents. Now she was having conversations with a goddess and being pushed toward Galla's throne. Having Nahir look at her with shock and awe was too much. Everything was spinning out of her control.

"Why are you here?" she asked again.

His face went hard. "You've been gone for two days. How could you just disappear like that?"

Two days? Her eyes widened in shock before she reclaimed her control and smoothed her features back to placid indifference. "Why do you care? You should be on the road east. You've completed your mission. I was delivered safely to Port Caspin." There was enough bitterness in her voice to sour a meal. She turned away and began to walk. He spun her around so quickly she didn't realize he'd grabbed her until she was facing him.

"Where did you hear that?" His eyes were narrowed and his chest was heaving; she'd never seen him so angry.

"From you. That's what you told your father, isn't it?" She stared him down.

"My job is to keep you safe. You're not safe."

"I'm fine. I'll make my own way back." She scanned the area, hoping to see the donkey she'd left. There was no sign of it. She smothered a sigh. Two days was a lot to ask of the animal. Could she hitch a lift? The King's Highway was a furlong ahead, down the rocky slope. She adjusted the bird and nest resting in the crook of her arm and began to walk, her feet crunching on the stony ground. Out of habit she raised her free hand to check her hair. She groaned. *Red earth!* It was uncovered. That would be a problem.

Nahir's steps crunched behind her, then he was grabbing her arm. "Get on the horse!" He pointed back at the caves, where two horses stood tethered to rocks.

Her fury was so hard and hot it stole her voice. Who did he think he was to order her around? She stared daggers at him.

"You can't just go wandering around here," he said. "You can get on, or I can put you on."

Her jaw dropped. She was so furious with him she prayed the ground would open up and swallow him. His face was unyielding; he meant it. She braced her feet and clenched the fist that wasn't supporting a legendary bird with its egg and nest. The urge to deposit her precious bundle on the ground and meet Nahir's challenge was overwhelming. She wished for her spear or a sword, or any weapon she could use to beat sense into him.

Nahir watched the thoughts flit across her face. He noted her clenched fist and seemed to understand the general direction of her thoughts. He raised a brow. "Really?"

His voice was soft. Challenging. *Red earth, he was infuriating!* It galled her to acknowledge that she'd never won a sparring match against him. Even when she was fully armed, rested, and not responsible for a fragile gift from the Goddess. True, he was injured too, but he was still the better fighter. It was a question of how badly she would lose. She pursed her lips, cut her eyes at him, and spun on her heel to march to the waiting horses.

SHE STOOD OUTSIDE THE THRONE ROOM AS SHE HAD TWO DAYS before. A guard announced her just as they had then. She hadn't changed her clothes or brushed the dirt and sand from her hair. But she had no intention of doing so. She wanted to drag dirt and grime over their polished floors. The doors swung open and she strode in.

A surprised hush fell over the assembly at her entrance. Whispers accompanied her steps as she marched through the room. She didn't care about the speakers or their words. They were a nameless, faceless mass. All her attention was on the four men seated at the front. She held the kori bird's nest to her chest, against her stained and bedraggled white dress.

Lord Suja's face was a picture of indignation and wariness, as though he was trying to understand the reason behind the confidence propelling her across the room. Lord Godmayne was fighting a grin. She saw Nahir had inherited his dimples from his father.

She stopped an arm's span from Lord Suja and held up the nest in one hand. "Who will be taking charge of the kori egg?"

Lord Suja struggled, unsuccessfully, to master his expression. Wariness had won over the indignation. "You expect us to believe..."

She lowered her hand and tilted the nest to reveal the kori bird, which was now fully awake and looking around warily. It pecked furiously at her fingers when she lifted it up to reveal the blue egg. The bird launched itself from her grip and circled the air above her head with unfurled iridescent wings and loud caws of annoyance before swooping to settle back atop its egg. Gasps ricocheted around the court.

"I've named her Sylvia," Kalothia declared. The gasps became exclamations and chatter, which rose in volume to a clamor.

Lord Suja's eyes were bulging, his lips trembled, but he remained silent. Kalothia watched him steadily, satisfaction warming her like a fire on a cold night. Lord Godmayne rose heavily to his feet. He stepped forward and signaled the back of the room. A series of drumbeats thundered out, silencing the tumult. "The princess has fulfilled the challenge." His voice carried. "We serve at your pleasure, Your Highness." He folded forward, bending until his right hand touched the floor in a bow.

The voices that had been silenced rose again in a wave. Alarm clanged through Kalothia like a rung bell. The warm feeling that had flowed through her turned cold. Then, as though a discussion had been held and a consensus reached, the voices faded out, as, one by one, the courtiers rose from their seats and kneeled. In seconds, the entire throne room was kneeling and silent. Kalothia stared at them. When she turned back to the lords, all of them, except Lord Godmayne, remained seated. None of them looked pleased.

Lord Woli was the first to rise, with the aid of his walking stick. His rheumy eyes met hers. "It may spell our ruin, but it seems the Goddess has her hand on you." With difficulty, he bent as much as he could, pointing his right hand toward the floor.

Lord Suja glared at her. "All it proves is that you are in league with dark forces." But, like an oak tree bowing under the force of a storm, he bent, slowly and reluctantly.

She thought Lord Caspin would refuse. "A woman has never led this country," he said. "The Goddess would never allow it."

"And yet she has," Lord Godmayne said. "You see, she has given Kalothia her bird."

Lord Caspin's stare was laced with such contempt that she was certain he would stare her down. But eventually he folded his short body to touch the floor. Her heart hammered. The enormity of her change in status finally hitting her. She was next in line for the throne.

LEARNING THE ROPES

KALOTHIA AWOKE TO VOICES. SHE OPENED HER EYES TO WHITE netting draped over her bed in the royal guest room she now occupied. The voices came from an adjoining room. Ye-Ye had been climbing one of the bedposts, but he scuttled down and ran to her when she pulled the netting open.

"Come on." She invited him with a cupped hand. He raced up her arm to his spot behind her ear.

Several wrappers lay draped over a bamboo chair against a wall. She took one and wound it over the silk nightdress she wore. Then she passed through an empty dressing room to the parlor beyond. There she found Bukki talking with a small, square man in a starched tunic and shokoto with sharp pleats.

"Your Highness." Bukki kneeled elegantly.

Kalothia froze. Bukki had dipped her a bow before, but this was a full bow, and it seemed to be delivered with a pointed significance.

The throne room, full of kneeling courtiers, flashed through her mind, igniting flares of anxiety through her body. She did not want to be queen.

The square man bowed too, pressing his right hand to the floor. He rose smoothly. "Morning greetings, Your Highness. I am the royal secretary." There was something square about his voice too. Every word precise in a tone as flat as a straight line.

The man gestured to a nearby stack of boxes with scrolls poking out in haphazard directions. "I've brought the royal correspondence. I will assign you a scribe to read the materials and write your responses. It will be very unconventional. Usually only the king and, if necessary, the prime minister, would be privy to these sensitive materials, but I've been told to accommodate—"

"Why would I need a scribe?" she interrupted the secretary's monotone stream of words.

He paused and looked at her. "Because you are illiterate." He spoke slowly, as though she might have trouble understanding.

"I am not illiterate," she replied just as slowly. "I will not be needing a scribe." She wandered closer to the boxes. *Red earth*, this was a lot of correspondence.

"You read?" Bukki asked, her voice high.

When she glanced back, they were both staring at her in shock and Bukki was looking her up and down as though searching for a tail or some other irregularity. "They say it makes women mad," she said.

Kalothia sighed and remembered the battles Teacher had fought with Aunty over her education. "I think I'm still sane, but maybe that's the madness talking."

"You're poking fun!" The secretary looked appalled. His calm reserve was gone. "Book-learning causes infertility in women! It's in the Goddess's precepts! A barren queen . . ." He paused to digest the horror.

Bukki nodded. "Even my mother—she's very rational—she says the Goddess forbids it. Women must be modest—"

"—and peaceful," Kalothia chorused with her. "'The burden of learning and leadership falls on men.'" She shook her head. These misleading teachings were truly seared into the minds of Gallans. She sighed then pointed at herself. "I'm not mad. I haven't grown a third thumb. I don't think I'm infertile. Aunty—the woman who raised me—believed all the things you do. They're not true."

The secretary gasped as though she'd just drowned a baby before his eyes. He floundered for a moment, searching for his lost composure. "You suggest the precepts are wrong?"

She nodded. "Two of them."

He looked around as though the walls had suddenly grown ears, then moved closer. "Please never say that again," he whispered. He rubbed a fist over his chest, soothing his heart. "We can't have two queens executed. Our neighbors would call us barbarians."

He sucked in a deep breath, closing his eyes as he breathed out. Having marshaled some composure, he began again. "I have made you appointments for discussions with the trade department, infrastructure, security, taxation, farming, and the former elders' council. The Oracle has been consulted. She is searching for an auspicious date for your coronation."

Kalothia's heart sank. Retrieving the kori egg might have kept her in the palace, but it was also going to complicate her investigations and make her a monarch, which she really wasn't sure she wanted to be.

The secretary bowed. "At midday you have a meeting with the lords." He bowed again and left.

What have I done? Kalothia thought to herself, her brain still reeling from the flood of information.

She bathed in a shiny copper tub with water that rushed out of a tap. Bukki had described the waterwheel that generated power for the palace, but they'd had nothing like this in the forest and Kalothia would have to see it for herself to fully understand how it worked. In the meantime, she enjoyed the luxury of not fetching water from a well and heating it over an open fire as she had grown up doing.

She was presented with three white dresses of escalating splendor and chose the simplest. When she asked Bukki about acquiring a tunic and shokoto, the girl looked at her in bewilderment. "The royal court is very conventional," Bukki said. "If you want to be taken seriously and form alliances, you won't dress like a man. If you want to be respected, you'll try to look beautiful. The courtiers are judgmental and shallow. That's why they drape themselves in fine fabrics and jewels."

Kalothia nodded. She had noticed. "What about you?" she asked.

Bukki had dressed for the day in a simple white dress that flattered her curves. She wore small gold ear studs and a necklace of varnished ash wood.

Bukki raised a brow. "During the Queen's trial, my mother spoke up so strongly in the Queen's defense she was accused of abetting the infidelity. She was exiled and we spent over ten years in my father's village. We only returned because we had no money and Mama said she'd rather take her chances in the palace than starve in a village. Mama has a medicinal garden where she grows herbs that she brews into health remedies and scented water. Her concoctions earn us enough cowries for food and clothes. The palace grants us accommodation. In short, though we live in the palace and seem to be part of the fabric of the court, we have no status. We are merely tolerated. It doesn't matter how I dress; I will never be acknowledged or respected. So, I do as I please."

Kalothia frowned. "That seems like a difficult way to live. Have you considered leaving the palace? Trying somewhere else?"

Bukki laughed. "Where would I go?" She gave Kalothia a patient look. "You haven't traveled much. Women can't live without the protection of men in Galla. My mother's father was wealthy, but women can't inherit land or money, so all his wealth went to her brothers.

"When my father took a second wife and stopped caring for us, we could barely scrape together a living. Nobody will give a well-paid job to a woman. If you run a business and it thrives, you can't invest the money in property, land, or gold without a man to sign the paperwork. If you travel the roads alone, you are molested. If you are injured, the courts will blame you for recklessly traveling without male protection." She sighed. "I live under the protection of the royal court. I would need to marry to leave, and trust my husband to treat me well."

Kalothia's mind pored back over Bukki's words. She felt embarrassed and foolish. She had dreamed of traveling and exploring, and had discounted Aunty's warnings about the expectations and restrictions for women in Galla. Now Bukki made the reality clear. Kalothia had noticed the differences between the lives of men and women when she'd passed through Illupeju with Nahir, but it had been a glimpse. She had been ready to launch herself into the world without knowing the basics, like where she'd live or how she'd earn money. It was as foolhardy as somebody strolling into her forest with no idea of how they'd source food and water, and no weapons for defense.

"It is so unfair that women's lives are so restricted," she said.

"Perhaps, with a queen ruling, things may change." Bukki gave her a pointed look.

Discomfort prickled between Kalothia's shoulders at the mention of the throne. Bukki's words echoed the Goddess's urging that Kalothia work toward more equality between men and women. The suggestion irked her. It made her feel pressured, as though she had a responsibility to rule. She didn't want that burden. If only Prince Olu had survived. No doubt he had been raised with all the skills a leader required. It was such a strange twist of fate that he had died in a palace while she had survived an assassination attempt in a forest.

"What was the prince like?" she asked. She realized Bukki would know a lot more about her brother—the word still sat strangely in her mind—than Kalothia had been told by Teacher and Aunty.

Bukki took a moment to consider. "He was a very dutiful son. He never criticized the king, he never overstepped, considering how little the king was said to do. I never spoke to him, but I saw him around a lot. I know he had ideas on how taxes could be reformed, how life could be made a little easier for ordinary people. People whispered that he was like Queen Sylvia." She took a breath. "The one topic he was vocal on was Padma. He thought more should be done to prevent the attacks that happened on border villages. But he never got to do more than talk about it before he died."

"The prince died in a fire. What caused it?"

Bukki shook her head. "They couldn't find the cause. He was staying at a royal residence in the west when it caught fire. It was reduced to smoldering rubble and the prince's body was burned almost beyond recognition."

The morning meal arrived, interrupting them. Ye-Ye was delighted to see the array of dishes. He grabbed a cashew nut as large as his paw and lay in a patch of bright sunshine to gnaw on it. Kalothia watched him, her mind busy.

"What are you thinking?" Bukki asked after several minutes of silence.

Kalothia chewed for a moment. "I'm just wondering how such a fierce fire started. Was the residence constructed in a way that made it vulnerable to fire?"

"They'd had no previous problems with fire. Not that I'd heard. But it was a particularly powerful fire. Why do you ask?"

Kalothia brushed her fingers over her pendant. "I don't know. I'm just curious. Was nobody here suspicious when the king's only heir died?"

Bukki canted her head to the side in thought. "The cook lived in the nearby village. I heard she was roasting a turkey that day and might have accidentally left the oven lit overnight. You suspect foul play?"

A forgotten oven. It sounded like a plausible explanation, still . . . "I don't suspect anything yet. It's just a strange series of coincidences. My mother was wrongfully executed, my brother died in a huge fire, assassins came to murder me within days of my father's untimely death." She met Bukki's eyes. "It's possible that my family is just cursed, but if they had succeeded in killing me, there would be no heir to the Gallan throne. Or none of the Osura line anyway."

Bukki nodded. "The court was curious about the fire. They investigated, but they found nothing untoward. The cook swears she doused the oven fire."

Kalothia sighed. "It's likely I'm chasing shadows. I suspect everybody right now. All the lords have the wealth necessary to fund assassins in multiple regions of the country, and any one of them would want the power and influence that came with ruling Galla."

"Yes. Under law they are supposed to rule together but they can't cooperate enough to share power that way. I don't think they want war. They know they'd all lose out. But they're jockeying for ways to gain an upper hand over one another. Eventually somebody will take offense or go too far. Then—*kaboom!*"

Kalothia raised an eyebrow. She could see how she'd be the simple solution. Unless somebody was really vying for power. In that case she became an obstacle. "I hear Lord Caspin has been very clear about wanting to rule. He has contacts in Padma through his trading connections."

"How is Padma involved in this?" Bukki asked.

"The assassins who came for me spoke Padman."

Bukki's eyes widened at the implications. "Do you think the Duchess of Padma is involved?"

Kalothia shrugged. "I don't see what she'd have to gain, other than to destabilize Galla."

"Could it be that's the goal?" Bukki wondered.

Kalothia considered it. "Someone at court knew I existed and found my location. Someone with resources. Then they recruited Padmans to kill me. But who? Lord Suja wants a deal with Padma to stop the attacks on the borders in his lands. Maybe that involves an alliance . . . collusion . . . an agreement to weaken Galla? Or . . . I don't know . . ."

They sat in quiet contemplation for the rest of the meal.

THE SECRETARY RETURNED SHORTLY BEFORE MIDDAY TO GUIDE them to the king's library for Kalothia's first official meeting. "You'll meet with the lords here," he told Kalothia, opening the door and ushering her inside. "I'll go and see about refreshments."

"I'll find you once you're finished," Bukki promised. They both disappeared, leaving her to enter the library alone.

A bank of windows flooded the large room with light. A long table filled the space. Behind it, bookcases lined the wall. Kalothia strolled over to the nearest one and ran her finger along the shelves. There were books on farming practices, on Galla's history, on ceremonial traditions, on the Gallan law and its evolution over time, on faith and how to honor the Goddess . . . It was exactly the kind of library she would have designed herself. She wondered which king had stocked it so well. She hoped it wasn't her father; she didn't want to admire anything about him.

She turned and found there were two portraits on the opposite wall. The first was done in bright splashes of color. It showed a girl with charcoal skin, almond eyes, and a wide mouth curved in an infectious smile. It was a side profile—her head was tilted back in a casual pose and her hair was wrapped in a gold scarf. Kalothia's heart jolted in her chest. It was Queen Sylvia. Her mother.

The painting beside it was more sober. A man of eighteen to twenty harvests, with dark red hair like her own. He had his mother's charcoal skin and wide, full mouth but larger eyes and sharper cheekbones. Her brother, Prince Olu. Nahir said they'd met a few times. That he'd been a good man. Surely, he'd have been a better king than their father. A better ruler than the lords.

"Your Highness."

She jumped at the unexpected voice and turned to see the man who'd shown her kindness during that first meeting in the throne room when he'd given her a stool. The man in her mother's sketchbook.

"Prime Minister Hadley?" she ventured.

He nodded and bowed. When he straightened, he gave her a warm smile. "Yes. I have been hoping to see you." He was aged well over sixty harvests, but his jasper skin glowed with health. Bushy gray eyebrows gave him a distinguished yet kindly look. "I trust you are settling in well."

His words had a pleasing musical flow, and the way he met her eyes and waited patiently for her response put her at ease. She hadn't realized how draining it was to live among people who clearly disliked her. Aside from Bukki and Madame Toks, he'd been the kindest to her of anyone here since her arrival.

She returned his smile. "I'm taking each day the Goddess grants," she said, giving the standard reply.

He turned to her mother's portrait. "The resemblance is uncanny. It was a tragedy to lose her so soon, but, with you here, it feels like the Goddess has sent a replacement." He nodded. "Your brother was also delightful. Full of ideas."

She returned her gaze to the portraits. It was comforting somehow to know her mother and brother had also been supported by this high-ranking man.

Lord Suja was next to arrive. He stalked in, caught sight of Kalothia, and gave a bow that somehow managed to be as mocking as it was deep. Kalothia watched him take a seat at the table and decided she was putting him at the top of her list of suspects. She didn't like him. He was rich, arrogant, entitled, and cruel. If he had an eye on the throne, or a contender for it, learning of her existence might have enraged him enough for murder. Could he be trying to prove himself as the youngest lord? Kalothia held in a sigh. Royal court politics were indeed complicated and draining.

Prime Minister Hadley joined them at the table as Lord Godmayne entered the room. "Are you well?" he asked Kalothia after touching the floor in a bow.

She nodded and watched as he took a seat. He was hale and hearty and at least sixty harvests. *What are his dreams for the future?* she wondered. So far, she hadn't really considered that he might have launched the attack against her and she tried to imagine his reasons for doing so. It made no sense, not after he'd kept her alive for sixteen harvests. If he'd wanted her dead, it could have been so easily accomplished during that time. Yet, she wondered, why had he protected her? Was it so he could rule as proxy through her? Was she simply a useful game piece for him?

"Princess?" It was Hadley's smoky voice. "Please rest. It is awkward for your subjects to be seated while you stand." He waved at the head of the table.

She smiled and sat. "Did you ever spend time in the North?" she asked him. It seemed he had no qualms about her leading the country. With his age, she'd expected him to have a more traditional attitude. It was a very Northern mindset.

"No, Your Highness. I am a Southerner from heel to skull top."

Lord Suja drummed his fingers on the table impatiently. Kalothia gave a sigh of relief when Lord Caspin and Lord Woli arrived. The quicker they began, the quicker the meeting could end. The royal secretary returned with a serving boy, who bowed and offered Kalothia a bowl of purple fruit.

"They are kola nuts," Hadley explained. "You peel and eat a segment. It is how we start and end official meetings."

She peeled the skin and bit into it. She chewed and immediately gagged. The nut was bitter and fiery hot. It burned her mouth and nose.

"See!" Suja's voice was a triumphant boom. "The kola nut rejects her. It is a sign. She will be a disaster."

Kalothia's eyes were streaming now. She struggled to draw air into her lungs while the lords ate their own nuts. Hadley brought her a glass of water. She gulped at it eagerly.

"Maybe the Goddess will have mercy on us and take her quickly." Lord Woli stroked his beard thoughtfully.

What did you say when people wished death on you? Kalothia didn't know. She put a hand to her neck and felt the glass of her mother's pendant beneath her fingers.

"Your Highness, nobody's first experience with kola nut is pleasant," Hadley reassured her.

"She'll adapt," Lord Godmayne promised.

She thought again of the agenda he might have for her and the throne.

The prime minister rose creakily to his feet. "May the Goddess grant us wisdom and courage," he prayed.

"Let her will be done," they all answered.

Kalothia lifted her palm to her mouth, sealing the prayer.

"If the girl is to be queen, she'll need an adviser to sign off on her decisions," Lord Caspin stated.

Kalothia choked on her water, insulted by the suggestion.

"My family worked too hard building the South into a powerful trade hub to have a chit of a girl destroy the country," he went on. His round face was impassive despite his ugly words, as though he'd said nothing unusual.

Kalothia flushed with anger at his words. "You don't believe a woman can rule Galla," she said.

"No, a woman cannot rule Galla," Lord Caspin said with a sneer.

"Padma has a duchess," Kalothia said.

Lord Caspin raised a derisive brow. "And look at them. Stealing from their neighbors, launching sly attacks, lying about their crimes. That country will never thrive under a woman ruler, the Goddess herself condemns it. 'The burden of learning and leadership falls on men,'" Lord Caspin quoted.

Kalothia gripped her empty glass and reached for calm. "How is it you pray to a goddess and hold her in such high esteem when you don't believe a woman can rule Galla?"

Lord Suja waved a dismissive hand. "It's not a goddess we'll be putting on the throne," he told her pointedly.

"The princess will have support," Lord Godmayne replied. "I will put together the new elders' council before the coronation."

"Men of your choosing, no doubt!" Lord Caspin turned on his peer.

Kalothia watched Lord Godmayne's expression curiously. He'd kept her safe all her life, but it was possible he wanted something in return. Would his selections for an elders' council be favorable to him?

"Sirs! You have capitulated too early. Are we not going to discuss the prospect of putting a woman on the Gallan throne and becoming the laughingstock of the region?" Suja demanded.

"We need to find a competent second son among the neighboring royal families and marry her off," Lord Woli chimed in.

Frustration boiled beneath Kalothia's skin at being talked over as though she were an object to be moved at will.

Lord Woli gave a long, deep sigh. "Prince Olu would have been perfect. Smart, authoritative, respected, handsome. We'd groomed him for years." He rubbed a hand over his white shock of hair. "Maybe the Goddess is punishing us."

"He understood the need to deal with Padma," Lord Suja agreed. Kalothia's attention sharpened at the mention of Padma. "The prince would have been brave and bold. Unlike the king—Goddess rest him—who sat on his haunches, enabled by advisers like you!" He pointed at Lord Caspin.

"Padma is an important trade partner. We must tread carefully. That is what I told the king," Lord Caspin replied, clearly irritated.

Lord Caspin had advised the king to protect the trade relationship with Padma. Kalothia tucked that piece of information away.

"Is trade more important than the safety of Gallan towns and villages?" Kalothia asked. Nahir had spent the last few years in the Eastern Territory, trying to protect Gallan communities from guerrilla attacks waged by Padman fighters.

Lord Suja clicked his tongue. "I've never heard a woman give her opinion so readily," he groused.

Lord Caspin gave a dry laugh. "Very outspoken, like her mother."

She imagined that, to certain men, a woman who spoke at all would be considered "outspoken."

Lord Suja went on before Kalothia could muster a response. "If it were that easy to cut off trade with Padma, don't you think we would have done so?" He rolled his eyes.

Kalothia wanted to ask him to explain, but she knew the question would just provoke more derision. She would have asked Nahir, but she was still avoiding him. She glanced at Lord Godmayne before swiftly looking away again—any help he offered might come with strings.

"Nobody is expecting you to rule Galla," Lord Suja told her. "Just worry about your dresses and we'll find a man to do the actual governing."

Lord Caspin nodded. "It will need to be the right man, of course. A man who'd built his own territory into the most profitable corner of the country, who had good trade connections with neighbor countries, who could be trusted to return the throne once a son and heir was produced . . ."

There was a moment's silence in the room. Then Lord Suja said archly, "My dear Lord Caspin, it sounds like you are volunteering for the role."

"If I am what Galla needs, I'm ready to serve."

The other lords exclaimed loudly. Lord Woli cleared his throat dramatically. "The rules around succession are . . . hazy because kings are notoriously paranoid. They fear a clear rule for succession will give their enemies a road map of loopholes to undermine them. Let's work with what we have. If there is no heir, we the four lords hold the country until such a time as one is found." He cast a disparaging glance at Lord Caspin. "There is no need for anybody to step into the void."

Lord Godmayne sniffed. "Thank the Goddess this conversation is irrelevant. We have an heir. An heir who retrieved a kori egg and proved her suitability for the crown beyond any shadow of doubt."

They all turned to Kalothia.

"Of course." Lord Caspin bowed his head at Kalothia, but his eyes were sharp and speculative.

Lord Suja huffed under his breath, clearly displeased.

Kalothia forced herself to take regular shallow breaths. She had the anxious sense of being surrounded by sharks in open water. A loose succession law meant a man intent on the throne could be creative about his route there. She had reason to fear every man at the table.

⇒— ◊ —⇐

SHE HAD NEVER BEEN SO RELIEVED TO MEET THE END OF THE day and retire from people. Those who said the country would dissolve into factions and wars without a ruler would judge themselves right if they ever had to sit in a room with the four lords of Galla, she decided. They had gone on discussing pressing policy issues, but there was no sense of unity. No working in service of a common goal. How had the king endured it? Then she remembered he hadn't. The lords had spent most of their time in their own territories and the king had spent most of his time in bed. It was Hadley, Caspin, and a council of elders who had managed the country. Now Galla needed a good leader; if not her, who? Surely not them.

The sun had set hours before, but she had excess energy to burn off. She took one of the many lamps and slipped out into the large garden, attached to the royal guest suite. Nahir hadn't made a single appearance. Not that she wanted to see him. But if he had left for the East, why had he made such a fuss at the caves?

She positioned her feet for a drill workout and began punching and kicking the air in a steady rhythm. While her body moved, her mind worked. Her goal was growing more complicated. The more she saw the inner workings of the royal court, the more responsibility she felt to be the adult in the room, for the sake of ordinary Gallans. Women in particular. Women like Bisi, Chidera, and the other traveling traders she'd met on her journey. Women like Madame Toks who just wanted safety and equal opportunity to provide for herself and her daughter. If she could improve Galla for them as the Goddess and Bukki had suggested, was it selfish of her not to try? And the intrigue around the attack on her home seemed to grow ever more complex too. But one simple fact remained: if somebody was after the throne, the king's death cleared the last obstacle. Apart from her.

She twisted, kicked, punched.

"You need a new spear," Nahir spoke from the darkness.

She stumbled, jolted from her dark thoughts. Then warmth flared in her chest. He hadn't left yet. It was followed swiftly by the returning sting of hurt and anger, burning just as brightly as it had days before. She ignored him.

"Is it safe for you to be out here alone?" he asked.

She pivoted and kicked, irritated by his words. "I'm not your responsibility anymore. Shouldn't you be heading back east to rejoin your men?"

She heard his footsteps in the darkness. Then he was close enough for her to see his outline in the lamplight. "I told my father I'd stay until you decide what you want to do."

She paused. "What do you mean?"

"Are you planning to accept the throne? Become queen?"

Red earth, the Oracle could announce a coronation date any moment, which would set off a steady march to the throne. She desperately wanted to discuss it with somebody. But not him. "Why do you care? I was just a job to you!" Her chest hurt as she threw his words back at him. Tears threatened again. Goddess, why was she always crying over him?

He was silent. The breeze whispered through the trees. A woman's laughter floated on the wind from a terrace or garden. She resumed her workout. Kick, punch, pivot, kick.

"When I received the news about the king's death, I rode straight to the forest," Nahir said.

She stopped. Caught her breath. "So? You were ordered to keep me safe."

"The king dying didn't make you unsafe." He drew a breath. She wished she could see his face. There was something vulnerable in his voice that was foreign and strange and doing uncomfortable things to her heart. "I wanted to see you because he had been your last living family member. I felt sorrow on your behalf." He paused.

She crossed her arms and waited.

"We should have told you. But I think we all wanted to protect you from the world. From the tragedy of your family. Your life before ours."

It was the mantra Clarit had often rattled off. Kalothia sniffed back a tear. She could be mad at them, but she couldn't pretend they hadn't cared for her, that they hadn't done their best to keep her safe. Something loosened in her throat.

"I'm sorry I lied to you," he added.

"All my life."

"Yes, all your life. I'm sorry."

"All right."

"I don't like you being here."

That surprised her. She crossed to the lamp and turned it up to its highest setting. Now she could see his face painted in shades of orange. "At the palace?"

"At the palace. In Port Caspin. In the South."

She frowned. "Where should I be?"

"Somewhere that makes you happy." He looked away and cleared his throat. "You didn't answer my question. About the throne."

She sighed and began to pace. This was another part of her life that had grown complicated over the last few days. "If I don't take the throne, who will hold the country together?"

"There are four lords and a prime minister who are supposed to figure that out."

She snorted. "Everybody is concerned with their own territory. With power for the sake of power. But there are problems that must be fixed." She thought of Padma and the attacks on border villages she kept hearing about. "And there are changes that must be made." Her mind went to Bukki and how Gallan laws kept women dependent on men. "I don't think the lords can be trusted to do that."

Nahir frowned. "You are considering it."

She shook her head, trying to shake off the thought. She'd wanted freedom, not to go from a forest prison to a job with so much responsibility, where there were rules at every turn and constant scrutiny. Still. "I'm just saying, we need the right person on the throne."

He pursed his lips.

She changed tack. "After you heard about the king's death, you didn't ride to me because you thought I was in danger. Yet I was. Don't you think that's strange?"

His raised a brow. "The timing? It could be coincidence."

"The local villagers near the forest rarely ventured past the tree line." She let her mind range backward over the moons. "But last harvest, Clarit and I noticed hunters moving deeper and deeper into the forest. We had to change our hunting routes for a while to avoid them. They disappeared eventually, but now I think they were scouts and their assignment was to locate me. The attack came so soon after the king's death that whoever planned it must have known exactly where to find me."

Nahir rubbed the back of his neck, his eyes thoughtful. "That makes sense."

"I'm sure whoever tracked me down in the forest still wants the throne. I'm still an obstacle. It would be foolish for me to leave Port Caspin without discovering who has been orchestrating all this.

"Lord Caspin said pretty clearly in today's meeting that he feels more qualified to rule than me. He's been managing many of the king's responsibilities along with Hadley, so he probably believes he's already been doing the job. Lord Suja hates the ground I walk on. Lord Woli points out the rules of succession aren't as clear as I thought." She didn't mention her worries around his father and the ambitions Lord Godmayne might harbor. "I have plenty of enemies to choose from."

Nahir gave her a quiet look. "You have supporters too. Keep that in mind."

She nodded, but the distribution of power between those two groups seemed to work against her.

THE ORACLE

THE NEXT DAY WAS FILLED WITH ADMINISTRATIVE MEETINGS with men who spoke to Kalothia as though she had the understanding of a mosquito. She grabbed Ye-Ye and Bukki and made a beeline for the king's library once her obligations were finished so she could page through the scrolls there and enjoy some respite.

Lord Woli happened to be walking the same way. She caught up with him. He was reading a letter and jumped when she spoke to him. "Oh, it's you." He sounded disappointed. He nodded at the letter. "Dictated by my daughter. She's troublesome too." He looked pointedly at Kalothia.

"I hear you have eight children," she said.

"Yes, and they are all useless. Over the last thirty harvests I have built our territory up. All my sons see are the spoils of my labor. Everything I give them they fritter away. The king and I used to discuss our hopes for our children." He shook his head and seemed to drift off into a reverie.

"You discussed children with King Osura?" she asked, somewhat surprised. She didn't know they were that close.

"No, not him. Not your father." He clicked his tongue disapprovingly at her ignorance. "Your grandfather. He was so proud of Osura. A good thing he died before he saw what your father became." He caught her curious look. "Your father was a fine king at first: fair, sensible, brave, and decisive. Then your mother happened and he went from blinded by love to bitter, distraught, and broken." He shook his head. "Women are a beastly creation. Luckily, he had Hadley to keep him somewhat functional. He'd known Osura since the prince was a boy. When Osura started sinking beneath the waves, Hadley managed to keep his head above the water. A very loyal man. Unlike the queen." He glared at Kalothia again.

Kalothia felt the heat rise in her. She was about to retort, but they had reached the entrance to the library and Lord Woli hurried off, muttering about the dangers of ambitious women.

Kalothia and Bukki exchanged a look of suffering endurance.

"No wonder he finds his daughter troublesome. Poor thing has to live with that," Bukki grumbled.

Kalothia thought again of how much a female leader might be able to address the inequality in men and women simply by giving women permission to say and do things men considered "troublesome."

She went into the library, and the royal secretary tracked her down there soon after. He rushed in brimming with excitement. "The next quarter moon!" he declared. "The Oracle has chosen your coronation date!"

A wave of nausea washed over her. Everything was happening too fast.

"Lord Suja says we should hold a pre-coronation ball," the secretary went on. "It will be an opportunity to introduce you to the country and Galla's neighbors."

Kalothia carefully put down the quill she had been using, mindful not to let the ink drip. She looked around the library at the scroll-littered table and the lamps that burned brightly. Bukki was weaving a colorful wrapper at a loom, her fingers flashing back and forth. She had started to feel comfortable, she realized. Now reality was intruding. She pushed back the panic triggered by the Oracle's news and considered the idea. "Will the guests include all of Galla's neighbors? Padma as well?"

"We will be inviting dignitaries from most of our neighboring countries," the royal secretary said. "Padma was included. But I doubt they will send a representative; they haven't done so in years. Maybe they'll be curious enough about you to attend. Relations have been sour since the start of your father's reign."

Ye-Ye hung from a scroll shelf surreptitiously, reaching out toward the set of keys that hung at the secretary's waist. Kalothia snapped her fingers, and when his round eyes met hers, she gave him a firm admonishing look. He swung up to a higher shelf, looking innocent and unfairly accused.

"You will need new dresses!" The secretary shot Bukki a significant look as though entrusting her with this sacred duty. "Beautiful dresses! We will show our foreign neighbors that Galla is the brightest star in the Goddess's firmament." He sucked in a breath. "I have sixty score things to organize. I will return tomorrow to discuss this further."

He blew out of the room in the same whirl of energy he'd entered with.

Kalothia looked at Bukki, who shrugged, her hands busy at the loom. "This palace loves a celebration. You've just given them an excuse for two."

Kalothia sighed. She looked down at the scrolls on Galla's legal framework and knew it was a lost cause. The Oracle's news had scrambled her brain. "Let's leave this for tonight," she suggested.

Bukki led them along a new route through the palace. Kalothia enjoyed discovering new quirky features in the sprawling building. There were mirror pools tucked into alcoves, color-blocked hallways, open-roof washing rooms, a drying room for the cow-hides to be stretched and dyed for drum-making, and an aviary where birds were trained to deliver messages across the kingdom. Walking through the palace was always an adventure. However, when they turned down an austere corridor tiled in white, Kalothia paused in surprise at the sight of imposing, life-size bronze statues. Lemongrass burned in small bowls, purifying the air.

"Goddess bless!" she breathed, transfixed.

The statues were cast with the same care and expertise as the one she'd found of Queen Sylvia. She studied them as they passed. OJOMO 832, OMONISI 891, OLATUN 925 . . . She had observed three statues before she realized what they were. "The kings of Galla," she murmured.

"King Okun started the statue tradition," Bukki said. "He was the twelfth to live in this palace. He put in most of the gardens too. I'm sure you'll have noticed the palace has a very"—she raised an expressive brow, which somehow made Kalothia smile—"*eccentric* mix of styles. You know how men are. Each new king had to make their mark. *Red earth!* There's a missing lamp," Bukki complained, looking down the corridor, where the line of lit lamps was broken by a patch of darkness before resuming. "The girl who maintains this corridor is already on her last warning. I'll go and get a replacement candle. Wait here with your ancestors."

Kalothia turned back to the bronzes. These men were indeed her ancestors. She stepped closer to the casting of Otunbi 941, ran her fingers over the cold metal that had been cast to imitate clothing, limbs, and skin texture. She searched his face for glimpses of herself and found none. At Ye-Ye's impatient grumble, she stepped back and moved on. The lamps stopped where the statue of King Osura 1019, her father, would soon stand. She was staring at the empty spot, recalling the rigid face of the deceased man she'd seen in the temple on the day of her arrival, when she heard the shuffle of footsteps. She looked up. The corridor was empty. Had she misheard? No, there was the sound again. The prickle of warning at the back of her neck was an instinct she'd learned not to ignore.

Ye-Ye rumbled against her ear, his body stiff.

Her breathing slowed. Her heart began to pound as her body came alive, steeling itself for action. Somebody was watching her. The weight of their surveillance raised goose bumps on her skin. She turned back the way she had come, the way Bukki had gone in search of a candle, and studied the deserted hallway. A lamp hung suspended from the ceiling above each statue, illuminating the bronze figures, but also casting pools of shadow. The life-size statues obstructed her view and offered convenient concealment to anyone who wished to hide.

A crack of breaking glass shattered the silence, followed by a shower of glass onto the stone, tiled floor. A statue three figures away from her plunged into blackness. Kalothia flinched. She pulled up the voluminous skirt of her dress and slipped a hand under, drawing the dagger she wore there. She palmed the weapon and considered her options. She could make a run for it, back toward the library. But the smashed lamp was a warning. There was somebody hiding between herself and safety in that direction. Was that person big or small? A skilled fighter or an amateur? Armed or not? There were too many variables to risk it. Another crack of glass rent the air; another statue snapped into darkness. Another warning. Her stalker was herding her in the other direction. She turned to look behind her. The corridor was completely empty; there were no statues for a person to hide behind, but it ended at a blind corner that led who knew where. What choice did she have? She began to walk, quietly enough to hear any movement behind her.

The footsteps began immediately. Her stalker was no longer trying to be stealthy. That couldn't be good. She began to run. Her feet slapped lightly against the tiled floor. Behind her, the footsteps were heavy.

As she flew around the corner, she risked a swift backward glance. She saw the outline of an arm, but the person was keeping to the shadows.

Beyond the corner she found herself in a new corridor, one even quieter and dimmer than the last. She briefly considered standing her ground and facing whoever was on her heels. Her dagger was solid in her hand, but if they had a sword or any long-range weapon, she'd be outmatched. She increased her pace until she was running full speed. Her feet slapped against the floor. Her heart pounded in her chest and sweat ran down her back. She clutched Ye-Ye against her chest.

20

UNDER ATTACK

AT THE END OF THE CORRIDOR THERE WERE TWO CHOICES. A SET of spiral stairs and a doorway just before it. The stairs descended into blackness. She didn't fancy her chances there. The doorway led to a large unlit room, but at the end was a rectangle of light. Through it she could see a familiar staircase that she knew led back to her rooms. She sucked in a breath, held Ye-Ye firmly with one hand, and sprinted for the doorway and light beyond.

She swung into the room, skidding slightly on the polished wood floor, then bent her body and raced for the door that led out to light and safety. Her ears strained for noise behind her; she caught the faint taps of footsteps over the wheezing of her breath and the pounding of her own feet. The doorway grew larger, the light brighter as she neared it. Without warning, a hand grabbed her hair and wrenched her off her feet. Her scalp burned as though it had been doused with fire.

She crashed onto her back with bone-jarring force, her skull cracking on the hardwood floor. Her body skidded like a wagon wheel across the smooth surface. Then pain exploded, assaulting her from so many directions it all blurred into one ball of agony. She whimpered, trying to swallow down the anguish so she could move. Footsteps sounded on the floor, stopping beside her head. Terror filled her chest. Ye-Ye screeched in distress. When his cry cut off then resumed as a howl of pain, her heart stopped. *No!*

"Ye-Ye," she moaned. Her voice ricocheted in her ears. She had to help him! She forced her head up, tried to roll up to sit, but pain made her insides clench and her stomach turn. All her senses felt jumbled and scattered.

Somebody crouched beside her. She turned her head to see a heavyset man outlined in the meager light from the open door. She couldn't see his face; she had the impression of a mask but it was hard to tell in the gloom and with her blurred vision. Her heart began to race, every beat vibrating through her body. She flexed her hands and found them empty.

The man reached for her slowly. At least his movement seemed slow with her scrambled senses. Moments later she felt the warmth of his large hand as he grabbed her neck. He forced her head back to the ground, then began squeezing, crushing her throat. She slapped at his hand, scratched, yanked. The hand only tightened. It was impossible to draw air. Her chest burned. She swung her arm for his face, wanting to claw, but the reach of his arm was longer than hers and her hands met only air.

She kicked and connected with nothing. She bucked and writhed, but the hand just squeezed tighter.

"No use fighting," the attacker warned her in Padman.

Her mind began to fog. Fear engulfed her, threatening to drag her into despair, into giving up. She fought back. Her hands scrabbled along the wooden floor searching for something, anything! She was weakening, her chest ready to explode, when her hand touched cool stone. A pedestal. She could sense something wobbling on it as she pushed. Could she summon the strength to dislodge it? Her throat was burning; flickers of light swam through her vision. She pushed against the pedestal harder.

Something fell with a clamorous crash.

The hand loosened for a moment. She dragged a pull of air that felt like nails across her throat, then shouted *"Help!"* with every ounce of strength she had left.

A pair of feet running sounded in the hallway. *"Your Highness!"* Bukki's worried voice called.

The man beside her grunted and his hand tightened again. But Bukki's searching voice was closer. The hand released her. The man leaped to his feet and raced off in the other direction just as footsteps clattered in. *"Your Highness!"*

A moment later yellow lamplight flooded the room. Bukki stood in the doorway, her eyes wide with shock. Kalothia lay on the ground panting and shaking. Her attacker had vanished.

BUKKI FOUND GUARDS TO ESCORT KALOTHIA BACK TO HER suite. Nahir came barreling in a few minutes later. "Are you all right?" he demanded.

Kalothia sat on a sofa in the parlor draped in a wrapper against the cool evening breeze that rolled in through the open windows. She was cradling Ye-Ye, who lay quivering in her arms.

Nahir crouched before her. He put his hands on hers. The warmth of his large, calloused hands seeped into her. "So foolish of me! To assume you were safe within the palace walls."

She shook her head gingerly, careful of the bruising around her neck. She'd been just as complacent. How ridiculous to let her guard down in the palace despite her certainty that whoever had ordered the attack on her home was part of the royal court. "I heard him speak," she whispered. The words scraped at her damaged throat like shards of glass.

"Padman?"

She nodded.

Nahir's jaw tightened. "I'll have all the staff questioned and I'll examine the visitor logs at the gates. They must have left a thread we can pull."

She nodded. "The good news is we learned something. What they did tonight was reckless. Impatient. Careless people make mistakes. That's how we'll catch them."

He put a hand to her hair. "None of that is good news. It's the kind of discovery that makes me want to bundle you up and spirit you away." His eyes were fierce and she knew he meant it. He closed his eyes and let out an exhausted sigh. "I'd rather we didn't use you as bait." He opened his eyes and stared at her. "We'll catch whoever it is some other way. Prepare to have every step you take in this palace dogged by a legion of guards."

NEW ALLIES

KALOTHIA WOULD HAVE IMAGINED IT TOOK MOONS TO ORGANIZE a ball. She was surprised to find they could be thrown together in a handful of sunrises. Between plans for the ball and the coronation, the palace became a hive of activity while Kalothia became more anxious. It seemed she was on a pendulum swinging toward a future she could not avoid while she was no closer to discovering who had murdered the only family she'd known. She monitored Lord Caspin's movements through Bukki's helpful palace staff, but their behavior was innocuous and offered no clues. Nahir's conversations with the palace staff and investigations into palace visitors produced no useful leads. She spent her evenings in the library, reading up on Galla's framework of laws to better understand how the justice system worked, planning for the day when she could face Aunty, Teacher, and Clarit's murderers, while her days were spent at meetings or enduring dress fittings, approving menus, and other ball-related chores. Her footsteps were dogged by multiple guards and though this made her feel stifled, she was also grateful. The attack in the palace had shaken her. She was used to looking out for danger yet she had let her guard down. It was foolish to be caught unawares that way. The close encounter made her feel vulnerable in a way she never had in the forest. It had dented her confidence in her ability to protect herself. She'd been stupid to be so complacent about her safety. Somebody wanted her dead, and they had gone to extreme lengths to achieve it, seeking her out in the forest and coming for her on the very same day that the king died. She paused as an idea unfurled in her mind. Why had the attack occurred on the very same day the king died? Was it coincidence, or had the person behind the attack planned to wipe out the entire royal line in one day? But that would mean that the king's death wasn't natural. The hair on the nape of her neck rose at the alarming thought. Was that possible?

In the days that followed she brooded on the possibility. Two sunrises before the ball she woke early with the idea of speaking with Prime Minister Hadley. Hadley was among the few people who'd seen the king regularly. He might offer insight or a perspective that helped her find a pattern in the strange deaths that had plagued the royal family. She enlisted Bukki to help her.

"His rooms are close to King Osura's suite because he spent many nights there keeping the king company when he struggled to sleep." Bukki shared the nugget of information as their retinue of guards flanked them down a series of corridors to an even more opulent part of the royal wing. "The king suffered from acute insomnia and often slept only a few hours a night."

Kalothia appreciated Bukki using the king's formal title and not referring to him as her father. It helped maintain a distance between them. Though the palace courtiers spoke of the late king either with sympathy or respect, she couldn't think of him as anything other than the man who'd murdered his wife despite believing she was pregnant.

"The royal secretary says he had melancholia."

Bukki nodded. "He barely ate, he slept little, he moved slowly— like a man three times his age. The maid who tended his rooms says he spoke in a whisper, as though it sapped his energy to do more. Here it is!"

A guard knocked and announced their presence before ushering them inside the prime minister's suite.

Hadley came forward to greet them. He was dressed for the day in a pale green shokoto and tunic. Kalothia liked that he favored simple styles just as she did; it was a contrast to most of the royal court, who liked to be as ostentatious as possible.

"Your Highness," he welcomed her, bending to press his right hand to the floor in a bow. "This is an unexpected gift."

Kalothia smiled, feeling at ease. There was something authentic and warm about the prime minister that reminded her of Aunty and Teacher and helped her imagine how they and her mother had fitted into the bloodthirsty royal court.

"I hope we're not disturbing you, Prime Minister."

"Impossible!"

Hadley led them to a pair of sofas that overlooked one of the gardens. Kalothia took in the elegant simplicity of his rooms, white-washed walls, and dark wood furniture. The color came from the numerous plants that flowered on every flat surface and the vibrant tapestries that covered the walls.

Ye-Ye leaped down from her shoulder and set off to explore.

"Be good!" Kalothia called gently after him. She was pleased to see him back to his curious self. He'd been quiet and fearful immediately after the attack.

"There isn't much for him to disturb," Hadley reassured her. "What prompts this honor of a visit?" he asked as they settled on to the plush seats.

Kalothia hesitated, unsure whether to bring up her questions about the king and wondering what exactly she should ask. Something clattered to the floor across the room where Ye-Ye was picking his way over a desk wedged into a corner.

"My apologies!" Kalothia rose to her feet and hurried over to extract her pet.

The desk was cluttered with scrolls, quills, bottles of ink and some loose keys. She was grateful to see Ye-Ye had only upset an empty tumbler and some sheets of parchment. She picked up the items and noted a parchment with diagrams on crop rotation.

"Do you farm?" she asked, holding up the parchment.

Hadley shook his head. "Just part of my state work. Some farming communities are finding their soil is yielding fewer crops. I'm thinking about a national strategy."

Kalothia smiled. There was such a contrast between the prime minister and his quiet hard work and the lords with their squabbling.

"I forgot you read," Hadley observed. There was admiration in his voice, not the alarm and censure she'd had from the royal secretary. She shot Bukki a speaking glance. *See! Somebody appreciates my skills.* Bukki smiled and nodded. "It's unusual but pleasant speaking with a literate woman," Hadley added.

It was an unexpected compliment, but it made Kalothia smile in a way she rarely did at court. Maybe this was a good segue.

She recalled Lord Woli had said the prime minister had known King Osura since boyhood. She was eager to know more. "Where did you grow up, Hadley?"

"An unremarkable town near the border."

There was a note in his voice—wistfulness, she thought. It made her suddenly homesick for the peace of the forest. "Was it hard adjusting to the grandness and pace of palace life?"

He smiled at her kindly. "It's hard to leave home. I've been here many harvests. With the right friends, a new place can become special too. I didn't have much time to get to know your mother, but I know she also longed for the familiar at times. Please call on me whenever you need."

Kalothia plunged on, having found that unexpected questions often produced the most honest responses. "You served the king for many years. Was there anything unusual about his death?"

"Unusual?" Hadley frowned in confusion.

"He was only forty-three harvests. It isn't usual for a man to die so young."

Hadley nodded. "Not the average man. But the king had been unwell for many years."

His words confirmed things she had heard. But still . . .

Hadley must have read her thoughts because he said, "Your suspicions are understandable. People are often wary when a king dies. But as for King Osura, I can assure you, he died a natural death."

"But if some kind of poison was used . . ." Kalothia thought of Clarit and Aunty.

Hadley's large gray brows flew up toward his equally gray hair. "If the king were poisoned, we'd have a serious crisis on our hands, Your

Highness." There was a gentle censure in his tone that made Kalothia immediately regret the suggestion. "If there was poison in the king's food or drink it would have killed the two servants who taste-tested all his meals."

Ah. She hadn't thought of that. "And the night he died . . . you were there?"

"I was." Hadley's expression was kind now. As though he were reassuring a grieving daughter and not a suspicious new royal. "Lord Caspin was also present, as was the whole elders' council. It is better not to have a whiff of doubt around these matters."

Oh. Kalothia's neck prickled with embarrassment. She really had launched herself down the wrong path.

"I understand the reason for your doubts," Hadley read her chagrin. "Especially in light of your own experiences. I was horrified to hear of the recent attack in the palace. I am glad Captain Godmayne has bolstered your security team with the best of our royal guards."

Kalothia rubbed at a headache brewing behind her eyes. Sensing her frustration, Bukki gave her a sympathetic look. If the king had died of natural causes that meant there wasn't a grand plot to end the royal line. Was she wrong about the prince's death too? It felt like she'd hit a granite wall. The only thing she could be sure of was that somebody wanted *her* dead.

She ducked her head in agreement, grateful for the few allies she had in the bewildering court. A suspicious rattle sounded above her. She looked up and sure enough, Ye-Ye had found a new spot to disrupt. He sat perched on the top of Hadley's scroll shelf, playing with whatever he'd found in there.

Kalothia laughed. "He seems to like it here." She did too. Hadley's rooms were comfortable. "We'll get out of your hair." She beckoned Ye-Ye down with a hand. Bukki rose from the sofa.

Hadley smiled, and the expression lit up his face. "I served your father well. It will be an honor to do the same for you."

She nodded. It was nice to have somebody so high up in the court in her corner. "Let's go and trouble the cook," she told Bukki and Ye-Ye as they left.

22

REHEARSAL

IT WAS THE DAY BEFORE THE BALL AND IT SEEMED TIME HAD passed in the blink of an eye. Kalothia stood in a palace ballroom, trying to suppress a sigh. The fabric of her dress stuck to her back and sweat prickled on her scalp, making her head itch beneath her cornrows. Her feet ached and she simply wanted to lie down in a pool of cool water for the rest of the day and sleep.

Her dance tutor, a short man with three chins that wobbled when he moved, clapped his hands, signaling the drummers and string players to stop. "It is on the *three*, Your Highness!" he said, the exasperation stark in his voice. "Then arms on the four and rock." He demonstrated the rock with a back-and-forth sweep of his pudgy hands.

Kalothia closed her eyes and kneaded her forehead, where a headache was throbbing. They had been practicing the four-step since sunrise and now it was lunchtime. Her stomach felt hollow as a calabash bowl, her body was sore, and her command of the dance seemed to be getting worse instead of better.

She opened her eyes. "Master Fletcher, if we could try it without the counting, I know I could—"

"No!" He looked appalled. As though she'd suggested they strip and dance in the nude. A snicker came from behind her and she turned a baleful eye on her newly appointed ladies-in-waiting. Nahir had insisted she accept at least three in addition to the expansion of her royal guards. The girls had lost interest hours ago and sat on chairs against the ballroom walls playing cards and napping in the soggy heat.

"The count is the heartbeat of the dance. Without a heartbeat, there is only death. Or terrible dancing. Come! We will try again." He snapped his fingers at the musicians and they launched immediately back into the mid-tempo piece of music they had been playing for hours.

Kalothia took the hand of the poor servant who'd been assigned as her dance partner. Sweat swam down his face, though he swabbed it frequently with a towel whenever they paused. She put a hand on his shoulder and ordered herself to get the stupid steps right this time so they could be released from this torture. At first, it seemed the pep talk had worked. One-two-three, she stepped back exactly half a foot, stepped to the side, rocked and—

"Stop!" Master Fletcher chopped his hand in signal to the musicians. "The kick, Your Highness, should be graceful. You are not a donkey, kicking to remove fleas."

Kalothia sighed. It wasn't that she didn't know the steps. She did. Aunty and Teacher had made sure she knew all the national dances. But Master Fletcher was demanding precision and perfection. She didn't know how to dance like that. She only knew how to dance for pleasure.

"You're not doing badly," Bukki whispered, handing her a glass of water. "If you relax a little, it will help."

Kalothia rubbed at her forehead. "If I could stop counting maybe I could relax," she grumbled. "I think we're going to grow old and die here."

Bukki chuckled softly. "In that case, we should eat."

"Did somebody say food?"

Kalothia jumped at the sound of Nahir's voice. He was suddenly standing right behind them. She hadn't seen him in days. Her heart rattled in her chest and she felt a tremor in her legs. She told herself it was simply because he'd startled them. But he looked as fresh and appealing as the glass of water she held. His locked hair was neatly tied back, his face was freshly shaved, and his skin looked like polished chestnuts. Once her nerves settled, the smile bloomed from inside her.

"You look exhausted," he said, his eyes narrowed with concern. "What's wrong?"

She sighed. "Just struggling to get this dance right."

He frowned in confusion. "You're a beautiful dancer."

Kalothia cocked her head, surprised at the compliment.

Nahir's hand went to the back of his head. "What I meant was—"

Kalothia jumped again, startled by Master Fletcher clapping loudly beside her ear.

"Enough talk," Fletcher said. "Maybe you need a change of partner." He pointed at Nahir, either oblivious to the colored string of beads around his wrist that told the world he was a high-ranking captain, or uninterested. "You know the four-step, I'm sure. Partner her." He waved at Bukki and the servant, shooing them from the dance floor.

Nahir raised an eyebrow.

Kalothia sighed. "He's been like this all day," she murmured.

Fletcher snapped his fingers at the musicians and they launched back into the music.

Kalothia winced; apparently the dance teacher was rude to everybody, not just newly arrived princesses. "It's fine, you don't have to . . ."

Nahir held out his hand. Kalothia blinked at it in surprise. Nahir would dance if he was in the mood, but he didn't like to be the center of attention and he didn't usually bend to whimsical requests. She'd expected him to decline. Instead, here he was, bowing slightly, his hand out in invitation. He gave her a questioning look. She realized she'd hesitated too long and shook herself out of her stupor. She took his hand.

His grip was firm. He slipped a hand on her waist. She stood straighter. Looked into his eyes. It was impossible not to. She was in heels and they were almost the same height. His face was serious, as usual. But there was something in his eyes. Amusement? Curiosity? Whatever it was, it put her at ease.

A pause, a breath as they waited for the rhythm to loop, then they stepped together. She took a step back, he forward, then sideways together. They dipped, hips rocked side to side, then straightened and repeated in reverse, she forward, he back, to the side then rock.

The four-step could be a sensuous dance if you stood too close, but with an arm's width of air between their bodies, it was respectable and dignified.

Nahir rotated them slightly and they repeated the steps. Kalothia smiled with relief. This was how dancing should feel. When you didn't have to count, didn't have to think about the steps, just let the music thrum through you and move your body however felt right.

They moved through the sequence again. The familiar movements left Kalothia's mind to wander. She marveled at the ripple of muscle under her fingers as she held on to Nahir's upper arm. He had dressed simply, a white tunic and black shokoto. She could feel the warmth of his body through the cotton of his tunic, and as they moved, her hands slipped naturally against the fabric, sliding over his biceps.

She forced her attention back to his face and found him looking at her curiously. Did he know what she was thinking? She ducked her head to hide her embarrassed smile. She was looking down when Nahir added in an extra half step before he rocked his hips. Kalothia grinned, and on the next sequence, mimicked the step, bookending his move, keeping the symmetry.

Where she should have rocked in the next sequence she stepped and turned. Nahir loosened his grip on her waist, letting his fingers graze her dress as she turned, then pulling her back into his body when the rotation was over.

They went on this way, a kick here, a half turn there, improvising and modifying, watching each other for changes then adapting. It was easy to fall back into their old rhythm. To anticipate each other's moves. When he nudged her, she knew to let her body bow backward, knew he would catch her. When she put her hands on his shoulders, he knew to lift her, that she would wrap a leg around his waist while he swung her in a circle, her dress billowing out like a cloud.

Kalothia had forgotten their audience after that first sequence. All she heard was the pulse of the baseline, the beat of the drum. All she saw was Nahir's eyes on hers and all she felt were his hands on her hips, his body against hers. Everything else, the heat, the headache, Master Fletcher, her ladies, time—none of that existed. She laughed when Nahir did a complicated three-step and complemented it with a graceful glide. Nahir grinned, his dimples, so rarely visible, popped into view like a celebration.

They might have continued like this if loud clapping hadn't filled the room. Nahir stopped abruptly. He caught her by the waist when she would have stumbled, righted her firmly, then stepped back. Kalothia felt dazed. She turned to the door and found Lord Suja standing there, clapping. He looked delighted, which immediately made her wary.

"Princess." He bowed dramatically. "I do hope you plan to delight us with this dancing at the ball. Your interpretation of the four-step is so energetic and . . . uninhibited." There was something suggestive in his tone, a quiet leer in his expression. She felt Nahir tense beside her.

Lord Suja gave a short bow then strode off, chuckling.

He left silence in his wake. His interruption had snatched the joy out of the room so suddenly that the grand walls and high ceilings seemed to echo with moments-ago mirth.

She felt rattled, as though she had been caught doing something wrong. But they had just been dancing. She looked to Nahir for help, but he was staring after Lord Suja, his mouth pressed into an annoyed frown. He turned to her. "I didn't mean to—" He cut himself off, then stepped closer to her and lowered his voice. "I've made things harder for you. I apologize."

She opened her mouth to protest, bewildered, wondering what he meant. But he had stepped back.

"I should . . ." He indicated the door, then bowed sharply and marched out.

"Magnificent!" Master Fletcher's voice slashed through the air, jarring her unsettled nerves. His hands were raised, open palmed, in prayer pose, while his eyes stared at her with wonder. "You dance magnificently, Princess. What have you been doing all day?" His chins wobbled and a line stood out on his forehead as though he were truly perplexed by the question. The musicians were packing up behind him.

"We're finished?" Kalothia wondered, dully. The exhaustion from earlier swamped her, made every muscle ache, as though fatigue had been waiting for the right moment to invade her body.

"Of course we're done!" Fletcher's chins wobbled a little harder. He pulled out a square of cloth and mopped his face. "You weaved all four national dances into that performance. It was magnificent! You are gifted by the Goddess."

Kalothia turned away from his exuberant praise, to Bukki, who stood waiting beside her with a cool cloth and a glass of water.

"Your Highness, you and Captain Godmayne . . ." She paused, her eyes round with wonder. "You dance as though you've been dancing together your whole lives!"

Kalothia felt her cheeks heat with self-consciousness. She remembered the feel of his hands on her skin, the press of his body against hers. Her skin heated even more and she gulped the water to cool the flames.

23

THE MARQUIS

IT WAS THE DAY OF THE BALL. DIGNITARIES FROM THE surrounding countries had been arriving all day. Kalothia knew because the palace staff dashed to and fro as though chased by wild dogs. She knew because the rattle of carriage wheels merged with the soft swish of the sea, giving the palace an urgent atmosphere.

She dug her spoon into fluffy, orange-tinged rice and diced fried plantain and gazed out the window. She couldn't wait for all this to be over, but she was even more terrified about what came next: her coronation. She hadn't yet sorted through all her feelings about becoming queen. It was a question of sacrifice: allow the lords to rule Galla with all their arrogance and misguided ways while she lived the life she wanted away from scrutiny, or take on the responsibility of ruling Galla herself. Self or country. The dilemma made her head throb.

Bukki brought her a glass of mint water. "The hairmaker is ready to start once you've eaten," she told her. She smiled at Kalothia's pained expression, unaware of the thoughts her friend wrestled with. "The quicker the ball starts, the quicker it will be over."

Her new ladies-in-waiting flitted about the suite, chattering and laughing gaily. One stood on the balcony, commenting on the arrival of guests. Kalothia frowned at the mention of Padma.

"Who did they send?" she asked Bukki.

Bukki hurried over to the balcony to ask and then returned to report that the duchess's grandson had arrived with a small contingent.

Kalothia nodded. The royal secretary had said there was to be absolutely no talk of politics at the ball, but how could she pass up the opportunity to ask some pressing questions of the Marquis of Padma? Surely some of the answers to the riddle of the attacks on her home lay with the Padmans. She would feel out the marquis, she resolved, and learn what she could without creating a diplomatic incident.

A FEW HOURS LATER KALOTHIA EMERGED ONTO THE PALACE roof to find the night lit by a sea of candles suspended overhead in glass bulbs. The air was rich with the scent of burning patchouli, mint tea, and roasting meat. When her presence was announced, the drumming troupe fell silent and the spirited crowd of guests, dressed in colorful silks, satins, lace, and jacquard, turned to her and bowed. It was easy for her to spot the royals visiting from neighboring countries as they remained standing, only dipping their heads politely.

She counted four men and an array of women before the court rose, the babble of chatter resumed, and the drummers launched into a lively new rhythm. Prime Minister Hadley materialized beside her, dressed smartly in a soft blue outfit. A tall figure was with him. "Your Highness," the prime minister announced. "The Marquis of Padma. The Duchess of Padma's grandson."

"Your Highness." The man took her hand even as he inclined his head. He was tall and broad, and she could tell he was a decent fighter from the way he stood, his weight evenly distributed.

Kalothia took a second to collect herself. Discomfort rippled through every line of her body. It wasn't his appearance that disconcerted her. His face was inoffensive: well-balanced features, full lips, a proud nose, long-lashed eyes, smooth skin the color of cinnamon. She grudgingly admitted he was handsome. His hair was cropped and sat neatly beneath the wine-red cap that matched his outfit. He still held her hand, loosely it seemed, until she gently tried to draw it back only to find she'd have to exert an unseemly amount of effort to reclaim it. He was standing too close, she realized. She could smell tobacco and rose water on his skin. She didn't want to know his scents. She had become used to the buffer of space that always lived around her, and it annoyed her that this man was invading it, not to mention holding her hand hostage.

"I hope you take no offense at my grandmother sending a lowly second grandson," he went on. "She is tied down with weighty matters of state." The marquis smiled as he spoke, and his teeth were neat and even.

Lowly second grandson, her foot. It was obvious the man looking down at her held himself in high esteem.

"Your Grace," she said, snatching her hand back. "No offense taken at all."

"We were sorry to hear of the king's death. Padma stands ready to support Galla in whatever way we can."

Kalothia hesitated only briefly before seizing the opportunity to find out if the Padman royal family had been involved in the plot to kill her. "Our biggest worry is the recurring disturbances along our border with Padma." She watched his face closely but detected only mild interest in her words. "Particularly a brutal attack in a forest in the East a few sunrises back." His expression did not change. "Do you have any thoughts on that?"

Hadley cleared his throat pointedly, reminding her that there was to be no talk of politics.

"I was unaware of any disturbances," the marquis spoke mildly. "In the East or anywhere else, but I'll be sure to investigate once I'm home."

"We must move on, Your Highness," Hadley interrupted. He escorted her on through the crowd. "That was a curious topic for small talk," he noted with a terse clip to his words. She glanced sideways at him, surprised at his tone, but quickly put her puzzlement aside when he stopped and introduced the king and queens of Lasson.

Kalothia looked at the short, wide man, and the woman beside him, who was a head taller. A huddle of beautiful young women idled near them. Hadley had called them "queens," she recalled. The women's clothing reflected their status as the king's wives. They all wore a silver fabric with scarlet circles, while the king and—Kalothia assumed—the senior queen wore the same colors in reverse.

"Your Highness," the king said, with a slight movement of his head that would struggle to qualify as a nod. His gaze was assessing and almost discourteous in its intensity.

"Your Highness," Kalothia repeated, returning the same imperceptible nod. She guessed the king was another man who didn't believe women could walk and speak at the same time. She reminded herself that Lasson was Galla's largest trade partner for cassava and palm oil. She gave the king a warm smile then turned to the senior queen. "That is a beautiful fabric you are wearing," she complimented her.

The woman, ten harvests younger than her husband and flawlessly beautiful, smiled easily. "Thank you. I have been admiring your dress since you entered. And this palace is a wonder. I have never had a chance to visit."

"Thank you," Kalothia said with a genuine smile. Why was it women were so much friendlier than men? she wondered. "I can't take any credit for the palace; it was built lifetimes before us, but it does take the breath away."

"Your Highness!" A thick-set man with the same penetrating eyes as the king of Lasson lumbered forward and dipped his head in a bow.

"The king of Orewa," Prime Minister Hadley explained.

Ah, yes. They were brothers, Kalothia recalled. The resemblance was obvious when she saw them side by side.

"Your Highness," she replied.

The king of Orewa was swaddled in a painfully bright fabric that seemed to change color under the hanging lights. Trailing behind him were three silent women. "My wives," he announced proudly.

Kalothia nodded politely. Nahir would be proud of her, she thought. He always accused her of wearing her thoughts on her face, but she was doing a sterling job of concealing them this evening. What could these two men possibly need with so many wives? She was relieved when Hadley stepped forward to lead her away.

"Sixteen wives for one. Three wives for the other?" she murmured to him once they had moved off.

"It's very common," Hadley answered, ushering her up a short flight of steps onto a covered terrace for the evening meal.

⋙— ◊ —⋘

HER RELIEF AT HAVING CONCLUDED THE BRIEF MEETING WITH the marquis was short-lived as she soon discovered he had been seated next to her.

"Well, this is opportune," he said with a smile as they took their seats. He complimented the pepper soup effusively and offered a gracious answer when she asked about the colorful patterned scarf he wore draped over a shoulder.

There was nothing obviously wrong with him. Yet there was something about his manner that made her pull back a little each time he leaned toward her, that made her shoulders tense when he laughed. She couldn't put her finger on it. It didn't help that Nahir sat only a table away. His presence pulled at her attention, muddling her thoughts. She reminded herself that shoring up relations with Padma was vital for the Gallans living along the eastern border, that this evening could change the tenor of their relationship, and she tried to be more friendly.

Voices chattered around her as her fingers mechanically carried food to her mouth. She listened and responded to the marquis, but a sliver of her mind was on Nahir the whole time; he was doing an impressive job of not making eye contact. She thought she was managing the dinner well until the marquis said, "He doesn't speak much, does he?"

Kalothia looked at him. "Who?" she asked, genuinely confused.

"The young man you have been watching all night."

He raised a brow and took a mouthful of food while heat flushed through her body. She waited too long to laugh it off, seconds of

209

silence drew out between them. She opened her mouth to say something—she had no idea what—but at that very moment Nahir looked straight at them.

"Huh." The marquis chuckled. "It seems you're on his mind too."

Nahir's head cocked ever so slightly and his shoulders tensed. He was concerned. Kalothia looked down at her food and rearranged a few pieces.

"The two of you seem very close." The marquis smiled at her, a pleasant smile, no innuendo, just a plain observation. "I'm curious, what is it he does here?"

She swept her gaze over the table as she took a sip from her glass. Nobody was paying them any attention; why did she feel so exposed? She swallowed the palm wine that had been sweetened with spices, then wished she'd reached for the water instead as her head spun for a moment. "Captain Godmayne commands the Northern armies. He goes where he pleases."

"Mmmm." The marquis nodded as though taking her words in. "The Southern Palace is a long way from the North."

She didn't answer. Whatever he was driving at, she'd let him get there on his own.

"I guess you'll either need a very understanding husband or your captain will have to find his way back to his army."

She'd done enough for diplomatic relations, she decided. When the woman seated to her left said something that drew laughter, she took the opportunity to turn away and join their conversation. She did not speak to the marquis for the rest of the meal.

THE BALL

BUKKI CAME TO COLLECT HER AFTER THE MEAL. THE ENTIRE hall rose when she did and the heads of the non-royals bowed as she left the room surrounded by her guards and serving ladies.

"How was the meal?" Bukki asked as they made their way to a midsize anteroom.

"The food was delicious . . . I think." Kalothia wasn't sure she'd really noticed it. She had been so intent on finding ways not to speak to the Marquis of Padma.

"You didn't speak to your dinner partner much," Bukki murmured in a low voice as though reading Kalothia's mind.

Kalothia grimaced. Trust Bukki, sharp-eyed as ever. "We did not have much in common," she lied.

Her ladies helped her remove the sunset-orange gown she had worn for the meal. The royal secretary had told her that three dress changes was the convention for the host of a ball such as this. She'd agreed to two and blocked her ears to his pleas for more. As her ladies wiped her neck and arms with cloths soaked in rose water, then rubbed coconut oil into her skin, she was glad she'd stood her ground. It was taxing to dress for a royal ball, even when you had multiple people doing all the work.

Bukki touched up the kohl that lined Kalothia's eyes and restained her mouth with a concoction of beeswax and crushed flowers that gave her lips a vivid red hue. It took two ladies to ease her blouse over her head. It was an intricate fusion of black fabric ornamented with clusters of exquisite silver feathers sewn together with lacework so fine it was almost invisible to the eye. Once on, it contrasted with Kalothia's dark skin, complementing it the way the moon does a dark night. The lacework gave the impression that the silver feathers were floating against Kalothia's skin, held in place with nothing but faith and prayer.

The skirt was a long rectangle of black fabric studded with the same silver feathers. The ladies worked as a pair to wind it around and around Kalothia's waist, then tuck it at her right hip, fixing it firmly in place. She had to sit for Bukki to arrange her head tie. Bukki wrapped and tucked, tied and twisted a length of silver brocade fabric around her head until she'd created a design that unfurled with the pleated beauty of a fan. There was almost no reason to add jewelry since she was already wearing several pounds of silver, but they draped bright orange coral beads about her neck and wound them about her wrists.

She'd always hated it when Aunty fussed at her to wear dresses and jewelry, but when she saw her reflection in the looking glass, she was astounded. She looked like a woman who could rule a country on her own terms. She looked like a woman who might make men want to please her. She looked like a woman capable of achieving anything she desired. It was a heady feeling.

"Don't forget," Bukki coached her, "we enter the ball together, we dance for one song, then you can sit on the royal chair—it's the one painted with gold dust. After that you can dance again if you choose but you don't have to—unless you're asked by a royal, in which case . . ." She shrugged. "Probably a good idea. At the end of the ball, Lord Woli—as the eldest lord—will say a few words to close the ball."

Kalothia nodded. She was looking forward to the rest of the night now that the formal part of the evening was over. She loved music and dancing. The night was beautiful and the rooftop terrace glowed like a jewel.

When the sound of music leaked into the room from the terrace, Bukki decided it was time to rejoin the guests. As they left the anteroom, Kalothia caught sight of Nahir standing with her guards. Their eyes met and she smiled a little, but he maintained a neutral expression. The terrace was filled with bodies, some dancing to the band that played on a raised dais, but most standing and chatting.

The bandleader rapped sharply on his talking drum. The rest of the band finished the current musical phrase and fell to silence. Slowly the crowd noticed the music had stopped and conversations died down until only the sound of breaking waves and the whisper of the breeze could be heard.

As the guests began looking around for the cause of the lull, a high-pitched, quick march of a beat began. It set the pace for the bandleader to come back in, languorously, with a playful pattern that rang through the night, bounced off the stone walls of the terrace, and vibrated through limbs, begging them to move. Its spirited teasing was joined by more drums and a pipe swept in to twist through the patter of beats. The pull of the music was compelling, irresistible. Kalothia didn't have to think about the steps she had practiced as she and her ladies danced forward.

The crowd parted at their approach and they danced into the center. Kalothia let her body follow the pipe, let her hips follow the talking drum, her hands part the warm air, her feet stamp the ground. Her ladies danced around her.

She felt caught up in a whirl of energy and joy. They danced at the center of the terrace until the tempo kicked up, signaling a new song, and the guests poured back onto the floor. Kalothia found she didn't want to sit, not yet. They danced on. Kalothia danced until sweat trickled behind her ears and her breath became ragged. She caught Bukki's eye and nodded to the other end of the terrace. Bukki danced forward and led the group off the floor.

Two servers waited at the royal chair, one with glasses of water, the other with a tray of glasses filled with red, brown, gold, and clear liquids. Kalothia sat and accepted a glass of water. Nahir stood to the far left of her. He wore a fine tunic of midnight-blue silk, but he might as well have worn his armor, because his rigid posture and blank face made it clear he was working.

She looked out over the ball and smiled. Almost everybody was dancing. Royals, dignitaries, and courtiers all mingled with cheer and abandon. Maybe Lord Suja had been right to insist on a ball, she mused. Maybe it would clear some of the tensions in the palace. She was still enjoying the moment when a cool shadow fell over her. She looked up, the chill settling over her skin already informing her who she would find.

The Marquis of Padma stood before her. He bowed. "Your Highness, I would be pleased to have this dance with you."

The music still played, bodies moved in concert, laughter and chatter filled the air, yet she felt as though the weight of many eyes had shifted to them. The marquis held out his hand and she reluctantly took it. His skin was cold despite the warm air. She felt herself recoil a little. *Don't be foolish, Kalothia,* she chided herself. *One dance in full public view won't do you any harm.*

She forced a smile and stood. It was as he led her to the floor that she realized the band was playing the four-step, the dance she had practiced the previous day with Nahir. She told herself to relax. Did it matter if they played the same song? At least she knew the steps.

They took their places opposite each other. He stepped toward her and clapped a hand on her waist. There was a force to it, a possessiveness, as though he were clutching something that belonged to him. It made her frown, then, catching herself, she hid her displeasure swiftly. She gave him her hand.

She thought they would pause and let the music loop, but he stepped forward immediately, moving into her space. His right thigh pressed against her left. She stepped back instinctively, but it felt off from the rhythm, like a defensive move rather than a dance one. He stepped sideways and she followed. He raised a brow at her. They were out of sync. She felt as though she was hurrying to catch up, instead of dancing.

He dipped, hips rocking, and she followed, a little behind again, but it was all wrong, out of time, lacking grace; she could barely hear the music. He was making a fool of her. He straightened and once again she tried to get on the beat. She stepped forward as he stepped back, perfect, but he shifted his leg so that the inside of his thigh brushed hers. It was so unexpectedly intimate that she froze. Her eyes shot to his face, but it was a cool mask of disdain. Was he doing this on purpose or had it been an accidental touch? She couldn't tell. He stepped sideways and she missed the beat again. He dipped, pulled her down, and it was only his firm embrace that kept her from losing her balance and toppling over.

She tried to collect herself, to focus on the steps, but her equilibrium was completely lost. She spent the whole dance off-balance, held too firmly and too familiarly by the marquis and struggling not to let her discomfort show. By the time the dance had ended she was hot with embarrassment and exertion and fuming at the marquis's behavior.

The courtiers clapped politely at the end of the song, but she sensed the whispers ripple through the room. Were they talking about her? Her face burned as the marquis led her back to her seat. "I see you've been practicing," he murmured against her ear. "Let's hope these middling skills are not called upon too often."

Her hands clenched into fists and it took every ounce of her strength not to swing them at his head. He stepped back before she could channel her fury into words, bowed, and walked away.

She sat down. Her heart pounded furiously in her chest. Bukki appeared beside her with a glass of water. "Drink this," she ordered, gently.

Kalothia accepted the glass with shaking hands and took a long draft.

Bukki watched her with concern. "Are you all right?"

Kalothia wanted to shout. She watched the marquis moving through the crowd and had to fight the desire to throw her glass at the back of his head. *You are the Princess of Galla, the highest ambassador of this country, you cannot behave like a girl in the forest,* she lectured herself sternly. But, oh, how she wished she could let that girl roam free.

"The captain is coming!" Bukki warned. "Be careful! Everyone is watching." Bukki moved off to the side before Kalothia could ask what she meant.

Then Nahir was there. His face was completely blank, but a vein ticked ominously at the side of his jaw. He was furious. When he handed her a square of cloth, she looked at him quizzically.

"You're sweating," he said. His voice was gruff and barely sounded like him.

She blotted her forehead as he watched. He stared at her until she hissed, "What?"

"Are you all right?"

Her breathing had eased. Her heart had resumed a steady beat. The burning fury had given way to angry indignation. But there was something about the tension she could feel vibrating off Nahir that warned her not to say too much. "I'm fine," she lied.

He bent down under the guise of taking the cloth back and gave her a swift but thorough look. She squirmed under his penetrating gaze.

He straightened. "You're lying."

She opened her mouth to reply, but she didn't know what to say. It didn't matter; he'd walked off before she could speak. She sat fuming at the marquis while she watched her guests. Lord Suja was dancing energetically with a young woman from the king of Lasson's entourage, Lord Woli was doing a gentle shuffle with his elderly wife, and some of the courtiers were cheering on the dancing of a woman

Kalothia recognized from the royal court. The guests seemed to be enjoying themselves, which was the key thing, she figured.

When Lord Godmayne asked her to dance, she had calmed enough to follow him onto the dance floor. Her serving ladies joined them and thus, safely surrounded, she was able to enjoy two songs. By the time the king of Lasson cut in, she had recovered enough of her humor to appreciate the traditional dance steps he showed her. Though she laughed and danced, she was aware of the Marquis of Padma circling the floor. It seemed whenever she caught sight of him, his eyes were on her and his face wore that same cold, hard expression.

Kalothia noticed that Prime Minister Hadley kept trying to approach the marquis. Poor man. Maybe he was working on improving the relations between their two countries. His efforts would be wasted on someone as cold as the marquis.

Meanwhile, Nahir stood by the royal chair watching her too. He wore the blank expression she could never read. She sighed. What had started as a bearable night had quickly deteriorated. She was more than ready for the ball to be over.

A few hours later, when the sky was pitch-black and filled with stars, Lord Suja stalked over to the musicians. He bent to speak to the bandleader and the music came to a smooth end. Kalothia watched keenly from her chair. She prayed this announcement would bring the event to a close so that she could finally climb into her bed. Then she saw the Marquis of Padma making his way decisively through the crowd in her direction, and her stomach clutched with tension.

"What's he doing?" Bukki whispered.

Kalothia frowned. "I don't know. But we are definitely not dancing."

"Not him." Bukki nodded at the musicians' dais. "Lord Suja."

Kalothia looked at the dais. "Isn't this customary?"

Bukki shook her head as Lord Suja cleared his throat.

"Distinguished guests," Lord Suja began in a slow, deliberate way. "On behalf of Galla, I must thank you for your attendance tonight. Galla has experienced some difficult events lately, but it is good to see so many of our friends here to celebrate with us."

The marquis reached Kalothia and nodded at her. Bukki took a polite step back and Nahir turned to watch as the marquis leaned comfortably against the wooden armrests of the royal chair. Nahir began to walk toward them and Kalothia was suddenly certain that these two men should not be within reach of each other.

She shook her head at Nahir. He frowned. She widened her eyes expressively and nodded to the spot he had just left. Still frowning, he stopped where he was, crossed his arms and stared at the man beside her. She sighed. Goddess, she just wanted to get through these last few minutes with no diplomatic incidents or bloodshed.

"We are grateful to our neighbor countries for joining us in celebrating the return of our lost princess. Let us raise a glass to Princess Kalothia. To the princess!" Lord Suja toasted.

"To the princess!" the guests chorused.

Kalothia watched the proceedings with dismay. Lord Suja singing her praises? Something was wrong. She could feel it in every part of her body.

She looked over at Nahir. He was speaking to a guard who then made a beeline for the dais while Nahir scanned the room, his hand resting lightly on the dagger at his waist.

Lord Suja was still talking: "Now, as happy as we are to have a descendant from the royal line preparing to assume the throne, ruling a country is not a job we can expect a woman to do."

The crowd tittered. Eyes swung toward the royal chair for her reaction. Kalothia tensed, braced for whatever trick Lord Suja might be working up to. Instinctively, her hand moved to her dagger. She cursed under her breath when her hand touched nothing but the smooth fabric of her skirt.

"There is nothing we would like more than for our future queen to find her king," Lord Suja said.

Kalothia felt anger and humiliation merge in a nauseating mix that roiled in her stomach. Blood pounded behind her eyes and her hands shook. Lord Woli was watching her with a look of satisfaction while Lord Caspin was whispering to a companion, his eyes also on her. She couldn't see Lord Godmayne in the crowd. She felt trapped. Something terrible was about to happen. She moved to stand but the marquis wrapped a hand around her wrist and held her in place. "Not yet, my dear," he whispered.

Lord Suja was still talking. "We were therefore delighted when the marquis of our esteemed neighbor, Padma, asked for our lost princess's hand in marriage."

A gasp of surprise rolled over the terrace.

"We've had our difficulties, but an alliance with Padma would enrich both our peoples and give our beloved princess a fitting partner. What could we say but yes? The duchess has given her blessing to the union. We look forward to peace on our borders."

The guests burst into loud applause.

Kalothia rose to her feet, ready to march up to the dais. Fury whirled through her like a gale force. But the marquis held her with a steely grip that bit into her skin. She could break the grip if she wanted to wrestle with him in front of hundreds of strangers. While she considered the idea, he bent toward her. "Peace on our borders."

He repeated Lord Suja's words with emphasis, then he released her and raised a brow.

The musicians launched into an exuberant praise song. The guests began to sing along. Some approached her, loudly sharing their congratulations.

Kalothia felt overwhelmed by the voices, the reaching hands, the smiling mouths, and cold eyes. She tried to turn away but there were bodies everywhere. Suddenly, Nahir was there, clearing a space and pulling her out of the throng as he drew her hand over his elbow. She heard him politely but firmly telling guests, "The princess is very tired."

Her head spun. Even if she did decide to take the throne, she had no intention of marrying the Marquis of Padma. But what could she do to prevent it now? It had been announced without her permission. If she rejected his proposal, Galla would be left with all kinds of diplomatic and reputational problems. Possibly drawn into a war.

The noise of the ball died away and she realized Nahir had led her into the anteroom where she had changed earlier. He stuck his head out the door and had a short, murmured conversation with somebody—presumably one of the royal guards—then closed the door and turned to her.

"Are you all right?" His brow was creased in a frown and his jaw was hard with tension.

She shook her head. "No. This is such a mess."

Nahir crossed his arms. "Suja tried this nonsense with Prince Olu too. Tried to persuade the king to marry him off to a Padman girl in return for peace on the border," he hissed. "You can't marry him. It's very simple."

She closed her eyes, feeling the strain of the night sap the last of her energy, and sighed. "Of course I'm not going to marry him. But how can I get out of it? You know as well as I do that if I refuse, relations between Padma and Galla will deteriorate further."

She heard Nahir stride away, and she opened her eyes to see him turn and pace back. He didn't deny her assessment. Wonderful.

A loud argument erupted outside the door. She had just recognized the measured tone of one of her guards and the loud, demanding voice of the Marquis of Padma before the door swung open and the marquis marched in. "Captain Godmayne," he sneered. The cold serenity was gone, his face now an angry mask of sharp edges and furrowed lines. "Why am I not surprised? Where the princess goes her . . . 'bodyguard' goes it seems. Your services are not required here. I would like to speak to my betrothed."

Nahir stepped toward the marquis. There was an energy radiating off him that worried Kalothia. He was taller than the marquis and broader. "Your betrothed?" His voice was a dangerous growl that Kalothia had never heard before. She stepped forward and put a hand on his arm.

The marquis glanced down at her hand and his sneer deepened. "I'm sure it's hard to believe that somebody might actually want her hand. I'm nothing if not generous. After all, where did she grow up? Not in the royal court. Not among refined people. Nobody knows. There's little difference between her and a street girl—"

Nahir moved so quickly that he had crashed a fist into the marquis' face, shoved him against the door, and pressed his dagger to the man's throat before Kalothia could intervene.

She took in the altered scene with horror. Outside, somebody was banging on the door and trying to push it open, but each shove brought the marquis in closer contact with the dagger. The marquis's eyes were wide with terror. His nostrils flared as he tried to breathe. Blood dripped from his mouth where his lip had been split by the punch.

"Let him go!" she hissed at Nahir.

He turned a burning look on her. His eyes were pinpricks of rage. She was certain that any second, he would drive the dagger home. What was wrong with him? Had he been drinking? It was obvious the marquis was trying to provoke a reaction. Swiftly, she reached and wrapped her fingers around the blade of the dagger, trying to tuck them between the sharp edge and the marquis's skin. Immediately, Nahir pulled the dagger back, as she'd hoped he would. Her body sagged with relief.

The marquis stumbled away from them. "You'll hang for that."

The door burst open and Kalothia's royal guards poured in. "Your Highness?" one of them asked, his sword drawn.

"I'm fine," she said absently. Her eyes were on Nahir. She had never seen him lose control like that. He was being very meticulous about reholstering his dagger and avoiding her eyes.

"He will hang for this!" the marquis shouted. Another of the royal guards was using his large frame to herd him toward the door. "As for you," he spat at Kalothia, "not even a shepherd's son will seek your hand once I start talking. Maybe I'll accept you as my fifth wife. After you beg!"

Kalothia glimpsed a wide-eyed server, who stood frozen in the hallway. She sighed. How long would it take for this story to circle the palace?

The guard closed the door on the marquis's threats, then stood sentry at the door. The other soldiers had taken up defensive positions around the room.

"Your Highness, are you all right?" Bukki asked. She must have slipped into the room with the soldiers.

Kalothia noted that each time she had been asked that question, the evening had become a little worse. She sighed and shrugged.

Nahir moved toward the door.

"Nahir?" she called after him.

He turned back, bowed low enough for his fingers to brush the floor, then straightened and trained his gaze over her head. "Your Highness. I will leave you for the night." He looked at the guard beside her. "I leave her in your care."

The guard ducked his head in his own bow.

Kalothia watched, bewildered, as Nahir left. For Goddess's sake! First, he went crazy and tried to kill the Marquis of Padma, now he was doing his cold and distant act again. "Ass!" she called after him. She pressed both hands to her head, fearing it might explode. "What is wrong with him? Did he hit his head?"

"I'll go see to him," one of the guards piped up. He followed Captain Godmayne out of the room, leaving Kalothia frowning at his back.

Bukki put a hand to the back of Kalothia's neck, loosening the head tie and an unexpected pressure in her head. "Is it possible he's jealous?" she asked quietly.

"Of what?" Kalothia tore the head tie off completely, letting cool air massage her scalp.

"Of the marquis."

"I hate the marquis! Why would he be jealous?"

"Maybe you should ask him."

She shook her head. "No! When he's ready to be an adult, he can come and tell me what demon has jumped into his body and is making him act a fool. I have other problems to solve."

Exhaustion had been gnawing at her for hours, but now that this ridiculous night was over she was too frustrated to even think about sleep. She had to find a way out of her betrothal without starting a war, and the person she would have gone to for advice had just stomped off into the night.

25

CONFESSION

KALOTHIA SAT AT HER DRESSING TABLE STEAMING HER FACE over a bowl of rose water and trying to regain her calm while Bukki unbraided the intricate cornrows that circled her scalp. Somebody rapped on the dressing room door. Bukki moved to answer it. The guard on duty spoke softly but Kalothia caught Nahir's name. Bukki returned to her side. "Captain Godmayne is here. Would you like to see him?"

No, she would not.

"Your Highness?" Nahir called. She could hear the impatience in his voice. After the trouble he'd caused, he had the nerve to be impatient?

"Oh, give it a rest!" she yelled back as he stepped through the interlinking door and she scowled at him through the looking glass. "Stop with the 'Your Highnesses'! Especially if you're planning on doing whatever ridiculous thing you want anyway."

Bukki winced. "I'll just leave you two, then . . ."

As she slipped out, Kalothia swiveled around on her stool. Ye-Ye lay curled on a nest of fabric on the table. He raised his head, looked at Nahir, yawned, then lay back down, uninterested.

Nahir was slightly disheveled, but nothing obvious—just a few creases in his tunic, a looseness to the band that held his long-locked hair. But since he was always so faultlessly together, the slips struck her.

No. She would not be concerned about him.

"Do you think I don't have enough to worry about without you threatening the marquis of a neighboring country? One that already hates us?" She glared at him, still baffled at his behavior. *"Never make an aggressive move without thinking,* isn't that one of your sayings? Were you thinking at the ball?"

Irritation prickled like fire ants beneath her skin as she recalled the confrontation. Needing to direct the energy somewhere, she began pulling the remaining cornrows out of her hair. "I don't know why you even care. You disappear for days, when we meet you barely speak, then you show up here and—"

He stepped forward and knelt so they were eye to eye. Kalothia froze. It wasn't his posture; there was a strange energy about him. She smelled the sweet scent of palm wine on his breath. That explained his mussed state. He'd been down in the soldiers' quarters.

"I'm sorry." His voice was low and grave. He stared at her intently. It was impossible to look away.

She swallowed. "Have you been drinking?"

He nodded, his eyes locked on hers. "A little."

He put a hand on the edge of her stool. She jerked as though he'd touched her. Her breath had become choppy. She realized her hand was still in her hair and lowered it to her lap.

"You're acting strangely." Her voice was a whisper. The air seemed to be filled with an electric current, something that made it difficult to breathe or move or turn away from him.

"Sorry."

Red earth, two apologies within minutes from a man who believed everything he did was justified. The warmth of his hand beside her, the hand that wasn't touching her yet was somehow burning her hip from inches away, riveted her. What was happening?

He sighed. Then he raised a hand and put his palm to her cheek. She gasped. The sound ricocheted around the silent room.

"I should be back east with my men. But I don't like the thought of being away from you. I can't stand people speaking ill of you. I can't bear that you're in danger here. I think I'm going crazy." His thumb slid against her skin in a caress. Her skin burned where he touched it. Her head became foggy.

His eyes searched hers, then moved across her face, as though he were taking in every detail. "Your skin makes me think of midnight. Dark and clear and serene." He chuckled. "Which is funny because you are the furthest point from serene." He grinned at her, his dimples deep as caverns.

"I can be serene," she protested feebly through the fog.

His hand, the one not holding her cheek, went to her hair. There was a gentle tug, then another and another.

"Are you . . . unbraiding my hair?" Maybe she was the one going crazy.

Another flash of his white teeth, a deep wink from his dimples.

"Your hair is exactly like your personality. Curls, twists, strong, unpredictable, beautiful . . ." His eyes were back on hers, even as his fingers kept working in her hair.

Suddenly she wanted to be touching him. To put her palms on his cheeks, her fingers in his hair, her lips against each of those incredible dimples. Her heart hammered in her chest. She balled her hands into fists on her lap, fighting the urge to surge forward.

There must have been something in her expression because his eyes darkened. A shiver ran through her.

"Are you cold? Did I scare you?" He slid his fingers from her hair, withdrew his other hand from her face. Suddenly he was awkward with nerves.

Her body went cold as he pulled back. She wanted him close again.

"I didn't mean to . . ." He blinked as though he'd lost his train of thought. "Erm . . ." He rose, straightening until she had to crane her neck to look at him. "I came to say . . . I should go."

She rose too, suddenly anxious. "You came to say . . . what?" Her heart was still pounding. The urge to touch him grew stronger as he pulled back. It was as though the top layer of herself had been stripped off, exposing her feelings to the elements. She had to know what he'd been about to say.

He looked down at her. She stepped closer. The toes of her bare feet met the leather of his shoes. He stepped back. "Um, I . . ."

She stepped closer again. She could hear the steady rhythm of his breath. See his chest rising and falling. Without thinking, she put a hand on his chest, desperate to feel his warmth again. His breath hitched. As though her action had been a signal, he bent down and placed his hands on either side of her face, holding her in place. They stood like that for a moment, clinging to each other. Kalothia didn't know she'd curled her hand into a fist on his tunic, that she was tugging him toward her.

"What did you come to say?" she demanded in a whisper when his face was inches from hers.

He stared down at her. His eyes darted down to her lips then rose back up to meet her gaze. "That I'm yours."

Her heart turned over in her chest. His words swimming through her veins as sweet as sugarcane. She pushed up on her toes until her lips met his.

26

ACCUSATIONS

KALOTHIA DRIFTED UP FROM A DEEP SLEEP AND OPENED HER eyes to soft sunlight. A smile spread over her face as she recalled the previous night. She touched a finger to her lips and laughed softly to herself. Nahir was hers.

Her smile widened until it felt like it might split her face. Happiness was a tide rolling through her, filling every inch of her body with warmth. Each memory of Nahir's touch, his kiss, filled her further until she felt flooded with bliss. He loved her!

A soft clatter caught her attention. She turned her head to see Ye-Ye sitting on the window ledge playing with a small key. She huffed out a breath of exasperation.

"Bring that here," she ordered her pet.

Goddess knew who he'd filched it from. She would check with the royal secretary first.

Voices drifted from her washing room. She heard the steady splash of water hitting copper. Her maids were filling her bath. She had a few more minutes. She yawned and snuggled against the smooth silk of her sheets.

Padma.

The thought of the marquis's proposal stole the smile from her lips. She sighed. She would have to speak to the lords. Usually, the thought of disappointing Suja and Woli's plans would give her pleasure. But the stakes were too great for petty personality feuds like theirs. They would have to find a diplomatic way to break off the engagement without stirring up even more hatred from Padma.

She let her eyes drift to the ceiling. She still hadn't found out who murdered Aunty, Teacher, and Clarit and she didn't know how she would. She didn't know who had orchestrated her mother's death. She was surrounded by questions. But she wasn't giving up. There were still six sunrises until the coronation. Could she walk away from the needs of the women of Galla? From these unanswered questions? The alternative was the crown, and that thought still made her stomach roil.

A cock crowed loudly outside. She listened again and found the sound of running water had stopped. She pulled in a breath, braced herself for the day, and slid out of bed. She would speak to the lords about ending the betrothal that morning. Lord Godmayne would be on her side. She didn't fully understand his motivations, and she was wary of such a powerful man, but he'd cared for her mother and he'd kept her safe and surrounded by people who cared for her. She trusted him to help her find a solution. After they sent the marquis on his way, she'd go riding with Nahir in the afternoon. Her cheeks warmed when she thought about him. The anticipation hurried her through her scented bath.

HER DRESSING MAID WAS HELPING HER INTO A PATTERNED PRINT
dress of blue and red when Bukki came running into the room in
a rustle of skirts and a flurry of anxious energy. Her usually calm
friend held open the door that separated the dressing room and the
private parlor and flapped a hand at the dressing maid. "Please," she
said, "I need to speak to the princess."

Kalothia watched the woman hurry out with surprise.

"What's wrong?" she asked Bukki as soon as they were alone.

Ye-Ye grumbled plaintively from where he sat on a corner of the
table. She ignored him.

"Captain Godmayne has been arrested."

Kalothia froze, stunned. "What? Why?"

Bukki sighed. "The Marquis of Padma is dead. He was stabbed
last night."

Kalothia blinked slowly. Was she dreaming? Was she still lying in
bed and imagining all of this? Was that why she couldn't seem to complete a train of thought? "The marquis is dead?" she parroted, confused.

Bukki took one of her hands. She rubbed it sympathetically. "Yes.
Captain Godmayne has been accused. We have to go." She tugged on
the hand and took a step toward the door.

It was as though Kalothia were hearing the words through a fog.
Nothing made sense.

"But he was with me," she argued. "Last night. It was nearly dawn
when he left here. Not that he would. Kill the marquis, I mean. He
wouldn't . . ." Her voice petered out as her mind filled with an image
of Nahir pressing his dagger against the marquis's throat. Once
again, she saw his enraged face and recalled how the expression in
his eyes had chilled her. Oh Goddess! Would he? But no, he had been

with her, he'd been happy, he'd kissed her and told her he loved her. Why would he leave her room to go searching for the marquis?

"He was with me!" she said again, firm and sure.

Bukki shook her head. "I know. But you can't tell them that."

The foggy feeling in Kalothia's head grew. She was hearing the words, but she couldn't seem to understand any of it. She put a hand to her throat, wrapped it around her pendant. "Of course I'll tell them he was with me." She spoke slowly, hoping that her mind would clear and the conversation would start making sense.

Bukki turned back to her and squeezed her hand emphatically. "If you spent the night with your bodyguard after accepting the marquis's proposal"—she raised a hand against Kalothia's protest—"I know you didn't accept, but the court thinks you did. You could be accused of treason. You would have endangered the country. Or maybe you conspired with the captain to kill the marquis. Your enemies won't hesitate to suggest it. Or maybe you're simply lying for him. Covering up. Telling them the truth won't save him. It'll just implicate you."

Kalothia sat down heavily. "This is madness!"

Ye-Ye cried out again, louder.

Kalothia absently placed her free hand on the table and he scuttled up her arm to his usual spot. His soft weight comforted her. "What do I do, then?" she asked desperately. Her mind was whirring. "His father—Lord Godmayne. I need to speak to him!"

"Lord Godmayne is in the throne room. Everybody is there. Waiting."

"What?" It was as though the fog were getting thicker, things were making less and less sense. "Who's in the throne room?"

"The whole court. Lord Woli summoned them."

Of course. Of course the lords would be involved in this.

"We have to go now, Your Highness. Things are moving quickly. They might hold the trial this morning."

Trial?

Kalothia closed her eyes, breathed deeply once, twice. Then she opened them. She would get better answers down in the throne room than she could expect from Bukki.

"Let's go." She stepped toward the door.

Bukki shifted in front of her. "Your Highness, you mustn't go in there with emotion riding you. Somebody has orchestrated this. Watch, listen, and understand before you make a move." Her eyes were intent.

Kalothia nodded. It was the kind of thing Nahir often said. "Wait!" She turned and hurried back into her sleep room. Lifting the feather mattress, she felt underneath it until her fingers touched the warm leather of her dagger handle.

Her dress fit snugly around her torso, leaving no place to conceal a weapon. "Bukki, hand me a ribbon." Moving quickly, she tugged up the hem of her ankle-length gown and used the ribbon to tie the dagger to the outside of her thigh. If they wanted a fight, they would get one.

CEREMONIAL DRUMS POUNDED AS THEY MADE THE JOURNEY TO the throne room. The rhythm was ominous, a slow ponderous pattern that Kalothia had not heard before. The scent of food drifted through the corridors, reminding everyone that it was time for the morning meal, not a meeting of the royal court.

Guards swung open the heavy doors of the throne room and the court rose in a flurry of bright fabric. Kalothia's usual discomfort at entering this room when all eyes turned to focus on her was gone. Her only thought was of Nahir.

She marched in, her eyes searching for him.

The drums fell silent. The only sound was the rustle of fabric, the ripple of movement as the courtiers bowed. They were ranged as usual along both sides of the room. They had clearly dressed in a hurry. Ladies' head ties were misshapen, tunics were wrinkled. There were no glittering necklaces or boulder-size rings.

As Kalothia neared the front, she saw that, beyond the courtiers, Nahir stood with his back to her. He was still in the midnight-blue outfit he had worn to the ball. It was wrinkled but presentable. His locked hair was still neatly tied. He was flanked by two royal guards. It wasn't until she moved past him to reach the throne that she saw his wrists had been bound with thick iron manacles.

Horror and disbelief rolled through her. Her hands shook so hard she had to clench them into fists. "Release him!" she ordered the guards beside him. They looked toward the lords, uncertain. *"Who has the key?"* she shouted, forcing their attention back to her.

Those courtiers who were still folded in bows straightened to watch the drama.

"Your Highness." Nahir's soft call was an admonishment. She met his eyes. His strained but unemotional expression made her recall Bukki's advice to remain calm. Fire was burning in her veins and the sight of the manacles was fueling it. She couldn't calm down until they were gone. She turned to the lords.

Lord Woli rose to his feet and leaned heavily on his walking stick. "We appreciate your concern, Your Highness, but with the Marquis of Padma lying murdered, we must follow protocol."

Kalothia's body shuddered at the word *murdered.* Gasps erupted in corners of the room as some of the courtiers heard the news for the first time. Lord Woli seemed unaware of the stir he was causing, though he did partially turn toward where Lord Godmayne sat beside him and bowed slightly out of respect before retaking his seat.

Lord Godmayne's face was hard and devoid of emotion. "With what evidence are these charges laid against my son?" He didn't acknowledge Lord Woli's bow or address his question to anybody in particular.

It was Prime Minister Hadley who stepped forward, his steps stiff and reluctant. "Lord Godmayne, the evidence will be presented at the trial in a few hours as the rules dictate."

Kalothia opened her mouth to demand he explain further, but he continued without prompting.

"In the trial, we will present the server who overheard the Marquis of Padma angrily threaten to see the captain hanged and saw his face had been bloodied during an altercation after the ball, we will bring out the patrolling royal guards who saw the captain traversing the palace corridors in the middle of the night and again early this morning, we will show the court the captain's dagger, still bloody—"

The court had fallen silent, the courtiers leaning forward to catch every grisly detail. Kalothia heard the list with growing horror. Nahir *had* argued with the marquis; he'd even threatened him. He *had* moved through the palace late at night and again at dawn. Goddess knew he had numerous daggers. How difficult would it be to steal one and plant it?

"The captain will have several hours to prepare his defense before we begin." Hadley bowed to Lord Godmayne, then retook his seat.

He made it sound so reasonable. But it was not reasonable at all. Yet Kalothia did not know how to stop this boulder that was rolling downhill and picking up speed. Were these the same protocols they had followed when her mother was accused of treason? That rushed trial had ended with her death. Would the prime minister listen to reason? He'd been supportive of her so far, even kind—but Kalothia also knew he was a man of the court and had to observe the law.

It was Lord Caspin who rose next. Kalothia steeled herself for whatever blade he would plunge into the proceedings. "The captain must account for his whereabouts and provide witnesses. The duchess will be distraught to hear of her grandson's death. We must preempt her hunger for retribution by showing that justice has been served. Nobody can be above the law. We must try the captain swiftly and carry out the sentence, no matter how unsavory."

His eyes were steely. The face of a man who saw an opportunity and was determined to exploit it. She recalled how he'd outlined his suitability for the throne in her first official meeting with the lords. His words buzzed in her ears like mosquitoes.

She needed a moment out of this room to think. What should she do? What course of action was most likely to save Nahir from this noose that was being tightened around his neck? Thoughts and questions rattled noisily in her head. She closed her eyes, drew a breath, and did her best to push back the noise, just as she would in the forest when faced with danger. She just needed to buy them some time.

"We will meet for the trial at midday," she declared. "Until then, the captain will be held in his own rooms." She raised a hand when Caspin began to rise in protest. "Post as many guards as you want but hold him in his rooms." She pointed at one of the royal guards beside Nahir. "You will find the key to those chains and remove them."

The guard looked uncertain.

Nahir shot her a look. "Your Highness, I will be fine with whatever these men decide."

Hadley bowed low. "The captain is an excellent swordsman. Better than any man in here, I'd warrant. But he is also a man of honor. I'm sure we can remove the chains without worry."

Kalothia breathed a sigh of relief. Yes, he was still on her side. It was a tiny balm in the horror of the morning's events. She nodded at Hadley. "I'll leave him in your care."

She gave Nahir one last look, drank in his features, then marched out while the court scrambled to dip into bows. She had a few hours to discover who had really murdered the marquis.

27

SEARCH FOR ANSWERS

SHE STEPPED OUT ONTO A TERRACE NEAR THE THRONE ROOM and breathed in the crisp dawn air. Drew it into her lungs. Let it cleanse her. The sky was a sweep of pale blue. The manicured palace grounds looked serene. It was hard to reconcile the ugly machinations in the throne room with the gentle beauty outside.

"Who wanted the marquis dead?" She voiced the question aloud, turning the problem over in her head.

"Who didn't?" Bukki suggested from beside her.

They exchanged a grimace. The marquis had not been a pleasant man; it was not inconceivable that he had enemies. But who knew him well enough in the Gallan palace to hate him with murderous fervor? As Bukki pointed out, it could be any number of people, and without any clear sense of the motive, finding his real killer would take too long. Kalothia needed a simpler way to prove Nahir's innocence. She turned to Bukki. "Surely if I just tell them Nahir was with me last night—"

"It would only give Woli and Suja more wood for the fire they are building against you," said a man's voice behind them. They hadn't noticed Lord Godmayne on the other side of the terrace. He sketched a bow then approached them as he spoke again. "You would only compromise yourself, and to no good end. Your mother's word counted for nothing. Women are not respected in this palace. I have sent word for the Northern soldiers to be on guard. In your mother's time, we foolishly trusted that the truth would prevail. I will not make the same mistake twice."

Before she had digested his words enough to reply, he had turned and begun to walk away. The anger and sorrow had been stark on his face. Kalothia didn't try to stop him.

Kalothia lowered her voice and said to Bukki, "If the Northern soldiers enter the palace to protect Nahir, the other lords will instruct their soldiers to follow suit to enforce their sentence. It will end in a fight, the North will be outnumbered, the violence will spill out of the city—" She stopped.

"Civil war," Bukki finished for her.

"And then there's Padma and the duchess." A shudder ran through Kalothia as she thought about the duchess's reaction to her grandson's murder. Tensions between the two nations were already high. If the duchess wasn't satisfied that her grandson's murderer had been caught and brought to justice . . . She pressed a hand to her throat to grip her pendant in shaking fingers. None of her fears could be allowed to materialize, otherwise Galla would end up fighting both an internal and external battle.

If Kalothia wasn't able to give Nahir an alibi—and she did reluctantly see how doing so would be dangerous and futile—the only other option was to find the marquis's real killer.

"Where is the marquis's body?" Kalothia demanded, deciding on a starting point. "Maybe we can learn more there."

"It'll be in the crypt. I know a shortcut."

The four guards assigned to Kalothia's protection trailed them as they left the terrace and reentered the palace. As they walked, Kalothia had a sudden urge to undertake her search away from the watchful eyes of the palace soldiers. They were stone-faced as usual, but their presence made her uneasy for the first time. A guard had testified to seeing Nahir near the marquis's room in the early hours. It wasn't untrue—Nahir had been in the royal wing after leaving her rooms—but it just reminded her that whatever she saw and learned, they would too. Nor were they always honest—her mother had been betrayed by one of her guards, after all. It would be better if she carried on searching for the information without their presence. An idea flickered to life in her mind. Didn't her room share the same baked clay wall as the guest room she'd used on her first night? She was sure it did.

"Let's make a stop in my rooms," she announced loudly to Bukki. "These aren't the best clothes for our activities."

Bukki gave her a curious look at the suggestion but nodded in agreement.

Once inside her rooms, with the guards stationed in their usual places outside, Kalothia grabbed Bukki's arm and towed her into her sleep room. "Let's visit the crypt without the guards," she whispered, scooping Ye-Ye onto her shoulder, then rummaging through her drawers for an item she had not expected to use again.

"You suspect the guards?" Bukki wondered.

Kalothia pulled out the climbing hooks with a relieved sigh and moved over to the window. "We don't have much time. I want to follow my instincts wherever they lead without four burly men dogging my every step." She held up the hooks. "You don't have yours, do you?" Bukki shook her head. "It doesn't matter," Kalothia said. "The guards won't follow you anyway. Just tell them I'm resting and then let's meet on the floor below."

Bukki nodded, quickly accepting the plan. She left the sleep room to take the stairs.

KALOTHIA'S SLEEP ROOM WAS MUCH HIGHER UP THAN THE BASIC guest room she had stayed in on her first night in the palace, so she was careful not to look down at the long fall to the ground as she sat on the windowsill and swung her legs over the edge, Ye-Ye clinging tightly to her shoulder. The climbing technique came back to her easily, and she was soon at the window of the room below. She entered, crossed the room quickly, and found Bukki waiting in the empty hallway holding two lamps.

Bukki led them through the quiet corridors to a nondescript door near one of the many ballrooms. It was clearly rarely used as Bukki had to jiggle the door handle in a particular way to coax it open, which it did with a shrill creak. It opened onto a narrow stone staircase that led down a few steps before disappearing into deep blackness.

Stepping into the stairwell seemed to strip all warmth from the air, replacing it with a musty coolness. They each held an oil lamp, but the circles of yellow light offered a feeble response to the darkness pressing in around them.

The staircase was narrow and enclosed on either side by stone walls. The echo of their footsteps in the dark and the cobwebs that brushed against her skin reminded Kalothia of the Ibeso Caves. Ye-Ye clutched tightly at her neck, clearly feeling as jittery as she was. She was grateful when the stairs ended, and they were able to follow a slightly wider corridor until it turned into a large circular space with several doors off it.

"He'll be in one of these rooms," Bukki explained.

They found him on a stone table covered in a white sheet from his shoulders down. The air smelled like lavender, perfumed by the bowls of dried plants arranged around the perimeter of the room. But underneath the delicate fragrance there was something rank. Kalothia pressed her fist to her nose and approached the shrouded body on the table. Ye-Ye chittered nervously.

The marquis's cinnamon skin looked waxy in the orange light. Gold pieces had been placed on his closed eyes. The metal glinted in the lantern light with an unnerving glow. It was unsettling to see the mouth that had twisted and spewed hateful words hanging slack and unaware. Blood had dried on his split lip, a jarring memory of Nahir's punch. The other sign of violence was a dark bruise that marred his forehead. What Kalothia needed to see was the wound that had killed him. She braced herself but her hand shook when she reached out to tug aside the cloth that covered him.

A hand touched her back, making her jump.

"That's a pitiful sight," Bukki said.

Kalothia nodded. "Have you ever seen a dead body before?" she asked, partly to distract herself, partly in response to Bukki's calm behavior.

"No. You?"

"Yes." Aunty, Teacher, Clarit, the kidnappers. Too many. She sucked in a series of bracing breaths, afraid that the horror whipping through her would grow. She didn't have time to fall apart.

She pulled the cloth down. His torso was narrow, with smooth skin. The only flaw was a knife wound, a gash on his stomach, above the loincloth that protected his modesty.

"That doesn't seem enough to cause a man's death," Bukki spoke behind her.

Kalothia considered the laceration. In her hand-to-hand combat training, she'd been taught that the most effective place to injure an opponent with a dagger was the throat. The stomach meant a slow, lingering death. If the wound wasn't too severe, the person might even survive.

"No, it doesn't," she agreed.

Unbidden, her mind rolled back to the arrow that had barely grazed Clarit yet somehow killed her. Poison. Was it possible a similar method had been used? That could mean the marquis's death was linked to the forest attack. Her shoulders tensed.

She turned to Bukki. "Can you speak to the palace staff? Find out which of them attended to the marquis after the ball. See if anyone else visited him. Or if he was seen speaking with anybody between the ballroom and his suite."

Bukki nodded. "What will you do?"

"I'm going to visit the marquis's rooms. See if I can learn anything useful there."

IT WAS DIFFICULT DODGING THE SERVANTS AS SHE MOVED through the palace this time. She stopped trying when she reached the hallway that housed the royal guests. Doors to the suites sat open as staff rushed in and out, holding bedding and cleaning supplies. They bowed, their faces revealing their surprise at her presence, but when prompted they pointed her in the direction of the marquis's suite.

His door was the only one that stood closed. It opened onto an airy parlor. Ye-Ye stayed unexpectedly still on her shoulder, seeming to sense the tragedy of the room. A side table lay toppled on the tiled floor, a dark liquid had soaked into the soft gray rug, and a glass tumbler had smashed into sharp pieces. Drops of rust-colored liquid made a trail across the center of the room, ending in a small, dried smudge.

It had happened here, she decided. Not far from the door. Surely, the marquis would not have admitted a stranger to his room. But who did he know in the palace beyond his own staff? She crouched by the smudge of blood for a closer look. It was with her head close to the ground that she spotted the torn shred of fabric peeking from beneath an overturned stool. She pulled it out and held it up to the light. It was a soft blue silk. The marquis had worn wine red to the ball. Yet something about the distinctive shade nudged a memory in her head. She rose to her feet with a frown. Guests had worn outfits of all colors to the ball, but one name sprang to mind when she looked at the blue fabric, and there was no harm asking.

"Let's go and find the owner," she told Ye-Ye.

EVERYTHING CHANGES

AS KALOTHIA HURRIED TO THE SUITE SHE NEEDED, CAREFULLY avoiding the guards and servants, she turned the scrap of fabric over in her fingers, feeling increasingly confused by what she'd found. The cloth might mean nothing . . . but something nagged at her, something she couldn't put her finger on. What reason could he have to hurt the marquis? Surely none. Yet her feet led her to his rooms.

When she reached it, she knocked. There was no reply. But she hadn't expected one. She assumed the occupant was busy preparing for the trial. A surge of anxiety swelled in her chest as she considered her options. She had to move quickly for Nahir's sake, and that meant exploring every option, however far-fetched.

She tried the handle. The door was unlocked. She glanced around the empty hallway then slipped inside. Ye-Ye gave a chirp of pleasure, remembering the delights he'd found in the room on their last visit. He leaped from her shoulder and went off to explore.

"Don't touch anything!" she warned him, distracted.

She moved deeper into the suite, opening a door to Prime Minister Hadley's washing room and then the connected dressing room. What she was thinking was absurd. It was perfectly reasonable for Galla's prime minister to pay the Marquis of Padma a visit. But so late at night? And how had that shred of fabric ended up on the floor? Did they fight?

She recalled again how attentive Hadley had been to the marquis at the ball and how the marquis had ignored him. It had seemed part of the marquis's naturally arrogant demeanor at the time, but now she wondered if there was more to it.

In the dressing room she opened a pair of clotheshouse doors and shifted through the many outfits that hung inside. None was the soft blue Hadley had worn the previous night. She pawed through drawers and opened clothes chests. There was nothing.

Ye-Ye came to join her. He nestled himself into a corner of the windowsill and sat playing with a cloth hat. She sighed at his antics, then she moved on to the sleep room. It was sparse and clean. There was another clotheshouse there. It was large and ran from the floor to the ceiling. She sniffed. A strange scent hung in the air, and it grew stronger as she moved closer to the clotheshouse doors. She opened them and frowned.

The smell of burning rushed out to greet her, bright and pungent.

She pulled aside matching tunics and shokoto and searched the floor beneath piles of sandals and leather shoes, then moved on to the side panels of the clotheshouse. She was running her fingers along the back panel when she felt the ridged, unmistakable shape of a lock.

Her eyes widened with surprise. She leaned in past the clothes and knocked against the wood. The sound was hollow. A secret room? Or a safe, maybe? What valuables could Hadley have that were so precious he needed to hide them in such a way? She paused for a moment in indecision.

Hadley hadn't done anything but show her kindness and acceptance. Did he deserve her going through his secret belongings? Yet doubt gnawed at Kalothia's insides. Something hot bubbled under her skin. Some understanding waiting to be acknowledged. She had to know what was behind the door.

She looked around for an implement she could use to break the lock. Then she froze. The image of Ye-Ye on the windowsill had sparked a bizarre idea. She reached under the hem of her dress, under the waistband, and drew out the key she'd confiscated from her pet that morning. It was unlikely to fit, she told herself as she jiggled the key around in the lock. They'd visited Hadley days ago, so he would have noticed if Ye-Ye had stolen . . . Her mouth dropped when the key slid home and turned with a loud click.

Her heart hammered in her chest, racing with anticipation. She pushed the door, and it swung open onto a black space. The burning odor was now so overwhelming she had to draw back to take a pull of clean air. The breath cleared her mind. She darted back into the sleep room and grabbed a lamp that hung on the wall. She lit it before bracing her shoulders and returning to the depths of the clotheshouse.

The lamp illuminated a small, windowless room. An ink-stained table ran along one wall, a stool tucked beneath it. At the back were tens of scrolls rolled and stacked neatly in cubbyholes. She glanced at them briefly before her attention was drawn to the small tin bucket on the floor. The source of the overpowering smell.

Kalothia crouched and held the lamp over the bucket. It was full of ash. She ran her fingers through the blackened remains. Among the black fragments were tiny scraps of soft blue silk. She placed the shred of fabric she'd found in the marquis's room next to a scorched fragment. It was a match, as she'd known it would be. Why was Hadley burning his clothes?

She shook her head, confused, then ran through the things she knew. Hadley had spoken to the marquis at the ball. That night he'd worn a blue tunic and shokoto that matched the torn fabric in the marquis's room. Hadley had burned his outfit the next day—the same day the marquis was found dead. Hadley had a secret room hidden in his clotheshouse. The facts were pointing her in a single direction, but how could it be? Could Hadley have killed the Marquis of Padma?

The idea sat like a stone in the pit of her stomach. Was it really possible? No . . . Surely not? Even so, a thousand questions filled her head: Why? More bafflingly: *How?*

The marquis was young, a third of Hadley's age. How could the older man have killed him? She considered the possibilities. If the prime minister was standing close enough and the attack was unexpected, or if the marquis had been drinking or was suitably distracted, it would not be difficult for an older, slower man to drive a knife into him. It had been a single wound. Had the marquis fought back? The overturned furniture and broken glass suggested he had tried. She thought again of Clarit, of how quickly the poison had worked.

She looked around the room. If Hadley had secrets, surely, she would find them here. Her eyes fell on the scrolls again. She rose and pulled one out. It was several parchments wrapped together.

Letters of correspondence. They were short, unsigned, and written in Padman. A shiver ran over her as she read them.

We received your details of the Eastern army's movements. We'll focus our efforts on the towns left vulnerable.

And in a different hand:

Success. The defense strategies were as you described.

There were also several maps, each one marked a couple of Gallan border towns. Kalothia's heart lurched when she realized that all the towns labeled had recently suffered Padman attacks.

How could it be? Hadley, Galla's prime minister, was helping their enemy neighbor attack Gallan towns.

Nausea rose inside her, and she had to suck in a series of deep breaths to keep her stomach from purging its contents. Why would Hadley betray his own country? She unfurled more parchments trying to understand.

The marquis is interested in the town of Ruki. It is beyond our agreed boundaries for attacks, but we've observed it is processing salt for the East. If you prefer that we do not touch Ruki, we'll need a border town with equally valuable resources we can avail ourselves of.

Did Hadley have some kind of deal with the Padmans that they could attack some towns and not others? She shook her head; it made no sense. She selected a different roll of parchments.

We have searched the Kumasi Lake area. There is no sign or whisper of such a girl.

She frowned.

No sign of such a girl in the Western towns of Gobe or Mudan.

Then—and Kalothia's heart raced:

We have found her. In the Faledi forest. How should we proceed?

Kalothia's legs nearly gave way, but she forced herself to stay standing. In a flurry of panic, she began to pull scroll after scroll from the wall, clutching at them and reading them as quickly as she could:

Eventually she saw it, a piece of paper, smaller than the rest, and in a very messy hand. It was dated the day of the attack on her home:

The men shifted from surveillance to attack immediately when we received the order. The girl escaped but we have sent men ahead to Illupeju. Her guardians were killed, as instructed.

This time Kalothia's legs did give way, and she spilled onto the dusty tiled floor in a boneless heap. Teacher's deep chuckle floated into her mind, the one he let out when Aunty scolded him for breaking a bowl or letting the chickens run wild in the yard. She pictured Clarit sitting away from the fuss, treating her cudgel with oil, pretending not to hear the commotion but hiding a small smile. A sob choked her throat. It was impossible to hold on to the good memories; just beneath them were recollections of that last day: of Clarit's wide, terrified eyes before her body went still, of Teacher's cracked glasses lying out of reach, and of Aunty foaming at the mouth and writhing. All this time Kalothia had been searching for her family's murderer and he had been right here. She had trusted Hadley. She had thought he was an ally, but they were dead because of him.

Her breath came in short, shallow gasps as she tried to absorb it all. Hadley had ordered the attack on her home, he'd wanted her and her family dead! He was responsible for the marquis's death, and it looked as though he had been passing secrets to the Padmans and helping them attack Gallan towns for years. She ran through his crimes over and over, as though forcing herself to believe them. But why?

She pulled herself together and sprang to her feet. She had to tell the court. She looked at the wall of scrolls. What should she take? As much as she could carry, she decided, and began to gather up the evidence.

She was so caught up in her task that she didn't notice the door to the secret room open until something moved in the corner of her eye. She whirled and froze.

Hadley.

He stood in front of the closed door. Loathing and fear skittered down her back at the sight of him. She backed away, feeling his presence too close to her in the tiny room.

His face was confused, but then his eyes darted to the tin bucket and the scrolls clutched under her arms, and his expression became distraught.

"Why have you done this?" he cried. "You've ruined everything!" His face crumpled, and it looked for a moment as though he might dissolve into tears. Then he marched forward and slammed his palm down on the table with a violent thump, sending the small key she'd left there and a new key both skittering across the stained wood. "Meddlesome!" he shouted. "Just like your mother! Just like your brother!" His eyes were wild, fierce. He looked nothing like the gentle man she thought she knew. Now she could see it. How the impossible could be possible.

"You killed them," she murmured, accepting the truth for the first time. "You killed them. Clarit, Teacher, Aunty . . . the marquis."

But Hadley seemed not to hear her. He was staring at the mess of scrolls and maps that she'd scattered about. He bent down to pick one up from the floor and looked at it, almost lovingly. "Everything I've ever done has been for Galla," he said. "Nobody has served the throne as well as me. I have kept the royal family's secrets for more than twenty harvests, and I have worked to protect you all. Though you never deserved it." He looked up at her. "None of you has ever appreciated me."

Kalothia took a small step backward. When had Hadley ever protected her? If these scrolls were to be believed, he'd tried to kill her, twice at least. His words seemed irrational, and the wildness in his eyes had grown savage.

But before she could speak, he went on, as though talking to himself, "When I first learned of your existence, I was sickened, but I waited. With King Osura on the throne, you weren't a threat. But when he died unexpectedly, I had to make sure Sylvia's daughter never took the throne, not after all the trouble she caused me."

Kalothia jolted at her mother's name.

Hadley swept on, oblivious to her reaction. "I was determined your mother's terrible failings would die with her, so I ordered for you to be executed, in the forest, along with anyone who'd cared for you. Of course, you escaped, like a mosquito dodging a hand"—he slapped his own hand down hard on the table, making her jump—"then you succeeded in reaching the palace."

He sounded so put out by her survival that Kalothia shivered and put a hand to her pendant for reassurance.

"I tried to end your life again. But it seems the men I keep here are better at listening at doors than executions. Once again, you survived. Strangely, that gave me time to get to know you." Hadley smiled at the memory, his expression shifting like the change from night to day.

Kalothia grimaced.

"I realized then how like him you are. Your hair, of course, but it was more than that. It's in your mannerisms too. You are a part of him, of my Osura." His eyes softened, and he reached out for her, as though he would touch her. She shrank back and his fingers closed on air before clenching into a fist. "I was grief-stricken by your father's death." He swiped at his eyes as though wiping away tears. "Getting to know you, it . . . it was . . . it was as though he'd come back." His voice broke. "As though he regretted leaving me here . . . alone."

The strange outpouring of emotion made Kalothia's skin crawl with discomfort. She loathed the intimate look of affection he directed at her just as much as the anger of moments before. "I'm nothing like him."

"No." Hadley's eyes glittered darkly. "I see that now." He glanced around his disordered room again. "You are *her*. Through and through. Your meddling, nosy mother. She was always poking around, asking about the letters I received, the meetings I attended. She urged Osura to take action about the border attacks, clueless that I had it all under control. That I was containing the Padmans to one part of the country. She *undermined* me! Osura started to distance himself, listening to the poison she spewed. That's why she had to go—"

Realization struck her like a fist to the stomach. "It was you . . . My mother. You orchestrated it all!"

He merely nodded. "I whispered a little poison of my own into your father's ear, and her life came tumbling down. It was that easy. She thought she was safe because the king loved her, but he loved me more. I was his confidant, his source of strength. They'd barely been married four harvests. She had no idea who she was taking on."

His fingers drummed on the tabletop while something in her chest tightened, making it difficult to breathe or think.

"It didn't take much to persuade Osura that she'd been unfaithful. He was besotted with her, and the rumor that she wasn't loyal to him pricked his ego like an overfilled waterskin. All I needed were some well-placed rumors; some cowries in the hands of an amoral guard. She'd made enemies, of course. She talked too much, like you. Always whining about 'the needs of the people.' Trying to lower taxes and get the king to give surplus grain to the poor. The royal court doesn't like an upstart. They want their cowries in their treasure chests, not in the hands of the lazy poor. Not to mention she'd come from the *North*." His nose wrinkled as if the word were a bad smell. "An outsider. And someone who doesn't even adhere to the Goddess's precepts correctly. But that worked in my favor. Her people were too far away to protect her; she had no allies here. They spoke against her. All of them. All the *lords*"—he spat out the word—"except Godmayne, and that was only because he arrived after the verdict."

Kalothia realized what she'd always known. Her mother had been betrayed not only by this one man, but by the whole rotten court, by the whole kingdom that didn't place any value on women. Hadley had merely used that prejudice to his advantage. Had Lord Godmayne known the pressure she was under? The North was a long way from the royal court, but surely he'd tried to keep tabs on the woman he'd promised his best friend he'd care for like a daughter. Maybe he'd learned of the severity of the attacks against her too late. But doubt gnawed at her and fury bubbled in her chest that her mother had faced so much alone with only Madame Toks, Aunty, and Teacher at her side.

"So you hated my mother. And you hate me because I'm too much her daughter. Because I talk too much and I have too many opinions for a woman." She shook her head. "But why sell Galla's secrets to Padma?" Kalothia dropped the scrolls in her arms onto the table.

Hadley scoffed. "You've been here barely a moon. What do you know about protecting a nation? Read your history. Padma has been a thorn in Galla's side for scores of harvests. From the start of this duchess's reign, they have plagued us, poisoning wells, stealing children to work their farms, hijacking fishing boats—picking at the country like locusts, jealous of our superior wealth and resources.

"The duchess and her good-for-nothing family would never stop eyeing what we had and what they could take. I brokered a deal with them that kept their nefarious activity to a limited geography; in return we sacrificed a few border towns."

Kalothia's mind reeled. How could he justify the destruction of so many communities? It was like handing a wolf one of your children to keep it from eating the rest. "Did the king know of this?"

Hadley puffed out his chest. "He would not have had the heart for it. It was a pain I endured on his behalf. It was ironic, really, that I was then able to use the same Padman fighters to track down his only daughter. Not that he would have cared. He would never have believed you were his, even if he'd seen you in the flesh, with all your red hair. The queen had to be an adulteress for him to live with himself after he'd allowed her execution. The child she'd carried had to belong to an unknown man, as her guard claimed. Even

Lord Godmayne knew enough to keep you hidden away all these years. The king would have executed you before he admitted you were his blood.

"You can't trust them, you know," he added, eyeing her carefully. "Lord Godmayne and your captain. I'm the only one you can trust. You think they protected you out of altruistic goodness? Rubbish! They wanted power over the last heir of Galla. That's why the captain has to go. I had a moment of panic last night when the marquis forced me to kill him. But then I realized his death was meant to be. It was a chance for me to dispose of two presumptuous suitors instead of one. We've only got each other, Kalothia. The quicker you realize that the better. Even the Padmans have got above themselves. Their marquis coming here, thinking he can marry you."

"That's why you killed him?" Kalothia said.

"He told me they were *reconsidering* our deal," Hadley said. "Can you believe it? He wanted to marry *my* princess without my permission and he called *me* a traitor. Me! After all my sacrifices!" He shook his head, and his hand slipped into the pocket of his shokoto. "I didn't even know I'd struck him until he fell to the floor and I found my blade in my hand."

My princess. Kalothia shivered. She had to get out of here. But the only way out was through him. Her eyes focused on the hand hidden in his pocket. He was no match for her in a fight, but if he drew a poisoned dagger the odds would shift. He'd managed to take the marquis by surprise; she would not underestimate him. She scanned the table for a weapon to defend herself and then remembered her own dagger. Surreptitiously, she drew it from beneath her dress.

Hadley gave a small, twisted smile. Then, without a word, he drew open a drawer under the table and pulled out an object. She frowned in confusion when he put the object to his lips and she saw it was a long, wooden pipe. Her fingers flexed on her dagger in anticipation of an attack, but he merely gave a quiet huff of breath.

A sharp pain stabbed her chest. She looked down to see a small needle protruding from a spot below her left shoulder.

"Wh—?" she said, as a wave of dizziness washed over her. She looked at Hadley with alarm. "What have you done?" She tried to take a step forward, but stumbled on suddenly weak legs. She threw out a hand and braced herself against the table, remembering with horror the poisoned arrow that had killed Clarit, and the marquis's lifeless body. "Have you . . . ? Am I . . . dying?"

He shook his head. "It won't kill you." He said the words almost sadly, as if he knew he should kill her but couldn't quite bring himself to do it. "It will just make you sleep for a while."

She shook her head and tried to edge in the direction of the door, but there seemed to be three doors now, and they were quivering back and forth.

Hadley watched her sink to the ground. "Why did you have to interfere?" he asked, his voice full of sadness. "It could have been you and me leading Galla together. But you came snooping in my rooms, and now it's all ruined! After everything I've done for our family."

It felt like fingers were pulling at Kalothia's eyes, forcing her lids closed. She fought to keep them open as she tried to process his words: *our family*.

She could hear Ye-Ye scratching and howling on the other side of the door. "I . . . I don't understand . . . Who are you?" She was on the ground now, the dust tickling her nose, the tiles cold against her too-warm skin. Nahir. She had to save Nahir.

Hadley crouched before her. "I'm your uncle, Kalothia, and I love you, just as I loved your father and his father before him. You've all caused me nothing but trouble. Still, I'll make it all right again, just like I always have. I'll look after you, and the throne. Sleep now. You're safe."

Uncle? The word forced itself through the drug. She struggled to sit up. But it was too hard, her eyelids were too heavy.

The world went black.

RECKONINGS

KALOTHIA CAME TO SLOWLY. SHE OPENED HER EYES TO PITCH-black and the lingering scent of burning. Her head throbbed fiercely. Her shoulder ached, but when she shifted to relieve the discomfort, she realized her wrists had been tied behind her back. As her senses returned, everything she'd learned rushed in on her, stealing her breath and driving her heart into a wild gallop. But one piece of information stood out more than the rest: Hadley was her uncle. Her grandfather had had a secret child.

The thought was overwhelming and swamped her mind with questions. Who else knew? Had her father known that his trusted friend was actually his half-brother?

She rolled into a sitting position, her mind racing, until panic pushed Hadley's revelation aside. Nahir! Was it midday already? Was she too late to stop the trial? Hadley had managed to keep King Osura isolated all those years, positioning himself as the only trusted courtier and carving out a position of power. From his words it was clear he'd planned to continue that pattern—he'd keep her alive but eliminate her supporters, and therefore retain his power. Nahir was first on his list of obstacles to be crushed.

She whipped her head around to check the table, remembering the two keys. Both were gone. The desktop was empty. Next, she ran her tied hands desperately across the floor behind her, searching for the dagger. When her hands found nothing but dust and smooth tile, fear and hopelessness overwhelmed her. Of course Hadley had taken her dagger.

She sat on the cold floor and sobbed until her head ached and her eyes grew sore. Hadley would see Nahir executed, or Lord Godmayne would intervene and there would be civil war, and then Hadley would either return and kill her himself or send one of the lackeys he kept in the palace; after all, she was no longer a route to power for him. She was a danger now. She wondered briefly why he'd never told anyone who he really was. Why he'd never claimed the throne for himself instead of relying on others. But now this was his chance to be king in his own right, if that was what he wanted.

Despair pushed those questions aside. She thought of all those she had loved whom Hadley had killed, and of Nahir too, facing execution for a crime he didn't commit, and she wailed her pain, the tears soaking the collar of her dress.

She was crying so loudly that she did not notice the door swing open until Bukki was standing before her holding a lamp and Ye-Ye was rubbing his face against hers. Was she dreaming? Maybe she was still lying unconscious from Hadley's drug.

"Your Highness!" Bukki crouched before her. "I've been looking for you everywhere! Are you injured?"

Kalothia felt the tug on her wrists as Bukki worked at her bonds.

"How did you know where to find me?" she hiccuped.

"Ye-Ye. He appeared alone and distressed. It was so odd to see him without you that I let him lead me here. I didn't know what to think at first, when he came into Hadley's rooms and raced to this clotheshouse, but then I saw the hidden door, and here you are."

"The door wasn't locked?"

Bukki shook her head.

Maybe Hadley had overestimated the strength of the drug he'd given her, or he'd been in such a rush he had forgotten to lock the door. Regardless, his negligence had saved her.

"What's happened, Your Highness? Why are you here?" There was a tremble in Bukki's voice that belied her calm actions, and her eyes flitted around the room. It was empty now. All the scrolls and maps had gone, only the table and the stool remained.

"Hadley," Kalothia blurted. "Hadley is behind it all." It still seemed incredible to her, despite what she'd seen and heard. "He killed the marquis, and he ordered Padmans to kill me and my guardians in the forest. He planted the rumors that led to my mother's execution too. Who knows, he may even have killed the prince!" It was hard to believe one man could be at the center of so much chaos.

Bukki's mouth dropped open in shock. "Hadley!" She shook her head. "I mean . . . yes, actually, I can see that. Well, maybe not all that. But my mother always said he had too much influence over the king."

Kalothia drew a deep breath. "And that's not all," she said. "He claims he's my uncle."

Bukki blinked. "He . . . What?"

"If it's true, his presence here, and how much power he had over King Osura, must have been my grandfather's doing."

Bukki nodded. "Why didn't he put himself forward for the throne?"

"Goddess knows. But he kept saying that everything he'd done was out of love for my father, and for Galla." Kalothia huffed in disbelief. "He was obsessed with anyone affecting his influence over the king. He killed the marquis because the marriage would limit his influence over me, and Nahir—"

Bukki's eyes widened. "You think Hadley was threatened by your close relationship with Nahir?"

"Yes. He used the marquis's murder to trap Nahir. I'm sure he'll try to go through with the execution, even though it'll do him no good now." She staggered to her feet. Ye-Ye clung to his usual spot on her shoulder, nuzzling against the side of her neck. "Where is Nahir? Has the trial started? We have to stop it!"

She opened the door of the hidden chamber and immediately began coughing as the scent of burning filled her lungs. She stepped out of the clotheshouse and followed the haze of gray smoke to an iron tub in the washing room. She didn't need to bend to examine the blackened scraps of paper in the tub to know that Hadley had burned all the scrolls, all the evidence. Her heart sank with disappointment. She touched the pendant at her throat and ordered herself to buck up. "Where are they holding the trial?"

Bukki caught her arm. "What will you do? How will you prove the things you've learned?"

Kalothia shook her head. "There were scrolls and maps"—she waved at the iron tub—"but he's destroyed them all."

"They won't believe you, you know." Bukki's eyes were distraught.

Kalothia nodded. "I know, but we have to try." She was prepared to say or do whatever was necessary to stop them. A pang shot through her at the thought. Hadn't Lord Godmayne promised the same? That he'd save his son, whatever it took. His Northern guards were probably in the palace already. Without evidence, the only way to prevent an execution was bloodshed.

"Come on, then. They're in the Sunken Garden," Bukki told her.

Kalothia had turned for the door when an idea struck her. It was a desperate, ridiculous idea, but it might be the only chance they had of avoiding war. She quickened her step, anxious to reach the trial.

NAHIR STOOD AT THE EDGE OF THE GATHERING OF COURTIERS IN the Sunken Garden, on the wooden ledge that jutted out over the crashing waves of the sea far below. It was a place where lawbreakers had been sentenced and executed for the many generations since the royal court had moved south. The very place that Kalothia's own mother had stood sixteen harvests earlier.

The sun was high overhead, but a sharp breeze whipped at the lords' fine clothes as they sat on raffia chairs to the right of an empty throne. To their left sat the rest of the royal court, on wooden benches, under a light silk canopy that thrashed around in the wind.

Hadley stood in the middle of them all, addressing the court with animated gestures. Nahir wasn't looking at the prime minister as he detailed the incriminating evidence against him, but at the entrance to the garden, as though he was waiting for her, as though he knew she would come, no matter how hopeless his situation seemed.

Kalothia's eyes locked with his as she burst into the garden with Bukki right behind her, Ye-Ye on her shoulder, and a scroll gripped in her hand. His eyes lit up at the sight of her, but the concern on his face did not clear, even as she ran toward him. Relief flowed like warm honey through her as she confirmed that he was unhurt and had even been allowed to change out of the bedraggled tunic he'd worn hours before.

A swell of chatter rose as the courtiers grew aware of her presence. Though her dress was dirty and wrinkled, the courtiers rose dutifully and dipped into bows, the motion rippling across the garden as word spread. The lords called out to her, but Kalothia didn't stop moving until she stood beside Nahir.

"What happened?" he demanded in a low voice. He glanced at Bukki, who'd stationed herself beside them.

Kalothia shook her head as though to say "There's no time to explain" and touched his arm, drawing strength from the warmth of his skin. She wanted him far from the deathly drop of the ledge, but until she could make that happen, she'd stand with him.

She turned to face Hadley and noted with satisfaction how his face had twisted with anger at her arrival. She forced herself to loosen the tight grip she had on the scroll in her hand.

"I'm glad I caught you, Prime Minister Hadley." Her voice rang clearly around the garden.

Hadley gave a small laugh. "I'm pleased you were able to join us, Your Highness. You just missed testimony from the server who overheard Captain Godmayne threaten the marquis yesterday."

Kalothia raised a brow. "Isn't this a waste of the court's time, Hadley? After all, you're the one who killed the marquis!"

A gasp ran around the Sunken Garden.

Hadley smirked, but his eyes remained cold. "Ah, so you have come to plead on the captain's behalf with any lie that comes to mind."

Kalothia waved the scroll in her hand and was pleased at the trace of alarm that crossed Hadley's face. "Nobody needs to take my word for it. You're not the only one who keeps correspondence, Hadley."

She turned to the court. "Our prime minister has been aiding and abetting Padma in their attacks on our Eastern border towns. I found the marquis's meticulous notes in his rooms. It's written in Padman, so I'll let"—she looked over at the lords—"Lord Suja read us the accounts. It was his lands that were terrorized, after all."

Lord Suja sat forward in his chair, his face a mask of shock as his gaze swung between Kalothia and Hadley.

"Bukki, would you . . . ?" Kalothia handed Bukki the scroll.

Hadley's eyes bulged. His hands clutched reflexively at his sides and his gaze followed Bukki with angry intensity as she crossed the garden.

"Hadley has been supplying Padma with our state secrets, enabling the attacks," Kalothia said. "Maybe he did it for money . . ."

"You ungrateful witch!" Hadley's scream startled her. Her heart hammered when she met his eyes and saw the fury and hatred laid bare. "I saved you from the marquis! His death saved this *country*! Yet here you are besmirching my name! How *dare* you! Nobody in this court is more loyal than me."

He marched over to intercept Bukki and snatched the scroll from her hands. He dragged it open, then whipped his gaze over to Kalothia, his mouth open in silent rage. The parchment was blank. He crushed it between his hands, understanding it was too late to retract his words.

Kalothia regained her equilibrium and pressed her advantage. "If you're so loyal, why did you lie all these years, *Uncle*? Why didn't you reveal you were the king's *brother*?"

An incredulous roar of voices filled the afternoon air. Hadley's rage became horror, as though she'd ripped the clothes off his back and left him standing bare before the crowd.

"After the king's death the throne was vacant. You could have seized it! Why didn't you?" She was trying to make him angry, to force something out of him as he lost his temper, but the question genuinely perplexed her. He'd reveled in the power her father had given him as a trusted confidant. He'd killed her mother to protect it. Maybe her brother, the prince, too for all she knew. And then he'd killed the marquis and been willing to kill Nahir to recreate the same with her. So why not just take the throne when he had the chance? It would have given him more power, undiluted power to rule Galla exactly as he wanted. "Galla was yours for the taking. I'm sure the lords would have preferred an illegitimate son over a woman on the throne."

Lord Suja guffawed cruelly. "Would we? Who was his mother? What proof does he have of this ludicrous claim?"

It was the same mocking tone Lord Suja had taken with her when she'd been dragged before the court on her first day. Yet Hadley did not bear it as she had. He seemed to crumple, to collapse in on himself at the question, his shoulders stooping, his back curving, his knees buckling.

Understanding struck Kalothia in that moment. She recalled how Hadley had brought her a stool during her ordeal. The sympathy on his face. The empathy. This was why he'd tried to rule from the shadows, why he'd kept his true lineage a secret all these years. It wasn't out of concern for Galla or loyalty to his father; it was all for him. He wanted power, he wanted the throne, but he knew the lords would reject him. His own father had never publicly acknowledged him, but instead had kept the truth of his birth a secret. He had allowed Hadley to stay at court but had never given him a position of consequence.

It was like kicking a dog when it was down, but Kalothia pressed on regardless. "You didn't try for the throne because you feared that the court would refuse your claim. Just as your father had. You never told your brother the truth because you feared rejection. You knew you would never truly belong here. That's why you were so scared of my mother usurping your position. You always knew you were superfluous. That the king didn't really need you—"

She got no further. Hadley's bowed head whipped up and, with an animal cry of fury, he launched himself at her. It was so unexpected she barely had time to throw herself out of the way, crashing into Nahir and sending them both tumbling to the ground.

She felt the whip of wind and the brush of fingers as Hadley flew past—but momentum kept him going. He tried to stop at the end of the platform, his feet skidding noisily on the wooden ledge, his arms wheeling.

She reached a hand out for him, some part of her thinking to clutch at his clothes and haul him back. But it was too late. He slipped over the edge and plunged out of view, his cry of anger and horror fading until a distant splash of water ended it.

GOODBYES

THE CALL OF CICADAS FILLED THE COURTYARD IN THE FALLING evening light. Kalothia sat on a bench staring at the bronze statue of Queen Sylvia. She wondered how her mother might have changed Galla if she'd had more time. If she hadn't been sucked into the maelstrom of Hadley's twisted world. Ye-Ye nuzzled against her neck, his warmth a gentle comfort. If her mother had been offered the opportunity to lead Galla, would she have accepted it? Would she have challenged the bars that limited the scope of her life? She sighed. There were only six sunrises left until her coronation and she had no idea what to do.

Padma would continue to be a problem. She'd had the marquis's body dispatched to the border. The duchess was sure to react to the news that her grandson had been killed by Galla's dishonorable prime minister. It helped that the two men had been in cahoots. What could the duchess say when her own forces had been systematically attacking Galla for years? No doubt she'd claim ignorance, but it wouldn't change the damage Padma had inflicted on Galla.

Kalothia wondered about Hadley. It seemed he had no family, nobody to inform of his death. Nahir, combing through his rooms, had found documents relating to a Padman orphanage. Had he been Padman? Had that partly informed his decision to betray Galla? Who was his mother? So many of his secrets had died with him. For a man who had craved influence so much, his passing had caused barely a ripple.

It took a while to notice the change in the air. That it had become difficult to draw a deep breath. Her head began to throb, and her eyes to water. She clapped her hands to her ears as the pressure in them grew and turned her head back and forth, searching the courtyard for the distinctive shade of indigo. She found the Goddess standing in the shadow of a cashew tree. The rush of power receded as smoothly as it had built, fading to a background buzz. Ye-Ye sprang from her shoulder and raced to the Goddess. She scooped him up, then glided forward in her boneless way.

Kalothia staggered slowly to her feet, exhausted from the day. Still, she stood and bowed her head respectfully.

"Sit before you fall down," the Goddess commanded in her melodious, dark coffee voice.

Kalothia complied gratefully.

"You are in better shape than at our meeting in the caves." The Goddess stopped a handspan away. Close enough for Kalothia to touch. Though she wouldn't dare. Her hand might well erupt into flames.

"I hope you're eager for your coronation. You'll see that I chose a day when the air will be cooler and the dust winds calm."

Kalothia stiffened. She did not like to be maneuvered. That had been her life thus far. How would she retain her personhood on the throne with so many people and an entire Goddess eager to control her? The thought surprised her: *Does this mean I've decided to become queen?*

The Goddess raised a brow. "Of course you have decided. But you have free will, Kalothia. I cannot control you. I can only offer limited assistance in reaching our mutual goal."

Red earth. She forgot her thoughts were as clear as glass to the Goddess. "Our mutual goal. Giving the women of Galla the same opportunities as men."

"Indeed. It won't be easy. Change is hard on the heart and mind."

Kalothia thought of Aunty and Teacher, who had dedicated their lives to caring for her. It was a sacrifice they'd made for love of her mother and in service to Galla. Could she do as much? After all, the freedom she'd dreamed of, the freedom to travel and discover herself, wasn't an option yet. If she truly wanted to live freely, she had to secure freedom for all of Galla's women.

A door opened behind them. "Ah." The Goddess smiled. "Somebody else is after your attention." She bent and set Ye-Ye on the ground.

"And one last thing."

A pair of warbling calls filled the air. It was somehow familiar. Out of the gray evening sky a pair of birds flew across the courtyard, their iridescent blue wings flashing. One was as tiny as a baby's fist.

"The kori birds!" Kalothia breathed. "The egg hatched!"

"They have been resting in your aviary, but they don't like to be cooped up." The Goddess waved a hand and the circling birds melted into the cloudy sky, their warbling cry fading to nothing. "They'll do better at home." The Goddess smiled again. "I'll see you soon."

She was gone by the time Nahir appeared.

Kalothia's heart gave a lurch. "I remember when seeing you had no effect on me whatsoever," she grumbled. "Well, apart from annoying me. Now my heart does all kinds of strange things."

He laughed and sat on the bench beside her. "If it makes you feel any better, you have the same effect on me." He took her hand and drew her closer. "I thought I heard voices out here." He looked about. "Who were you talking to?"

She tilted her head. "Would you believe me if I said the Goddess appears to me?"

Nahir rarely spoke of spiritual things—she wasn't sure he believed at all—so she was surprised when he stiffened and looked around warily. "Yes," he murmured.

"Really?"

He looked back at her. "I'm not sure you realize, but you're quite extraordinary. It would make perfect sense if the Goddess took a personal interest in your fate."

Was it fate? she wondered. The inexorable push toward the throne?

Nahir brushed a hand over her hair. "You look like you have the weight of the world on your shoulders."

She smiled tiredly. "Just the country."

He kissed her forehead. "Take the night off. Galla will survive until tomorrow." He pulled her gently against his chest and wrapped his arms around her. She breathed in his shea butter and sandalwood scent and felt safe and comforted.

After long minutes she tilted her head back. Their eyes met and he leaned down to brush a kiss across her lips. It was sweet and wonderful. As natural as if they'd done it a hundred times. She wrapped her arms around his neck and he obligingly bent his head and kissed her, slow and sweet. A languid unwinding. She lost herself in the sensation, in the taste of his lips, the strength in his arms, the warmth of his chest . . . and was jolted back to reality when he abruptly pulled away. She opened her eyes and blinked. Bukki stood in the dim evening holding a brightly lit lamp.

"Your Highness?" she said. Her voice filtered into Kalothia's consciousness as though from a distance. "Sorry to interrupt!" There was a wince in her voice. "But I've just come from the throne room and the lords are talking—plotting, really." She sighed. "I think you should hurry there before they get much further."

The joy of moments earlier evaporated. Kalothia gave a loud, gusty sigh and dragged herself to her feet. Ye-Ye cried out imploringly. "Come on, then!" she told him, and lifted him onto her shoulder. "Let's go see what trouble they're brewing."

THE RUMBLE OF VOICES IN THE THRONE ROOM WAS AUDIBLE from the stairs. Kalothia heard Lord Suja's voice ring out over the hubbub, demanding attention. "No Gallan king has ever presided over such indignity! A prime minister conspiring with enemies, killing foreign royals! My father would be ashamed to call himself Gallan! This is just the start of the chaos a woman will bring to the throne."

A chorus of voices cheered him, agreeing.

"The only option is marriage with a foreign royal who can steer the country until an heir comes of age."

Heat blazed through Kalothia's body as she strode toward the trees that marked the entrance to the throne room. She recalled her meeting with the lords and how their internal squabbles and narrow interest in their individual territories had prevented them from agreeing on anything. The gall of four men who struggled to think of the needs of the country as a whole daring to dismiss her as unsuitable to reign made her head spin. It was the same kind of thinking that had allowed her mother to be persecuted and pushed over a ledge. Emboldened by her anger, she swept into the room at a full march.

The room was full, as though somebody had called an impromptu meeting and failed to invite her.

Without the usual announcer on the door, it took them a few precious minutes to realize she had entered the room. She was halfway to the throne before the loud barrage of voices began to die down and the courtiers managed to spring to their feet and bow.

As she strode past the lords, Lord Suja shot her his usual mocking look, entirely unapologetic at being caught accusing her of incompetence. He bowed slowly. She ignored him, climbing the dais and striding toward the bloodred throne at the center of the platform. It was the first time she'd sat in it. The seat was large—built for a substantial man—it was ornately carved and surprisingly comfortable. It was strange to think that her father, her grandfather, and a long line of ancestors had occupied this same seat. She settled back.

Slowly the court straightened from their bows then sat. Their faces were eager, their eyes bright, like children caught in mischief. The day had been an adventure for them, she realized. A delicious piece of drama that gave them respite from the usual humdrum roll of their lives. Bringing about change in Galla would be challenging. It would be harder still to do it surrounded by a court eager to see her fail. An idea lodged in her mind. An audacious, grand idea. Maybe she could make a difference, but on her own terms.

"Your Highness. After the events of the day, it was in your interest that we gathered and sought to—" Lord Caspin said.

"Please sit down, Lord Caspin," she instructed, her voice quiet but firm.

His eyes widened, and his mouth continued to move as though he were unsure how to close it.

She waited. Silence rolled out across the room.

Eventually Lord Caspin stumbled back to his chair, his fists clenching and unclenching.

Kalothia looked around the throne room. Her hands trembled a little, but she was determined to forge ahead.

She raised a finger. "I am the rightful heir to the throne of Galla, and I say there will be no suitors." She let her gaze travel around the room. She raised a second finger. "There will be no marriage of which I don't approve." Her gaze stopped on the lords. She raised a third finger. "And once I am crowned, there will be no royal court . . ." Lord Caspin's mouth gaped. Lord Suja's face folded into a frown. All around her there was fear in the eyes of the courtiers. "In the South," she added.

The fear turned to confusion. "Galla is a great country, but it can be greater. It can be a place where every subject is treated with respect and given the opportunity to achieve their full potential. Where women are not diminished or held down by restrictive beliefs but allowed to participate fully in life and to contribute the full range of their skills. Where their voices are heard and they are not subjected to cruel and arbitrary punishments." A gentle storm of muttering had begun. The confused expressions became alarm and disgust.

Kalothia ignored them and went on, "Many lifetimes ago, King Osaju moved the royal court from the Eastern Territory to the South. But I will not be ruling here. The royal court will move to a territory more open to change. I will consider and decide on the location."

The tremble in her hand grew a little as she prepared to make her next announcement. She turned to her right and found Bukki in her usual spot beside the dais. The muttering had died away, shock throbbing through the room.

Into this silence, Kalothia added, "There are many talented people in Galla, and I will populate the new royal court with people focused on serving the country and not their own needs. For over twenty harvests a traitor and murderer served as Galla's prime minister. I couldn't do worse in my selection. I intend to do much better." She met Bukki's eyes.

Bukki stared back, her brow furrowed with confusion. Suddenly understanding dawned. She gasped audibly. Her eyes widened in disbelief.

Kalothia raised a questioning eyebrow.

Bukki took a deep breath, rolled her shoulders, then nodded.

"Bukki is strategic, knowledgeable, and passionate about Galla. She will serve as Galla's new prime minister."

The room erupted with noise. Kalothia surveyed the courtiers. Her legs shook and her heart was galloping like a horse. She glanced at Bukki and whispered, "Are you sure?"

Bukki looked like she might throw up but she nodded. "Yes."

Kalothia nodded back, then she sought out Nahir, who was standing just below the throne. She wondered how or even if she should ask.

He smiled and mouthed, *"I go where you go."*

She breathed a sigh of relief. They could do this. As a team.

LATER, SHE STOOD IN HER MOTHER'S COURTYARD, THE EXCITE-ment and noise of the palace shut out, and stared at the moon. The rush of energy that had powered her seeped away. Ye-Ye lay curled around her neck, and she stroked him affectionately: a piece of her past. She held another piece in her hand: the soft leather of the map book Teacher had given her. All the places it contained were open to her now. She'd come such a long way from her forest home. She didn't know where life would take her next, but maybe that was the biggest adventure: taking your skills and gifts and doing the absolute best you could with them. She'd do her best for Teacher, Aunty, Clarit, her mother, her brother, and herself. She'd make Galla better.

ACKNOWLEDGMENTS

Thank you to my parents, Grace and Soji Lapite, who restricted my childhood boundaries to Safeway and Camberwell Library, thus nurturing a love of supermarket aisles and books.

Thank you to my agent, Joanna Moult, who saw potential in my manuscript and gave it wings.

I've missed Lou Kuenzler's brilliant writing workshops at City Lit; they were invaluable in shaping the early versions of *Goddess Crown*. Thank you to my lovely editors, Annalie Grainger and Susan Van Metre, who helped untangle the plot threads and pull the final version together, with strong support from Jenny Bish.

Thank you to the Toronto Romance Writers group for providing a community generous with advice and support.

There aren't enough words to thank my many friends who have encouraged, motivated, and celebrated me on my writing journey, but I'm sending love to Ambur, Audrey, Alison, Yvette, Miriam, Maria, Dawn, Bukky, Ruane, Tahmina, Charmaine, Shantel, Temwachi, and Nadine and to my sisters, Nike and Tolu.

A final thank you to the authors I have loved who have written wonderful female characters and helped shape mine.

ABOUT THE AUTHOR

SHADE LAPITE is British-Nigerian and has drawn on her heritage to create the world of her debut novel. She spent a significant slice of her childhood nestled in the library, inhaling books by Diana Wynne Jones, Tamora Pierce, Lois Duncan, and Mildred D. Taylor. Her love for the arts led her to a degree in media arts at Royal Holloway, University of London. She now lives in Toronto and juggles writing with her career in digital marketing. Her blog, *Coffee Bookshelves*, celebrates writing and promotes titles by authors of color. You can find her fangirling over Korean dramas on Twitter @TheShadyFiles or sharing her favorite books on Instagram @shadelapite.